ALSO BY EMMA TALLON

*Runaway Girl*

# DANGEROUS GIRL

## EMMA TALLON

Bookouture

Published by Bookouture in 2018

An imprint of StoryFire Ltd.

Carmelite House
50 Victoria Embankment
London EC4Y 0DZ

www.bookouture.com

ISBN: 978-1-78681-515-6
eBook ISBN: 978-1-78681-514-9

*Dedicated to the centre of my universe, my strongest motivation and the person that all of this is for – my son, Christian.*

# PROLOGUE

It was pitch black. The only thing the scared young woman could hear was the slow, constant drip of water somewhere in the cold, damp room. Her tightly bound ankles ached deeply where the rope had bruised through to the bone. She took a deep breath in, the sound sharp against the silence. The action sent her lungs into spasm and she coughed harshly. Days she had been down here in this makeshift prison. She shivered, and another tear rolled down her face. Why was she here? Who was doing this to her?

The bottom of the door scraped against the floor, announcing her captor's arrival as she stifled a scream. Her eyes grew wide as she attempted to see him, to see anything. His tall, broad frame was outlined by the sliver of light that made its weak way through the door for just a second, before he kicked it shut again behind him.

She heard the sound of a chair being dragged along and the creak of a body sitting down on it. Her eyes darted about in the darkness until he switched on a torch. She winced in pain at the unexpected light. He kept it trained on her face, blinding her. He sat behind the light where she couldn't see, just like he always did.

'Please,' she pleaded. 'Please, just let me go. I won't tell anyone, I won't,' she begged her silent captor. The tears now streamed down her cheeks. There was no answer. 'I have money, you know; my family have money. If you tell them you have me, they will pay you well for my safe return. I'll say whatever you want me to. I wouldn't say a word about all this, if you just let me go, I swear on my own life. Please,' she beseeched, her voice thin and shaky.

He lunged forward, pushing the torch against her eyes so she had no choice but to squeeze them shut. She shuffled backward on the filthy bed until her back hit the damp wall behind.

'There are some things,' he whispered, 'that money cannot buy you.' His cold tone sent a chill through her heart.

He moved and suddenly she felt a sharp blade as he pushed it against the skin of her throat. She began to shake with fear, her tears falling faster. He pressed harder and dragged the knife slowly downward until it began to pierce the flesh.

'Please, oh God, please,' she whimpered, her cries turning to hysteria. Her whole body shook, and her thighs grew warm as she wet herself in pure terror.

The knife was raised to her mouth, covering it, pressing hard against her lips. She quickly stifled the noise she was making, her breath coming out in short, sharp gasps.

'Your God don't come to these parts,' the man whispered again.

Without another word he switched off the torch and stepped back into the darkness. He closed the door as he left, leaving the room in silence once more.

Resting her face in her hands a moment, the woman rocked back and forth.

Her cries echoed around the windowless walls as she screamed desperately for help. She screamed for all she was worth. She screamed for hours, until she finally passed out in exhaustion. Not a single person heard. No one came to save her.

# CHAPTER ONE

Ash Bentley slammed the truck door and shifted the weight of the small, heavy box he was carrying. Checking both ways of the busy London street, he crossed the road and headed towards the closed club. The jarring sound of a pneumatic chisel in the next street filled the air amongst the running engines, beeping horns and local chatter. The sky was bright blue above the tall buildings, and a sweet breeze drifted over the top of the $CO_2$ emissions and the smell of brake dust. He breathed it in deeply and smiled. It was going to be a nice day. His ex-missus was grudgingly letting him take his little girls out for the afternoon and he wanted to take them to the park.

Two young women out shopping for the day passed by and gave him an appreciative look. He winked and gave them a cheeky grin. They giggled and looked back a couple of times after he passed. Ash was a ruggedly handsome chap with dimples, muscles and tattoos. He also had the gift of the gab. A bit of a Jack the Lad, he could charm the knickers off almost anything. It was a pastime that had cost him his family after his ex had caught wind and showed him the door. He felt bad about that, as he knew he should have done better by her, but he was who he was, so these days he stayed strictly casual with women.

Reaching the black side door to Club Anya, Ash pushed the buzzer and waited. A couple of minutes passed, then it opened slightly and a salt-and-pepper head with a receding hairline poked round inquisitively. Seeing who it was, Carl grinned and pulled the door open wide, moving out of the way.

'Ash! How you doing, mate?'

'Yeah, good thanks. Yourself?'

'Ah, you know me – I'm good. Tickin' over, keeping things running smooth.' Carl smiled warmly as he spoke. Everyone knew that Carl loved his job. He was second-in-command at the club, after the two joint owners. Having no family or partner of his own, Carl pushed all of his time and efforts into the club and saw his employers and the rest of the long-term team as his family. He was good at what he did and was appreciated for it. A man who liked a simple life, he had no complaints.

They walked through to the empty club, and Ash's eyes immediately swept over to the attractive brunette seated at the other end of the long bar. Her slim legs were crossed and she was looking down, intently writing something in a notebook. His eyes roamed over her appreciatively. Her long hair was styled and glossy, and she wore an elegantly sexy black pencil dress. It was simple, but it showed off her impressive figure and her smooth, bare legs. If it had been anyone else, Ash would have sidelined whatever else he was doing and made it his mission to seduce her. You didn't see a fine specimen like Anna Davis every day. But that was the thing. This was Anna Davis. Club owner in her own right, but more importantly, she was Freddie Tyler's woman – and Ash didn't particularly fancy losing any fingers right now. No one in their right mind would show disrespect to Freddie like that, or to Anna herself either. She was off the table.

'Are you going to just stand there all day, Mr Bentley, or are you going to come over and show me whatever it is that you have in that box?' Anna's clear voice carried over to him calm but authoritative. Ash blinked in surprise; she hadn't even looked over. He hurried forward, and as he reached her side, she closed the book and swung the swivelling bar chair round to face him. Anna gave him a tight, professional smile, and once again Ash was struck by how attractive she was. Deep blue eyes bored into him intently and he gathered his wits.

'Sorry, Miss Davis. Was just thinking about something. This—' He placed the box on the bar next to her and tapped the top of it. 'This is just a little present from my boss to you. Not for the bar, just for your own personal collection. He thought you might like it. You know, like, at home or whatever.'

Anna opened the box, curious. She pulled out what appeared to be a large, gold Russian Fabergé egg on tiny wheels. Pulling a confused face, she looked at Ash for clarification. He leaned forward and took it from her. Placing it on the bar, he pushed the top half of the egg open on its hinge with both hands. Inside was a beautiful clear bottle that fitted the shape of the bottom half of the egg, with an elegantly designed lid. Around the lid hung four intricately decorated shot glasses.

'Oh, that's interesting.' Anna leaned forward and unhooked one of the tiny glasses. She held it closer and inspected it. She looked down at the writing – 'Imperial Collection Super Premium Vodka' – and pressed her lips together. She had seen this stuff once before, at a supplier fair. It hadn't been for sale, just an attraction at one of the stalls. It was expensive stuff. Seriously expensive. Much too expensive to give a client as a sweetener gift. This wasn't for her, not really. This was for Freddie's benefit. She shut the lid carefully and placed it back in the box.

'Fabulous. I love it. When will you be dropping off Tanya's?' She smiled broadly at him and waited. Ash froze at the mention of Anna's business partner. His boss had only given him one and told him to give it to Anna, to keep Freddie sweet; show him that they were properly looking after his missus.

'Er, thing is, there was only the one, so…' He fidgeted awkwardly. Anna laughed.

'It's OK, Ash.' She tapped his shoulder to let him know that she was just messing with him. She looked at the box again and rolled her eyes. 'I'm sure Freddie will appreciate the gesture.'

Ash visibly relaxed and smiled back at her. She knew the game, this bird; she wasn't short of a few brain cells.

Anna picked up her paperwork from the bar and indicated that he follow her through to the office. He took the box and carried it through for her. Once inside, Ash looked around as he sat in the comfortable leather seat offered to him.

It was cosy and neat with everything organised properly. Nothing like the cold, haphazard mess his boss resided in. There was a collection of paintings on the walls. He liked the biggest one: a beach at sunset with big splashes of oranges and reds throughout and the silhouette of two people sitting in the distance. This painting was set in prize position, in the middle of the largest wall. On the desk there was a framed picture of Anna and Freddie laughing together. He realised that Anna was watching him. He focused his attention on her, and she opened up the file that was ready in front of her.

'It's quite apt that John sent us vodka, really, considering that's the subject I want to discuss with you.' She eyed him, her face unreadable. 'You've undercut every other supplier out there. Initially by a little bit, but lately by a lot. Why?' she asked bluntly.

'Well,' Ash said with a shrug, 'guess we just have better deals set up, don't we? And we like to pass savings on to the customer.'

'Right.' Anna nodded slowly. 'Or,' she said after a few moments' pause, 'you're selling me the fake shit and trying to make me feel like I'm getting a great deal. Which does make business sense, I guess. Unless you're on my end of the deal, of course.' She folded her arms and waited for Ash to respond.

Ash licked his lips and settled back while he decided which way to go with this. He knew the deal on this account. From what he had heard, when they got together three years ago, Freddie had offered Anna a direct supply of all the fake booze that he imported into the country. It would have saved her a lot of money and upped the drinks profits tenfold, but she had refused. Much as she accepted Freddie's line of work, she determinedly kept her club squeaky clean. It meant that her profit margin on drinks was OK but modest.

Freddie had got one of his outlets to undercut her original suppliers by just enough that she couldn't refuse but not enough that she would suspect. Over time, the suppliers were to drop their prices again and again, and when the prices got too low for them to supply the real deal, they were to switch to Freddie's fake versions. He prided himself on the fact that the spirits were good-enough copies that they were still at the same strength and they tasted no different. As far as Freddie was concerned, Anna would get the profits she deserved, but she would be none the wiser to the less-legal products being sold and everyone would be happy.

Now, though, sitting here under the sharp scrutiny of Anna's gaze, Ash's faith in Freddie's plan was wavering. John had told him that if she was ever to question him that he was to deny any knowledge. It would get Freddie into trouble, and that was something you just didn't do. He frowned, as if the idea she'd presented was confusing to him, and played dumb.

'Fake? How can it be fake? It's Smirnoff we bring you, right? How could we be bringing you fake Smirnoff?'

Anna raised one eyebrow and held his gaze. Reaching down to the floor, she picked up one of the bottles and plonked it unceremoniously on the table.

'You know, that's just what I've been sitting here asking myself, Ash. I've even been over every single inch of this bottle this morning, looking for the differences.' She paused and casually ran her eyes over the bottle, studying it. Ash froze. Had she found something? Was there a giveaway? Were they going to end up getting Freddie Tyler in trouble with his missus? This was not good. He began to pale and swallowed, trying to think of a response to that.

Anna flicked her gaze over at him and saw his Adam's apple bob up and down as he floundered. She noted his eyes brighten and his muscular shoulders tense and pursed her lips together, smiling wryly. His reaction told her everything there was to know. She turned away from the bottle.

'But I didn't find anything out of the ordinary.' She watched him visibly relax. 'The thing is, though, I have this friend. She's a bit particular about what she drinks, because she gets this strange, itchy rash on her neck when she drinks cheap vodka. So she only drinks certain brands that she knows don't affect her. Smirnoff is one of them. Imagine my surprise' – Anna leaned forward, folding her arms on the table – 'when a big, blotchy red rash appeared on her neck in my club, at the VIP table, where I'd been bringing her Smirnoff all night from my own bar. Such a bad reaction, in fact, that my friend had to leave early to go and buy a pack of antihistamines. It was not the evening that I had hoped to give her.'

Ash didn't say anything. What could he say to that? He was dreading relaying this conversation to John.

'Aside from ruining her evening, it also made me look like a twat.' Anna's face was hard. 'I now look like a back-alley cheapskate, when all I've done these last three years is work damn hard to make sure that this club has a decent reputation; that it is known for its quality. And now look.' She held her hands out to the sides. 'What am I supposed to do with this?' Anna stared at him, her eyes wide in question. 'No? No answer to that?'

She stood up, agitated, and leaned back against a small filing cabinet. She drummed her fingers on top of it and bit her top lip, looking off into the distance.

'You know, statistically speaking, it's been proven that, on average, if someone has a good experience somewhere they tell three people, and those people pass what they've heard on to three more people, and so on and so forth. It's how reputations get formed through word of mouth. Unfortunately, the same statistics prove that for bad experiences, it's five people that get told. Five people that pass on to five more people, et cetera, et cetera. Do you see my problem here?'

Ash knew when he was beaten, but even so there was no way he could go back to his boss and tell him that he had admitted fault. He couldn't, not with Freddie so personally involved. It would be the end of their good reputation. He shook his head and pulled a sad expression.

'That's terrible, it really is. But I tell you now, it ain't that vodka. It's the proper stuff. It must have been a dodgy bottle, that's all I can think of. Maybe the seal broke and the air got to it or something in storage, caused it to go a bit funny. I'll have a look into it. In the meantime, I'll get another crate sent to you free of charge as an apology, Miss Davis. And I'll make sure this gets reported directly to John.' He stared at her, sincerely and unwavering. Anna stared back at him for a moment, then nodded softly.

'OK, Ash, you do that. But you tell John this.' She walked back to her desk again and leaned over it, putting her weight on her hands and her face closer to the man in the chair. 'I have no problem paying the higher prices that I used to, to make sure I get the quality I order. It's that simple. That is the new deal going forward, as of right now. I also expect one of your vans this afternoon, exchanging the rest of the shit I have here for the real deal. All of it. Tell John to invoice me the difference from what I've already paid for it. Then we'll say no more on the matter. If this isn't completed to my satisfaction by the end of today, I won't be quite so reasonable. OK?'

'Yes, Miss Davis.' Ash nodded curtly and stood up.

'One more thing: tell John I don't want him trying to push his cheap stuff through here again. I appreciate his thoughts were probably in the right place, passing on the savings and everything, but that isn't what's important to me here. Now he knows that, we can all stay friends.'

'Of course. I'll pop back this afternoon and see to the exchange myself.' He would have to text his ex and arrange to see the girls another time. He felt a pang of guilt, but this was more important right now. Neither he nor his boss could afford to alienate the Tylers. It would be business suicide.

Anna nodded as he left her office and scurried off to download their conversation to John. She chewed her lip. She should have fired them as suppliers, really. She had been furious when she realised what had been going on. Furious at herself, too, for not realising sooner. But they had been very good suppliers for almost as long as the club had been open, and there had never been an incident like this before, so she decided to give them the benefit of the doubt and a second chance. After all, they weren't doing it to try to cream loads of extra profit, not at the prices they were charging. A lot of clubs would be grateful for the arrangement. But not Anna. With the rest of her world a myriad of grey, she kept the running of her club black and white.

Sitting down in her chair, Anna folded her arms and stared off into the distance. Her deep blue eyes unfocused as she became lost in thought. It was quiet in her office, the soundproof door blocking the noise of Carl's stocktake in the main bar. It was so quiet that Anna jumped slightly when her phone rang.

Focusing back on the present, she looked at the screen. It was Tanya.

'Hi, how's it going? Are they any good?' She paused, listening. 'Oh really?' Anna's perfectly shaped eyebrows shot up in interest. 'It sounds like they're exactly what we need. Let me know what you arrange, when you've talked to them. My diary is pretty flexible all week. For that anyway.' She studied her shiny pink nails as Tanya talked. 'OK, great. Speak to you later then.' She clicked off the call and smiled as the framed picture of herself and Freddie caught her eye.

It was one that Thea, Freddie's sister, had taken at a party about a year ago. Anna loved it, because it had caught them in a candid moment of happiness. Every time she looked at it, she could see all the love, loyalty, happiness and friendship they shared, captured in one shot.

Three happy years they had shared together so far, and Anna hoped that they would continue to share many more. Freddie had been the first person she had met, after Tanya, when she moved to the area. She had been vulnerable and scared, running away from her tyrannical ex, trying to start a new life. Freddie had been kind and patient with her, offering friendship at a time she badly needed it. Little did she know at the time that Freddie would be the one who freed her from the violent, psychotic Tony for good. Freddie had saved her both physically and mentally, and enabled her to become the strong, confident woman she was today. She had a lot to be thankful to him for.

Anna touched the photo with the tips of her fingers. Thea had a good eye for photography. It was something she had been doing as a hobby for a while, but lately she had been talking about doing a college course and trying her luck professionally. Anna hoped she did it. It would be a shame for her to waste her talent and passion.

With one last fond smile at the photo, she turned back to the accounts. The sooner they were done, the sooner she could get back home to see Freddie.

# CHAPTER TWO

Michael Tyler walked into the bright sunshine and straightened his suit jacket. Smartly dressed and standing tall at just over six feet, he looked like a different person to the troubled teenager who'd returned home in disgrace three years ago after been expelled from school. Having being bullied for his common background and criminal siblings, Michael had turned to violence and drug dealing in an attempt to become feared instead of victimised. He had developed a deep hatred for the school and its rich, stuck-up students and a burning anger towards his brother – the one who had put him in such a difficult position. When he had finally been caught and sent home, the family had been devastated that he had suffered so much.

Freddie had hoped by sending him there, it would set him on a different path. He felt no shame at what he did. It was life. Freddie had played the cards he had been dealt, worked hard, built an empire. He stood proud and was respected. But Freddie also knew how dangerous the life could be. He had hoped to give his brother an easier path, a safer one. But Michael had ended up getting into illegal activities anyway. It seemed no matter where he sent him, there would only have been one outcome. Perhaps it was just in their blood.

Once Michael had calmed down and settled in back home, Freddie had taken him under his wing. If Michael was determined to get into the life anyway, then the best thing he could do was keep him close. Mollie, their mother, had taken some time to come round to the idea, but eventually she accepted it. It was what it was. The Tylers stood together, through thick and thin.

Three years on, Michael worked directly under Freddie and was known as the youngest of the respected and feared Tyler brothers. Freddie ran almost all of the organised crime that went on through East and West London. He owned the Central belt and everyone in it. If it wasn't directly his business, he had a stake and a say in it. His fingers were in all the pies. Nothing crept past him.

With a quick, smart head on his shoulders, Freddie had paid his dues and risen up respectfully in his younger years, before taking on the mantle from the older faces before him. Since that point, he had continuously added new ideas and ventures until he had doubled the number of criminal enterprises under their control. He had his brothers and a solid firm around him, making sure everything ran smoothly. Central London's criminal underworld had never been stronger.

Squinting up at the bright sky, Michael stepped down onto the pavement. He looked both ways down the busy street and then walked over to his car, parked almost directly in front of the betting shop he had just vacated. The envelope holding the thick wad of money he had just collected made a crinkling sound in his pocket as he bent down to slide into the sleek black BMW. Unfastening his jacket he reached into the inside pocket to pull the envelope out, frowning in annoyance. He had his suits fitted perfectly, by the best tailor on Savile Row. He disliked anything that messed up their perfectly cut lines. And this bulky package did just that. He opened the glove box and threw it in until later, when he would deliver it back to Freddie. Now, though, he had another few rounds to do.

Looking over his shoulder, he swung the car out into the road. The engine roared as he pressed his foot down on the accelerator. He turned his music on, and the deep electronic beats drowned out the sounds of life around him.

He stopped at the next traffic lights and waited for two girls to cross. They looked about eighteen or nineteen, not much younger than him. As one of them chatted away, the other's eyes glanced over him as she took in her surroundings. She immediately flicked her eyes back for a second look. Raising one eyebrow, she smiled flirtatiously and raised one hand to him. Michael half smiled back and nodded politely. The girl giggled something to her friend and the pair of them studied him together. Michael sighed deeply and waited for them to move on. It wasn't unusual this reaction, these days. He was the proverbial ugly duckling who had grown into a swan. Gone were the awkward days of pubescent acne and skinny arms. Michael was now trim and muscular from hitting the gym every day and was graced with the same brooding good looks as his brother Freddie. Out of the three of them, it was only Paul who seemed to have missed out on that front. He sported overly large, bulky features and a constantly awkward expression. Although not outright ugly, Paul didn't attract the sort of female appreciation that his brothers did.

The lights turned green and Michael moved on. As he pulled round to his destination in the middle of Soho, he bumped the car up onto the kerb and turned the engine off. He left it there, ignoring the double yellows. Locking the car behind him, Michael stepped through a brightly lit door with colourful neon light tubes flashing through the windows.

Inside there was a small waiting room with chairs around the edges and a reception desk. Several men were seated, waiting for their appointment. None of them looked up when Michael walked in, nor made eye contact with any of the other men in the room. Michael smirked. It always made him laugh seeing them here, looking away as if this meant they wouldn't be noticed by anyone. A bell had chimed as he walked in, signalling his arrival to Linda, the manager of this massage parlour.

She appeared through the doorway behind the desk, looking annoyed and flustered. She patted her mess of natural dark curls, which were piled up and pinned on top of her head. Even up there, it didn't help to make her look any taller than her five feet, two inches. In her late thirties, she was too old for his tastes but still a very pretty woman, Michael thought. For a tom anyway. Her high, girlish voice sang out as she appeared.

'Welcome to Heaven Sent massage parlour, what can I do you for tod—oh! Hello, love.' Her eyes crinkled up at the corners as she flashed Michael a genuine smile. 'You alright? How's things?' Michael smiled back. He liked Linda. She was a nice old bird, did her job well and was always straight down the line with you. She never put on any pretences – you always knew where you stood. He appreciated that about her. Too many women played games, and he didn't have time for that.

'Things are good, thanks. What about here?'

Her eyes flicked back towards the hallway, annoyance creeping back into them again. 'They're OK. Come through the back – I'll get you a cuppa.'

Michael nodded and followed her through. When things were running smoothly, Linda would just give him the side profits straight away. She didn't waste time with idle chitchat. When she was offering a cup of tea, it meant that she had things to discuss with him.

'Brenda,' she shouted through to one of the side rooms, 'come manage the front for a few minutes.'

They walked through the long, narrow hallway past a number of closed doors, and Michael could hear muffled grunts and groans through a couple of them as he passed. They reached Linda's office, and Michael closed the door behind them before he sat down in one of the two comfortable chairs situated either side of the tiny desk. Linda busied herself with pouring two cups of tea from the already boiled kettle on the side table, the first of which she handed to Michael.

'Cor, it's been a right day here.' She huffed and sat down in the chair opposite him. She took a deep sip of her tea before continuing. 'Sandy, you know the Northern girl we took on last month? Well, I've just finished introducing a bunch of regulars to her timetable, got these guys all comfortable with her, you know, a long-term girl and all that. They're decent spenders too, this lot. She's got a body to die for, so I gave her the good ones. It was all set up nice. Stupid girl's only gone and started using, ain't she?' She shook her head and rolled her eyes. 'Walked in on her jackin' up. In here too! Fuck sake. Imagine if I had been her next client!'

Michael shook his head and sighed heavily. He knew the girl she meant. While Linda was trusted with the recruitment of their girls, the family still carried out a final vetting process on them. Michael remembered inspecting her a few weeks ago, just before she started. She was a very attractive girl. And a stupid one, it would now seem. There were two rules upon being recruited into one of the Tylers' houses. The first rule was to keep schtum. If ever questioned by anyone outside, this was a straight massage parlour. The second rule was to keep clean. No drugs.

His brother Freddie didn't want any of the girls in his houses doing whatever was necessary to get enough money for their next hit. That made them desperate and cheap. That wasn't what they were about. These girls were prostitutes, but they were healthy and clean for the punters. Freddie also wanted to make sure they did it out of choice. He never wanted to be like the wankers out there who gave girls no choice. This was a business, not a slave market. The girls were well paid, looked after and could leave whenever they wanted. That was the score in the Tylers' parlours. She was lucky to have got a place, and she had fucked it up already.

'I've told her to pack her things and get on her way by tonight. I ain't having a smack-head around my other girls. Now I'm going to have to distribute her regulars to the others. Hope this chopping and changing don't piss any of them off enough that they stop coming.' She looked concerned.

'They won't. It might annoy them, but they'll stick it out. It's more hassle to move.'

'Hopefully you're right. Anyway,' she changed the subject, 'that's my problem to solve. What I really wanted to talk to you about is this new face on the beat.' She sipped at her tea again. 'I don't know if you're already aware of him, but he definitely ain't on your payroll. Fresh-faced boy, full of good intentions.' Linda rolled her eyes. 'He must be straight out of police school, or whatever it is they do. He's assigned to this area, keeps trying to befriend everyone, get to know the local community and all that. He's started to cotton on here, started questioning my girls when he sees them out. Good thing is, he's very by the book, so he's poked around but not tried to do anything formally yet. He can't, till he gets some evidence. It's becoming more and more of a problem, though. He's like a dog with a bone. He's started just standing there on the other corner, watching the place. It's putting the clients off. Can you ask Freddie to get him off our backs? The name's Reynolds.'

Michael sat leaning on one arm of the chair, absentmindedly stroking his index finger over the dark stubble on his chin. His bright blue eyes had stared at Linda as she talked but now glazed over slightly. Linda shifted her weight uncomfortably. His eyes were still locked with hers, but they seemed to be looking straight through her. As the seconds ticked on, she wondered if he had even heard what she'd said. She drew in a deep breath, about to repeat her request, but the action seemed to wake Michael up. His eyes refocused and, shaking himself slightly, he looked down at his watch as he stood up.

'Yes, no problem, Linda. I'll see him later today, ask him to get it sorted out for you.'

'Great. Thanks, mate. You got time to unwind a bit before you go?' she questioned. Unlike both of his brothers, Michael liked a visit with one of the girls now and then. He was a hot-blooded young man. Freddie, she knew, had a long-term woman. Paul she didn't know what to make of really. He was nice enough but a bit of an oddball in her opinion. He had refused every time she'd asked, so over the years she had stopped offering. She waited as Michael considered.

'Yeah, go on then. I've got a bit of time. Who you got?'

'I think I've got Carla free.'

Michael followed Linda down the hall, his expression eager. He liked Carla. Linda knew that. Carla was just his type. All long legs and pert tits, she was a cheeky thing and always knew how to get him going. He hung back as Linda knocked gently on the door. It opened almost immediately and a thin, pretty face popped round. As soon as she saw who was with Linda, the door was opened wide, and Carla welcomed him warmly into the small side room.

'Well, hello, you,' she purred, looking overjoyed to see him. Michael wondered if all her punters got the same greeting or whether it was reserved just for people with the name Tyler.

'I'll leave you to it. No rush, love, enjoy.' Linda closed the door behind him and Michael began to relax. The lights were dimmed and the dark burgundy walls gave off a cosy feeling. The air held a mixed scent of lavender and sex. It was sweet and heavy. Some people may have minded it, but Michael didn't. It did something for him; put him in the mood. Perhaps he was getting too used to whores, he thought briefly.

Undoing his clothes until he stood there naked, he then handed them to Carla, who folded them carefully and laid them out gently on the small chair in the corner. She knew his ways. This was one of the reasons why he liked going to her above some of the others. He lay on the bed, facing upwards, pulling one arm up behind his head. He watched her as she pulled off the plain white shift dress they all wore, a nod to the work they were actually supposed to be doing here. She wore nothing underneath, and he let his eyes trail appreciatively down her body. She gave him a filthy smile, which he couldn't help but return. Climbing onto the bed down by his feet, she looked up at him, preening forward like a wild cat.

'We'll skip the massage – I know you can't be arsed with that bit. Now, do you want naughty or naughtier? We both know I don't do nice.'

Michael's arousal grew in front of them, and he stared at her hungrily. She arched her neck teasingly, showing off her breasts. Michael's eyes narrowed. Patience wasn't his strong point at the best of times – she should know that by now. He had no time for her teasing. Something inside of him began to grow angry as she taunted him. He reached forward and grabbed her, pulling her to him in one swift move. She let out a quiet gasp as his cold gaze burned into her intensely.

A second later he grinned gamely and flipped the lithe young woman onto her back. He chuckled and ran his hands over her body, leaving Carla questioning whether she had just imagined the cold, dangerous look flash across his face. Opening her arms she pulled him close, reminding herself that Michael would always be a dangerous man. Because above all else, Michael was and always would be a Tyler.

# CHAPTER THREE

The shrill sound of the door buzzer went off and Freddie checked the video monitor. Seeing Paul standing there he pressed the button next to the speaker and the outer door to the building unlocked.

'Come on up, mate.' He clicked off, opened the front door in readiness for Paul's arrival and walked back down the hallway to wait in the large kitchen, where he had been busy pouring himself a whisky. He didn't usually start this early in the day, but he had experienced a particularly stressful morning. He downed a large gulp of the fiery liquid and then exhaled loudly as he leaned on the counter.

Since the demise of Big Dom, one of the underworld's most respected old faces, Vince, Freddie's mentor and business partner, had slowly begun to take a back seat. Vince and Big Dom had built their empire together over decades, and Big Dom's death had been a stark reminder to Vince of his age and the limited time he had left on this earth. He had been gradually turning most of the businesses over to Freddie, and now he was almost fully retired.

Freddie had gracefully accepted the mantle Vince had handed him and still made sure that the older man got his cut of the profits every month. He would always be grateful and loyal to the man who had taught him everything he knew. It did, however, mean that his workload had greatly increased, and the Tyler brothers were now busier than ever before.

Freddie placed the empty glass by the sink. The kitchen was brand new and top of the range; he'd had it fitted when he and Anna had bought the place two years ago. Black marble floor tiles complemented the white granite worktops. A centrepiece light fitting adorned with low-hanging Swarovski crystals hung over the square breakfast bar in the centre of the room. The light glinted brightly off the crystals and the granite below it, giving the whole room a sparkling glow. Freddie had chosen it because it reminded him of Anna. She always seemed to shine the brightest in any room.

Anna had suffered greatly in her past with a brutal and psychotic ex-boyfriend who had controlled every part of her life. He knew that it had scarred her deeply and tried not to take offence when her defences shot up against him. Instead he trod slowly and carefully through their relationship, respecting her limits even when they caused him extreme frustration. It had taken a year to convince her to even consider making a home with him. He knew it would be a long time again before he could convince her to take another big step forward.

Anna was the centre of Freddie's world now. He had wanted to buy this penthouse for her, to be able to give her a home and security. It was the only way he knew how to treat someone he loved. He had always looked after the rest of his family; it was how he was built. But she had stubbornly backed away from the gesture when he showed her around and let on his intentions. After a difficult conversation Anna had only agreed to the property if she went in fifty-fifty with him. Freddie had felt deflated at her reaction, but understanding why, he'd agreed and they'd bought their home as equal partners. So, in order to do something for her without overstepping the mark, Freddie paid for all of the renovations and made sure that everything inside was nothing less than the very best. He had expected another fight, but Anna had pursed her lips and let it go. It was a small win, but it was still a win.

The penthouse was situated at Royal Wharf overlooking the River Thames. The views were spectacular, especially after dark. Not that either of them got to appreciate this often – both worked late into the nights and were usually ready to collapse into bed when they finally returned home.

For Freddie, the flat was practical. Steel-enforced doors and a video monitor offered him the cautious defences that he needed in his position. There was easy access to the river, and he had a small boat hidden nearby, which Anna was not aware of. Should he ever need to disappear quickly, he could do so easily. London City Airport was just a short cab ride away too, perfect to monitor the runners he had going in and out of the country. Not that he would ever have any of them at his home. He kept his business strictly away from Anna. This suited her. They had a mutual understanding.

Anna knew exactly what Freddie did, and any questions she asked, he answered truthfully. But Anna rarely asked questions. Freddie kept his work out of her direct path, and Anna kept her nose in her own business. They both knew that if anything was ever to go wrong with Freddie's businesses, Anna would be in the spotlight. The police would surround her like flies on shit. If she wasn't directly involved, they couldn't touch her. This was how Freddie wanted to keep it. Just in case.

He refilled the whisky glass again, this time with just a small amount. He felt his first swallow of the burning liquid begin to take effect. That should be enough to take the edge off. He rolled his shoulders, trying to ease the tension in them.

Paul walked in, his large frame seeming to take up the whole hallway. His smiled at Freddie, and then his gaze landed on the glass in his brother's hand.

'Bit early for that, ain't it, Fred?' He smiled quizzically.

'Yeah, probably,' he answered, shrugging. 'Want one?'

'Nah, I'll give it a miss, thanks. So, what's 'appening?' Paul sat down on one of the tall breakfast bar chairs.

'Just got back from Den's unit. Seems we had a skimmer on our hands. Not a little bit either. Fucker was pulling a tenth of our shit out, cutting it with bicarb, then selling it over in Shoreditch.'

Paul frowned. 'What? Who?'

'Tom Rains. Idiot.'

'What a twat.' Paul shook his head in disgust. 'He had a good set-up there. What are we doing about it?'

'I've dealt with it. Few broken fingers and a battering. He'll think twice before crossing us again. Not that he'll have a chance. He's out. Not having snakes like that around. Put the word out to all our friends that he isn't to be trusted.'

'Sure, will do.'

Freddie crossed his arms and stared out the window, his hazel-green eyes glazing over. 'What I want to know is how he got access to skim such a large amount for so long.'

Paul screwed his mouth to one side as he mulled over Freddie's words. They sat in companionable silence. Freddie didn't particularly enjoy carrying out the violent side of things. But it was necessary to keep order and respect in their business. This way of life wasn't a game. One wrong move and they would all be banged up. One uncertain step and the hungry wannabes would take them down and step into his shoes. It was a dangerous position being at the top.

Eventually he walked forward and picked up his jacket from the back of one of the chairs.

'Come on, we need to grab Michael and go meet a man about a dog. I've heard about a new supplier – Spanish guy. Bill's going to set up a meeting. I want to do some background on him first.'

Paul frowned in concern. 'Is it that bad?' he asked. It was uncommon to shift such a large amount of business from a long-standing supplier. It would definitely get some backs up.

Freddie nodded slowly. 'Yeah, mate, I think it is. I don't give two shits how long they've had our business. It's gone south. They've got far too comfortable in their relationship with us. It's time to stir things up.' Freddie gazed off in thought. 'We're the fucking Tylers, Paul. We say what goes. And I say we're trying something new. They don't like it?' He shrugged and his piercing eyes grew hard. 'They can fucking stick it.'

# CHAPTER FOUR

Twenty minutes later Freddie and Paul pulled up outside the Tyler family home. Despite the fact that Freddie had moved out two years previously and Paul six months after, it was still the main hub for them all to meet at.

The door was open and they walked inside. Kicking their shoes off, they continued through the lounge into the kitchen where they knew Mollie would be cooking away, as she always was. Sure enough, as they entered the room they could see her bent over, pulling something out of the Aga. A rich smell of slow-cooked meat and gravy hung in the air, making their mouths water. Mollie placed a large pie down on the cooling rack next to the sink and turned, her smile wide as she saw her two eldest sons.

'Well, look who's here then. And there I was thinking you'd forgotten all about me and I was going to have a fall and die here on me kitchen floor, alone and forgotten,' she said dramatically.

Freddie raised an eyebrow. 'What, since yesterday morning?'

'You aren't even that old,' Paul added, sitting down at the big wooden table.

'Well, when your sons bugger off and leave you, a mother starts wondering about these things,' she said indignantly, sniffing.

'Michael's still here. And Thea,' Freddie said in a casual tone. They were used to these outbursts now and again, usually when one of the remaining two children had done something to annoy Mollie.

'Well, Michael may as well not be, he's never here,' she replied.

Ah, Freddie thought. This was what was bothering her. Still, his youngest brother was only twenty years old. He had his youth, good looks and money. He was hardly going to spend his time sitting quietly at home.

Freddie knew that he had set an unrealistic expectation for Mollie. It had been hard when they were kids. Freddie's father had died when he was just a boy, leaving Mollie with four young children to provide and care for. Freddie was the eldest; at the tender age of ten, he was young enough to still need Mollie's care but old enough to understand their family's predicament. He had taken it upon himself to work every hour God sent and be there to protect his family, just as his father would have done. If he wasn't at home helping Mollie with the younger kids, it was because he was out earning their passage to a better life. Everything he'd done back then was for the family, and he had always been there for Mollie. As he worked his way up the ladder, the only time he ever socialised was through the late hours of the night, after his work was done and when the rest of his family were in bed. It was only later on, when his siblings were older and Mollie had everything she needed, that he started filling more of his spare time with fun. By then, she was used to always having them around.

'Ah, come on, Mum. He's young. He's out enjoying life.'

'Well, you never…' She trailed off and closed her mouth. He knew she was remembering why he had always been around. 'Well, anyway. Coffee? I've got your favourite.'

'Sounds good.'

'I'll take some of that pie, Mum,' said Paul.

'Where is he anyway?' Freddie asked, peering through to the empty lounge with a frown. 'He knew I was coming. I've got stuff to do.'

'Like I said,' she replied tartly, 'he's never here. Still.' Her tone softened. She could never stay snappy for long. 'At least you can stay for a bit of food. I doubt you've had breakfast, have you? Doesn't Anna feed you at home?'

''Course she does. She's a great cook. As you know, from all the times you've been over for dinner.' Mollie just sniffed again and Freddie hid a smile. Two years on and she still wasn't taking Freddie's relocation very well. He knew she liked Anna. She just found it hard to accept that she wasn't the only special woman in his life anymore.

'That pie is for tonight, but I have some quiche and salad you can have for lunch. I'll go get you both some now. Paul, stop slouching – you'll end up with a hunchback.' She ambled off to the pantry. Paul pulled a comical face at Freddie, making him grin, then straightened himself up and cleared his throat as Mollie came back with two plates full of food.

'So, how you doing, Mum? What are you up to today?' He shovelled in a mouthful of food. The radio was playing in the background and she turned it down slightly as the news came on.

'I'm going over to Angie to get my hair done later, which will be nice. I haven't seen Angie in ages. Her son's just been promoted to an officer; you know, the one in the army. So she'll want to tell me all about that.'

Freddie began to frown and stopped chewing his food. He stared past her at the little kitchen radio.

'Then I thought I might pop into that furniture shop at the end of her road, as I'm down that way. My sofa's starting to look a little worse for wear.'

Paul also frowned and put his fork down, cocking his head to one side. Mollie looked at both of her sons, who were no longer paying her any attention. The cheeky buggers, they came in asking her questions and they weren't even listening to her reply! Is that what she got for being their mother these days?

'And then I thought I'd run down the street naked, swinging my knickers round above my head.' No response. 'Singing "God Save the Queen".' Still nothing. 'With my hair on fire.' She rolled her eyes and stepped forward, bending down and waving in their faces. 'What do you think?'

'What?' Paul blinked at her, then looked over at Freddie with a concerned expression. 'Hang on a minute, Mum. You need to get down there, Fred. Shall I come with you?'

'Yeah, er…' Freddie pulled his phone out of his pocket.

'What are you talking about?' Mollie asked. 'What just happened?' She was utterly confused.

'Don't worry, Mum, I'll tell you later. Love ya. Have a good day with Angie.' Freddie swiftly got up and swung his jacket back on in one fluid movement. 'When Michael does see fit to turn up, tell him to call me straight away, yeah?'

Paul clambered up from the table more awkwardly, shoving the last bit of the quiche into his mouth. Wiping the crumbs off his chin, he leaned forward and quickly embraced Mollie in a bear hug, then followed Freddie out.

Mollie watched her sons dart off and sighed heavily. She would find out what the big hurry was later, but judging by the looks on both of her sons' faces, she could tell that something very bad had just happened.

They got in the car, Freddie in the driver's seat. Paul tapped away at his phone, biting his lip in concentration.

'What's it saying?'

'In a nutshell, the girl stepped out of the club late on Saturday night and that was it, disappeared. The friend went off to get the coats, and she was supposed to wait for her but seems she didn't. No one has seen her since.'

'Well, fuck. Just what we need,' Freddie groaned, visibly annoyed. They hadn't really been listening to the news bulletin up until they named the club that the missing girl had last been seen at. A well-known club in East London – one of Freddie's.

Now the police would be crawling all over them and not just the local ones. The local police weren't a problem. Freddie had enough of them on the payroll that they would never pose a real threat. A highly publicised missing-persons case, however: that warranted the specials coming in. And the specials could not be bought. Not the ones that Freddie had come across in his time at least. With them poking around, they would have to be very careful. This was the last thing that any of them needed.

Tapping away at the controls on the centre console, Freddie rang through to the club on the car phone. After three rings the call was picked up.

'Ruby Ten, Jessie speaking.'

'Jessie, put Terry on.'

The line became muffled as Jessie put her hand over the speaker.

'Go change that barrel, I'm going to the office,' Terry said to the girl, his deep, craggy voice sounding stressed. 'Freddie.'

'Terry. What do you know about this Katherine girl?'

'Not much. The police only called an hour ago, not been in here yet. Soon as I heard what they were saying, I got DI Fraser on the line and arranged for them to wait until I spoke to you. Press must have got an early scoop somewhere. I saw it on the news almost straight after the call. I was about to head over to catch you at CoCo.'

Freddie nodded. CoCo was Freddie's largest club and where he based himself most of the time. Everyone who worked for Freddie knew that was where to find him if they didn't want to talk over the phone. Although they used burners where possible, a lot of their phones still got discovered and tapped. It was just good sense to be cautious when discussing illegal or sensitive subjects.

'Yeah, don't. I'm on my way to you.'

'Right, OK. See you soon then.'

Freddie clicked off the call.

'Well, at least Terry had the sense to get Fraser to manage the situation,' Paul offered.

'For now,' Freddie answered gravely. 'Fraser won't be able to contain it for long. It's too high profile already. Don't know why the press have jumped it up so much.' He frowned. A woman on the missing list, last seen drunk in a nightclub wasn't that much of an uncommon occurrence. It had only been two days. While of course the family would be concerned, it would barely even be classed as a missing-persons case yet. She must be someone of importance. Either that or she was related to a journalist.

Whoever she was, Freddie didn't care. He just wanted to get the CCTV footage and all the information over to the police as soon as possible. He needed to wash his hands of it before the specials found an excuse to start poking around too deeply.

# CHAPTER FIVE

Grasping a coffee in each hand, Tanya strode down the street with a huge smile on her face. She whipped her long, thick red hair back out of her face and sidestepped a pothole. High, strappy stilettoes accented her bronzed legs and matched her flattering fitted dress. From behind her dark, oversized sunglasses, Tanya noted the appreciative glances and smiles that were aimed in her direction. She was high on life already today, but knowing that she was turning heads always gave her a buzz. It had always helped to balance out her deeply ingrained self-doubt.

She let herself into the club through the side door, humming happily under her breath, and made her way to the back office. This was where she knew she would find Anna, buried under the constant mountain of paperwork that seemed to go with the running of their club. Sure enough, as she pushed the door open with her shoulder, she caught sight of her beloved best-friend-cum-business-partner.

'There you are!' she sang, putting one of the coffees down in front of Anna.

'You say it as if you didn't already know,' Anna replied. 'Thank you – I needed this. I've been staring at the payroll so long it's beginning to send me to sleep.' She drank deeply from the take-away cup, shooting her friend a grateful look. 'So, where were you last night, missy?' She began to laugh as Tanya dramatically melted in the chair.

'Oh my God, I had the best night,' she replied enthusiastically.

It had been Tanya's shift last night, but Anna had received a last-minute text asking if she could cover instead. Of course she had obliged, not minding at all. But now she was curious as to what had been so important.

'So?' she prompted eagerly.

'OK, so do you remember me telling you about that guy? The one from that restaurant that I got chatting to a couple of weeks ago?'

'Umm…' Anna racked her brain, trying to place exactly which man Tanya was talking about. She dated a lot and nearly always dropped them by the third date. She got bored quickly.

'Oh, come on! You know who I mean – the one with all his friends. The one who caught my coat under his chair?'

'Oh, I vaguely remember you mentioning it,' Anna said, trying to recall the conversation.

'Well, he asked for my number that night and so we got texting and stuff, right. Then a couple of days later we went for a drink, down at that little cocktail place in Archer Street—'

'Ooh, I like it there. The flapper bar?'

'Yeah, that's the one. We should go there later, actually, if you fancy a drink.'

'Mm, sounds good. But carry on about Mr Restaurant. What happened?'

'Well, here's the thing – I think I actually like the sod. We had a really nice time that night, talked about all sorts for hours, lots of flirting.'

Anna rolled her eyes. 'Shocker.'

Tanya ignored her sarcasm.

'So, then he's messaging me constantly, right? Like, all smitten and chatty and full of like, I don't know, beans or something. And he tells me we're going out to dinner, which was last night. Gets all alpha male on me, saying he's already booked the table, that we're going to Hakkasan and to be ready to be picked up at eight. Didn't even ask, just told me.'

'Wow.' Anna's eyebrows shot up in surprise. No one got away with just 'telling' Tanya what to do, even if it was something fun. A few had tentatively tried in the past and she'd laughed in their faces. Tanya was not someone that anyone could control. She actively pushed against authority. This guy must have a real gift with delivering orders if Tanya Smith had actually taken one. 'So you just… went?' Anna questioned, an amused smile tugging up the corners of her mouth.

'Well, I didn't just jump to it. I'm not some pathetic, soppy twat that just does what she's told,' Tanya came back defensively, 'but you know… I like Hakkasan. They do really good dim sum.' They looked at each other and burst out laughing.

'So, OK, you went. There's nothing wrong with that – it's nice sometimes to be wooed.' Tanya sniffed and pursed her half-smiling lips. 'And then what? Why are you so flustered?' Anna asked, laughing.

'I'm not flustered, I just… I actually like him. He's funny and interesting and proper hot. He's some wanker-banker in the city. Had me laughing the whole night. And then we got back to mine and turns out he's just as impressive out of the suit too.' Tanya's eyes twinkled mischievously.

Anna threw back her head and laughed heartily. 'Well, good for you. It's nice to see you excited about someone. Have you told him about this place and everything?'

Tanya knew what Anna meant by *everything*. She was checking that there had been no mention of her link to Freddie. It was the same with any new person who came into their world. They had to be careful never to discuss Freddie or his business outside of their inner circles.

'Yeah, I've told him about the club and that you're my best friend as well as business partner. But that's it – I've not told him anything else.'

Anna nodded and winked at her. 'Great. Well, I look forward to meeting this new amazing man. What's his name?'

'Daniel Sharp. I was thinking if it's still all kosher next week that I could maybe invite him to your birthday?' It was just over a week until the big birthday bash Freddie had arranged at Mollie's house for all of Anna's friends and family. Anna had just wanted to do something quiet, but Freddie wasn't one for letting a celebration go without taking full advantage.

'My my – thinking ahead and everything, Miss Smith. This certainly is new ground, isn't it?' she teased. 'Yes, of course. I'll let Freddie know.'

'Great, thanks.'

Anna was intrigued by the man who had managed to break through Tanya's hard outer shell. Tanya always appeared to be on top of the world and happy with being single, but Anna knew that wasn't the real reason she hadn't found someone special. Deep down, Tanya wanted somebody to share things with, but she was so damaged she tended to push people away. It was a self-preservation mechanism, built up through a neglected childhood and over years of being used and abused by men while she sold her body. Life had been very different for Tanya over the last three years though. These days she had friends who loved her and a successful business to run. Tanya was proud of who she was and what she did for a living. But it still took a special type of determination for anyone to pole vault over the walls that she had so firmly erected.

'Anyway, why don't I take over and you head off?' Tanya said. 'You've been here for ages. Where are you up to?' She stood up and walked around the desk to peer over Anna's shoulder at the laptop screen.

'Er, about here,' Anna pointed to the screen.

'OK, I'll finish it. Go on – piss off. Go enjoy your life. And get some sun. I swear you're so pale you're starting to look like a vampire.'

'Thanks,' Anna replied flatly.

'Any time!' Tanya flashed her a brilliant smile, then took her place at the desk as Anna stood up.

'I'll be at home if you need me.'

'I did say "sun",' Tanya mumbled at Anna's retreating back. She rolled her eyes and settled herself in to finish up the payroll.

Anna let herself into the building with her fob and made her way up to their penthouse. Turning the key in the front door, she heard two deep voices in conversation. One was unmistakably Freddie and the other she thought sounded like Paul. She made her way to the kitchen and smiled warmly as her suspicions were confirmed.

'Hey, Paul, how are you?' She reached up to kiss his cheek briefly and smiled over to Freddie. He looked tense, she thought.

'I'm pukka, thanks, Anna. Yourself?'

'I'm great. Are you staying for dinner?'

'No, I've got to get off actually. Have some things to do. I'll catch you later.' Paul shuffled towards the door.

'Meet me back at Ruby Ten after hours tonight. Bring Sammy – fill him in.'

'Got it.' Paul closed the door behind him, and Anna turned her attention to Freddie. He sighed heavily, as if the weight of the world was on his shoulders. Walking over to the dining table, he turned one of the chairs and sat down, pinching the bridge of his nose and closing his eyes. Anna ran her critical eye over him and pulled a sad face. He looked stressed and drawn suddenly. He had been alright when she'd left him this morning. Something must have happened.

'What's wrong?' she asked gently. 'Are you OK?'

He gave her a tired smile. 'Nothing you need to worry yourself about right now.'

Anna screwed her lips to one side as she studied him. She didn't probe any further. If he could tell her, he would. If it was something he knew she wouldn't want to know, he wouldn't. That was how they did things.

Walking over to him she let him wrap his arms around her waist and pull her in. She stroked his head as he rested it against her and felt the overwhelming wave of love for him that she always did. Freddie was her rock, the love of her life. Often when couples had been together more than a couple of years, the burning passion that first united them would fizzle down to something calmer, but not with them. The intensity and fire between them had never dwindled and, if anything, had grown even stronger over the years. Anna knew without words that Freddie felt the same about her. They had a connection not many people experienced.

Leaning down she kissed the top of his head and breathed in the familiar, musky scent of him. Closing her eyes, she once again thanked the stars that they had been so lucky in finding each other.

# CHAPTER SIX

It had been a week since the disappearance of Katherine Hargreaves and the pressure was on. It turned out that Katherine was the beloved daughter of Ben Hargreaves, the Secretary of State for Justice. She was literally the spawn of the man who ran the entire police force, and she had disappeared outside of Freddie Tyler's club. It could not have been a worse situation.

The day they'd first heard about the girl's disappearance, Freddie had cleaned out the club of anything at all that could link it to his other businesses. Not that there was much there to begin with, other than the imitation spirits. Freddie was sure that this wouldn't be noticed, but he replaced them with legal bottles anyway.

He was immediately glad that he had because not long after a frantic and unexpected visit from DI Fraser the next morning, the specials had arrived in force.

They weren't stupid – they knew exactly who he was, and their guesses at what he did weren't too far off the mark. But they couldn't touch him for any of it. For one thing it wasn't their objective, and more importantly they had nothing solid on him. But it did mean that they were going to be as difficult as possible, in the hopes that they could pin something on him in the hunt for Katherine. It was obvious that they thought he had something to do with it, much to Freddie's disgust. He was a lot of things, but a kidnapper of innocent girls was not on that list. That was the problem with straight policemen though. The world was black and white to them. You were either bad or you were good. They didn't understand the shades of grey in between.

Freddie had been as accommodating as he possibly could, providing the CCTV footage and access for questioning to all of the staff who had been working that night. He had also done some investigating himself on the side, hoping to give the police a lead that would take them away from his club. Nothing had come of it so far, and he was at a loss as to what to try next. The footage from the front door showed the girl happy and drunk, stumbling out of the club. She hung around next to the smoking area, playing with her phone for a bit, then wandered out of view. There was nothing else. She wasn't with anyone, at least not before she moved out of the camera's reach. The bouncers were busy at the time, keeping a careful eye on a group of high-spirited men who were beginning to argue between themselves. No one had seen anything. No one even remembered her. Freddie wasn't surprised. The bar staff had hundreds of people to deal with, a new face every minute or so and three other voices calling out to them at any one time. The bouncers focused on making sure the numbers didn't get too high and that the peace was kept, despite the usual club-related mix of testosterone, hormones and alcohol.

Yet still the police kept eyeing him and re-questioning him as if they were sure it was something to do with him. It was tiring, and Freddie's patience was starting to grow very thin. Wherever he was, whenever he tried to get on with the day-to-day running of his businesses, they turned up throwing more questions at him. At this point he wanted to find the damn girl more than they did. But there were no leads whatsoever. The girl had vanished without a trace.

As he walked down the old cobbled path to the Portakabin he kept on the docks, Freddie breathed in deeply. He felt stressed and frustrated. The air was filled with the sound of men loading and unloading crates on the boats moored there. None of the boats around him held any of his goods today. With the specials breathing down his neck and turning up uninvited wherever he went, he had rerouted the shipments to come in further east for the time being.

It was a warm day, the sun coming through a thin layer of cloud and sparkling off the murky water. He lifted his face to the warmth. As he passed each boat, respectful salutations were called out to him. He nodded politely back to each crew. Some of them worked for him on an ad-hoc basis; all of them knew who he was and that his word was law in the shipping lanes.

As he neared his Portakabin one of the dock supervisors hurried towards him. Alan was on Freddie's payroll and kept an eye on everything here.

'Freddie, you've got a visitor. She's in there waiting for ya; said you'd be down here soon.'

Freddie sighed exasperatedly. 'Fuck sake. How'd she know that?'

He raised his eyes to the sky as if looking for answers. Sarah Riley was the woman heading up the investigation. She clearly hated Freddie and had made it her personal mission to make his life hell until she found Katherine Hargreaves. DI Fraser had quietly informed Freddie that Riley hadn't been the original DCI assigned to the job. She had replaced whoever that was supposed to be, on special orders from Ben Hargreaves himself. Apparently she was part of a team directly under Hargreaves. She had turned up wherever Freddie was working every day this week so far. Each irritating time had been at one of his clubs though, which Freddie could understand. They were registered businesses – with a small spark of intelligence and a good police tail she could predict which one to find him in easily. He had no idea how she could predict his arrival at a small Portakabin on the docks though, at least not before he even arrived. He figured he had a small head start at least.

A confused frown crept over Alan's face. 'Sorry, Freddie. I thought she was OK, being family and all.'

'What?' Now it was Freddie's turn to be confused.

'Thea – your sister. I thought it was OK. I'm sorry, Fred.' Alan shifted his weight uncomfortably. He played with the worn flat cap in his hands and started to turn red, mortified that he had read things so wrong. Freddie suddenly laughed and Alan looked up at him, startled.

'Thea. Right, of course. Sorry, mate,' Freddie squeezed the older man's shoulder and a look of pure relief flooded across his face. 'Thea's fine, 'course she is. I assumed you meant someone else. On that note actually' – Freddie looked back up the path over his shoulder – 'I have a tail on me. There will probably be another woman arriving soon. Keep an eye out for her and shoot me a heads-up.'

He walked off towards the Portakabin, checking his watch. 'You'll know her when you see her. Brunette, angry, dresses like a plod who's trying not to look like one. Might growl at you. Bit like a bulldog after a bone. I'm the bone.'

Alan chuckled. 'No worries. I'll let you know when she arrives.'

Freddie walked in and found Thea spinning round and round on the office chair with her head laid back over the top, staring at the ceiling.

'Do you know you have exactly forty-eight of these polystyrene ceiling tiles?' she stated without looking up.

Freddie looked up at them and shrugged. 'No, I didn't. Thank you for that insight.'

'Yeah, you really should stop hiding your books up there. It took me exactly three minutes to find them. And I wasn't even looking.'

Freddie narrowed his eyes. 'They were there temporarily, and besides, I have eyes on this place all the time. Anyway' – he took a seat opposite her – 'to what do I owe this pleasure?'

Thea stopped spinning and sat up, grinning. She leaned forward on the desk, eagerly. 'Well, you know I've started this photography course?'

'Yes.'

'I'm loving it. I really am. I don't think I've ever been more excited about anything,' Thea enthused. 'It's like I've found my passion. And Edward, my teacher' – Freddie made a mental note to vet Edward – 'he says that I have a real gift, that I see things other people don't. He says that's what makes a successful photographer.'

'Well… that's great, Thea,' Freddie offered.

'Thanks. I've done a few shoots on my own lately; just been wandering through the city taking pictures of the things I want to capture. I have a few prints here to show you.' Thea reached down by her legs and pulled up a thin folder. She handed it to Freddie and he opened it up, spreading the contents over the desk. They were mainly in black and white with a few in colour.

'I was hoping I might convince you to help me showcase my work, maybe put some up in your clubs? And I was thinking maybe you could see if Anna might put some up in hers? You know, only if she wants – she don't have to feel obligated or nothing. I was just wondering, you know.' Thea bit her lip anxiously as she waited to see what Freddie thought of her work. She had always looked up to her older brother. He had always helped and supported her in every way; his opinion mattered to her greatly.

Freddie looked over the prints slowly, one by one. He was impressed. He had always admired Thea's photos when she'd shared her hobby before, but these weren't just pretty pictures snapped on a fun day out – these were works of art. The pictures were moody and dark and truly captivated him. One of the prints looked down one of the older streets in the East End. Freddie guessed it to be early evening by the way the light fell on the brickwork. There were big grey clouds rolling in and a lone little boy playing in the road. Another was looking up through the ironwork of a bridge from the road underneath, with the blurry image of a train driving overhead. He went through each one, becoming more and more impressed. Eventually he put them down and nodded slowly, his face not giving anything away.

'Well,' Thea prompted, 'what do you think?'

'I'm not going to let you try and flog these in my clubs, Thea,' he said finally, shaking his head. Her face dropped. He grinned. 'I'm going to buy them from you and put them up as paid-for works of art. With all your details underneath, should anyone wish to follow in my good taste.'

Thea laughed with glee as she realised what he was saying to her. 'Oh you bugger!' She reached forward and slapped his arm playfully. 'Thank you. I'm so glad you like them. I picked these ones specifically for you.' She looked down at her work, smiling from ear to ear. 'You ain't paying for them though. You already paid for my course and all my camera equipment. This can be my payback.'

'Bloody expensive pictures then,' Freddie joked, laughing.

'Oh shut up, you. You know what, when I was—'

There was a frantic knock at the door and whoever it was opened it straight away, cutting Thea off.

'Sorry.' Alan looked flustered as he tried to get his message out quickly. 'It's just – it's – she's here.' His eyes darted back over his shoulder. He pulled a face at Freddie.

'Right. Thank you, Alan.'

Alan stepped back and a few seconds later a new figure appeared at the door.

# CHAPTER SEVEN

At five feet eight and with a broad, almost Amazonian frame, Sarah Riley was a formidable sight. The fitted designer trouser suit flattered her athletic physique while giving off a no-nonsense air. She had an interestingly handsome face with a strongly defined jawline and high cheekbones. Her dark hair was set perfectly with not one strand out of place. She would have fitted in well with any given military group, Freddie thought. She stepped into the Portakabin, seeming to fill the small space, then looked around slowly and deliberately, her nose in the air and an expression of cold curiosity on her face. His intense frustration began to bubble towards the surface and he pushed it down, faking a polite, casual smile.

'Miss Riley, what an expected pleasure.'

She smiled at him, narrowing her eyes like a cat. 'Well, I wouldn't want to disappoint you, Freddie, let you think there was a little corner of your empire that I couldn't reach now. What is it that you do here anyway?' She cocked her head to the side and raised one eyebrow.

'Here? Well, I just happen to really like watching the ships coming in and out,' he replied innocently. 'This office exists purely for my own self-indulgence.'

Thea sat silently, waiting for Freddie to let her know what he wanted her to do. She had figured out that this must be the DCI that was breathing down his neck and took an instant dislike to her, bristling at the way the woman looked down her nose at her brother.

Freddie's fingers moved slightly and she stood up. He had given her one of their signals, asking her to leave. They had a series of signals that only the family-in-the-know knew. They were so discreet that no one else would realise that they were communicating. Which was something they often needed in their line of business. Although not directly involved and technically classed as a civilian, Thea was kept aware of all the business dealings and ran the books for Freddie privately. She had been his personal accountant, hiding and laundering his money for years.

Thea's movement drew the DCI's attention to her.

'Ah, the sister. What are you doing here, princess? Come to pick up your pocket money?' Riley taunted. 'Don't actually work, do you? You just seem to live off your brother's generosity as far as I can see.' She waited for a response but received nothing but a stony look. Narrowing her eyes, she continued. 'Or perhaps I've missed something. He runs whorehouses, doesn't he, your big brother? Is that where you come in? Do you work as one of his girls?'

Thea's mouth and eyes shot open at the insult. 'You what?' she cried, incredulous.

Freddie stood up abruptly and turned his back to the detective, facing his furious sister.

'Thea, I'll catch up with you later. Leave these here – I'll send them to the framers and get them sorted out. If you have a preference for how they're done, text me.'

Thea breathed deeply, ready to tear the smug smile off the DCI's face. Instead she listened to Freddie. She knew he would deal with it. He wouldn't accept that sort of talk towards his sister. Bigger men would lose a limb for insults like that. She might be the filth, but she would still face something.

'Right. Yeah, I'll text you what to tell them for the mounts and that. See ya later.' Picking up her handbag, Thea walked round the table and paused by DCI Riley. 'I earn every penny I have by using my brain rather than lying on my back. But perhaps you know more about that sort of thing than me. After all' – she looked her up and down – 'you might look like the back end of a bus, but you're an expensive one, eh? I doubt a pig's wage would have been able to wrap you in Dolce & Gabbana. You knocking off the boss for some extra cash?' Thea smirked, then leaned in and curled her lip. 'You wanna watch who you're talking to, you smug cunt. You think you know who he is.' She shook her head slowly, her mouth forming a hard smile. 'You don't.'

DCI Riley smirked and watched as Thea left, the door shutting behind her. She laughed lightly and folded her arms. Turning back to Freddie with another quip fresh on the tip of her tongue, she was met with a large, strong hand connecting with her neck. Taken by surprise she was slammed backward onto the desk, on top of the prints that Thea had left behind. Freddie's vice-like grip tightened around her neck, and she grappled at his wrist, trying to get him off. Her eyes were wide with panic, and she kicked her feet out trying to connect with him. Freddie positioned his body so that she was unable to do so. He leaned over her helpless figure, venom in his eyes.

'Like my sister said,' he said through gritted teeth, his voice hard, 'you think you know who I am. You don't. You don't have the first fucking clue who I am or what I'm capable of. No one talks to one of mine the way you just did.' He tightened his grip further and the panic in her eyes grew to outright fear. She was beginning to realise that she was way out of her depth. She had poked the wrong bear. 'You ever insult my sister or anyone else in my family like that again, you won't even live to regret it. Understand?'

With one last cold stare into her frightened eyes, Freddie let go. Riley immediately fell to the floor and began coughing, her lungs desperately straining for oxygen. She grasped her throat, where Freddie's hands had been. He removed the gloves that he had put on as Thea left. An action Riley had been too overconfident to notice.

'Whatever you think you know about me or my business, let me make something clear – you will never gain an upper hand with me. So you may as well stop wasting both our time and start focusing on your actual job,' Freddie spat. 'I mean, let's be frank shall we, Detective? Finding that bird is in my interest too. All this is bad for business. Like I've told you already, I had nothing to do with it. Even if I was into kidnapping women, which I'm not, drawing attention to myself – in my own fucking club, more to the point – is not exactly something I like to do. Think about it, for fuck's sake.'

Freddie pulled a cigarette out of the box in his pocket and lit it, before drawing deeply on it. He exhaled the smoke loudly and opened the door. Sarah Riley sat on the floor, her back against the desk and one hand still at her throat. She seemed to have calmed down, though, and was actually listening to him for a change. He stared out at the boats being loaded and the scene around them.

'I do actually like watching the boats, you know,' he said absentmindedly. Turning back to look at her again, his face was hard. 'I will help you in any way I physically can. If I find out anything, even the smallest detail, you will be the first person to know. If you have a genuine question to ask me, you can phone me or Terry at any time. But other than that, you can fuck off and leave me and my business alone.'

He watched as she stood up awkwardly and straightened her suit, regaining her composure. 'Next time,' he added as she walked towards the open door, 'I might not ask so nicely.'

She paused and narrowed her eyes at him hatefully. 'I could arrest you for that – have you banged up before you could even blink,' Riley said through gritted teeth.

'But you won't,' Freddie replied, his voice calm and confident. 'Because not only did you leave whoever you're with back out there at the car, giving you no witness and opening yourself up for questioning as to why you wanted to speak to me alone, you'd look like a prize twat too. And we both know your ego won't allow that.'

Freddie stared her out, his gaze casually level. Riley's eyes burned for a second before she looked away.

'The only reason I won't be arresting you today is because I think you may be of more use to my case on the outside. But that was still a bad move, Tyler.' She nodded to herself. 'You won't be of use to me for very long, and I make a very bad enemy. I'll be seeing you.'

'Good day, Detective,' he replied as she left.

When she disappeared from view, Freddie sat back down in his chair. His anger towards the woman still flowed through his veins. She was lucky that all he'd done was threaten her. He had known she wouldn't arrest him. She was too proud, and there was something about her that told him she didn't quite play things by the book. She would try to get her own back, however, of that he was sure. But that wasn't anything to worry about. Freddie had lived and breathed this life for a very long time. He protected himself from threats every day. Sarah Riley was playing a game that she was completely unprepared for. There was no way on earth that she could actually win.

*

Sarah Riley scowled furiously at the men around her as she walked back through the docks and up the cobbled path towards the uniformed colleague she had left in the car. She should have taken him in with her, really, but she had wanted to bait Freddie; she had wanted to put him on the back foot, make him uncomfortable. It had totally backfired. She had assumed that he would be scared of her, less powerful than her, the way criminals should be. But he wasn't. Instead he had shown her how foolhardy she had been and had literally slammed her back in her place.

*Scum, the lot of them,* she thought bitterly. The fact that they ran around London in plain sight, living as though they were some sort of royalty, burned through her. How dare they? How dare they have the gall to say or do anything to her? They were criminals. She was a bloody DCI, for fuck's sake, and she gets treated like that?

'No way,' she muttered angrily under her breath. Freddie said she had no idea who he was; well, he had no idea who she was either. 'No fucking way. That was a big mistake. I will get you for that, Tyler. Not right now, oh no. But I will get you, if it's the last thing I do.'

# CHAPTER EIGHT

Tanya walked into the restaurant and scanned the room for her date. Daniel waved his hand to catch her attention. The head waiter flew over, having just realised that there was someone waiting to be seated. It was a busy night and he was a waiter short.

'So sorry to keep you waiting. Have you—'

'No worries; I'm with him.' Tanya pointed.

'Ah, perfect. I will be with you shortly to take your drinks order.'

'Great, thanks.'

The waiter scurried back to what he'd been doing before, and Tanya began to wind her way through the crowded restaurant. Eventually reaching the table she sat down.

'Christ, it's busy in here, ain't it?' Her thick East End accent came through clearly as she laughed.

'Yes, I was lucky to get a table,' Daniel replied. He grinned at her eagerly, bright white teeth shining evenly. Expensive teeth, Tanya thought.

'I ordered some wine, but I can get you something else if you would prefer?' he asked politely.

'No, wine's fine, thanks,' Tanya replied, squeezing his hand happily. He always made her feel so warm inside, being so polite and gentlemanly towards her like this. It wasn't something she was used to. She liked it.

She looked him over fondly. His floppy, public-schoolboy haircut was, as usual, falling forward over his forehead and he flicked it back into place. His long nose and high cheekbones gave him a classically handsome look, and his clear-cut Home Counties accent captivated Tanya. She could listen to him talk all day.

Daniel was not her usual type. She didn't come across people like Daniel a lot – genteel, educated, gorgeous and single all in one. When she did, they never wanted to date her. They looked, of course – all men did, but when she opened her mouth and revealed her East End roots they turned their attentions away, back to the girls their posh mothers would approve of. Daniel, though, he was different. He liked Tanya for who she was and didn't seem to notice or care about their differences.

'So, how's your day been?' Tanya asked.

'Stressful. Better now that you're here.' He grinned. 'Had loads of management meetings today. Utter ball-ache. Just a waste of time that keeps me from doing my actual job, you know?'

'I do. I feel the same about my paperwork. I would much rather be coordinating the acts and running the club, but it's always there, staring me right in the boat race. To be fair, though, Anna does most of it. She's one of those people who would rather be tucked away in the office on her laptop than out with the punters or dealing with the front-of-house stuff. It works well. We're a good team, Anna and me.'

Daniel poured the rich red wine into Tanya's glass and handed it to her while she talked. She took a sip and pulled an appreciative face.

'Mm, that's pukka. What is it?'

'This is a rather bold Malbec from Mendoza, 2012. It's won quite a lot of awards apparently; thought we could try it.' He swirled the liquid around in his glass and tried some himself. 'Yes, this does go down well, doesn't it?' He switched his attention back to what Tanya had been saying. 'So, it sounds like you've found your perfect other half in Anna, business-wise.'

'Yeah, definitely. Couldn't be without her.'

'I'd love to meet her sometime. Maybe come and see your club too.'

'Oh, yeah sure, you can come any time. And I can't wait for you to meet Anna – she's my best friend,' Tanya said excitedly. 'Actually, as it happens I have an invite for you.'

'Oh?' Daniel raised one naturally defined eyebrow in question.

'Well, it's Anna's birthday on Saturday, and Freddie, her other half, is throwing this big party for her. There's going to be loads of people there, food, drink, music. It should be really fun. Would you like to come?'

'Ah, Saturday.' Daniel grimaced at her apologetically. 'I have to work next weekend so I won't be around. I'm sorry, Tanya. If I were here I would have loved to come. Maybe another time?'

'Oh right. Yeah, of course. No worries.' Tanya shrugged, trying to hide her disappointment. Asking a man to meet her best friend and come to a family event was a big thing for her. When Anna had been brought into the fold of the Tyler family, so had Tanya. They came as a package and were accepted as such. For the first time in her lonely life, Tanya was treated as part of a family with Anna and the Tylers. They meant everything to her. Introducing someone new, even just for a party, was a big deal. But she knew that she had to respect Daniel's work. He had already told her that he worked away most weekends. It was part and parcel of his job. Not many women would be happy spending their weekends alone, but it actually suited Tanya. Weekends were her busiest time at the club.

Daniel reached forward and squeezed her hand over the table, apology still showing on his face.

'How about I book something fun for Monday night, when I'm back?'

'Sure, yeah, that sounds good.' Tanya smiled, not wanting him to feel bad. It wasn't like he was being an arsehole. Work was work; she fully understood that.

'OK.' Tanya straightened her back and flicked her thick, wavy hair over her shoulder. She picked up the menu and began to check out the contents. 'So tell me, Mr Hotshot, what's good to eat here?'

Daniel slowly ran his eyes down her body.

'I can suggest a good starter and main, but what I want for dessert is definitely not on this menu.' His eyes burned into hers intensely.

She felt herself melting under his gaze and took a deep breath. She cleared her throat and tore her eyes away. 'Well, I'm sure I have something back at mine that would suit your tastes.'

'Oh yes. You most certainly do.'

# CHAPTER NINE

The rest of the week seemed to pass quickly for Freddie. Sarah Riley had backed off since his last conversation with her. Other than one phone call to Terry asking if there was any update, there had been a blissful silence. Finally free from constant scrutiny, Freddie had a lot of catching up to do. The businesses that had been put on hold were started back up again. Shipments that had been hidden or moved were rerouted back on track with extra men and caution, in case this was only a brief respite. Meetings that had been cancelled were rearranged and sites that Freddie had avoided in order to keep them hidden were visited.

Freddie was working on a new plan with Sammy to expand their gambling dens with an underground boxing ring. He'd always loved boxing. It would be an exciting new direction, and one that could bring in a lot of money.

He stepped across the busy street and entered Dot's, a small sandwich shop he often visited when he was over this way. There was a customer in front of him, but seeing who'd just walked in, the chubby woman behind the counter clicked her fingers at the teenage girl next to her. The girl looked up, her eyes widening as she saw Freddie. She quickly looked away and quietly took over the first customer's order from her boss.

The chubby woman wiped her hands on her apron and moved down the counter with a big friendly smile. 'Freddie, sorry to keep you; what can I get you today?'

'That's alright, Dot. I'll have the salt beef today, I reckon. Looks good.' Freddie pointed to the large cut of meat under the glass. Dot picked it up and took it over to the chopping board.

'I'll do you one nice and thick, Freddie. This is fresh in this morning, really tender.'

'Thanks, Dot.' Freddie smiled at the girl, whose eyes had crept back over to him under a set of long lashes. She immediately jumped and bowed her head, her cheeks turning scarlet. Freddie's smile faded slightly, and he turned to concentrate on Dot again.

He had spent most of his life building up a reputation that was both respected and feared by all who knew of him. It was how he had risen to the heights he had. Without that hard level of respect and fear, the wolves would descend. Most of the time it served him well. Sometimes, though, when a slip of a girl like this had heard of him and looked at him as though he was the monster who might steal her in the night, it felt like a heavy weight on his shoulders rather than a shield.

'Here you are, love. And take a drink from the fridge, too – it's a hot day out and that salt beef will make you thirsty. No charge.' The older woman smiled at him and waved her hand in protest as he tried to hand her a ten-pound note.

'Ah come on, Dot, you know I'm not going to allow that.' Freddie grinned and placed the note on the counter in front of her. 'Keep the change. Best sandwiches around, these are.' He opened the fridge and took a bottle of water out.

'Oh, bless you, Freddie. Thank you.' Dot beamed gratefully and put the money into the till. 'You have a good day now. See you soon.'

'Bye, Dot. Bye, Cassie.' Freddie didn't look back at the girl. She was probably shaking from his use of her name. He didn't want to see.

Dot's was not a business that he took protection money from, but he made sure that she knew she had his support anyway. It was a small business that she had started up from life-insurance money she'd received from her husband's death. It hadn't been a lot to begin with, but she'd used it wisely. Freddie respected her for that. At the time, she had two small children to look after and no family around to help. The business didn't make a big profit, and she worked all the hours God sent, but it provided her with enough to look after her children comfortably and she was grateful for that. Dot's situation reminded Freddie of his own mother's, back when his father had died. So Freddie made life a little easier for people like Dot, wherever he was able to. Even if it was just making sure people knew that she was protected. With all the bad things he did in his line of work it made Freddie feel more human, helping people who needed it. It felt like somehow it evened out the scales a little.

Turning down a side road towards his car, Freddie mulled over what else he needed to do that day. He needed to tie everything up as quickly as possible. It was Anna's birthday tomorrow, and he wanted to head over to his mum's house to check everything over, make sure it was all in order. He knew she wasn't a big birthday person, but he wanted to spoil her, celebrate her.

She would love it tomorrow, especially after a glass or two of champagne. He had a great present picked out too, though that was something he would give her at home, in private. He had chosen to hold it at Mollie's house because of the nice big garden, and he knew it would make her happy to be involved. Two birds, one stone.

He was just thinking about how Anna's face would look as she walked into her party tomorrow when he heard the low rumbling of a vehicle behind him. He stepped off the road onto the narrow pathway running along the side of the buildings. He carried on walking, holding his arm in; it was a very narrow back street. The car didn't pass but slowed down instead. He frowned. It was narrow, but he was practically hugging the wall. He couldn't exactly climb the fucking thing. They should be able to get past him fine as he was.

A door opened and Freddie turned, about to say as much to whoever was behind him. He opened his mouth but never got the chance to utter a word. He felt something heavy and hard connect with his skull; heard the sickening crack of wood against bone. He felt broad arms catch him as he fell, and then there was nothing.

# CHAPTER TEN

Anna woke up, her eyes blurry and heavy from a restless night's sleep. She buried her head back under the covers for a moment, too comfortable in her cocoon and too tired to get up just yet.

Remembering that Freddie had not been there when she last woke up, she reached out to his side of their king-size bed. It was empty and the sheets were cold. Disappointed she pulled her arm back and began to doze off again, not bothering to look at the time. She had worked at the club until late and so felt entitled to a bit of a lazy morning.

It wasn't unusual for Freddie to return home in the early hours of the morning or even the next day, depending on where he needed to be. It wasn't unusual for her either – they both worked through the night. Theirs was an unconventional lifestyle, but it worked.

Anna never doubted Freddie when he didn't come home. She knew who he was, and she knew how fiercely loyal he was to those he cared about. There had never been any cause for her to worry on that front.

Her phone began to buzz away on the dark mahogany bedside table. She groaned and ignored it, trying to get back to sleep. It rang off and she relaxed into the luxury mattress she had chosen with care, to enjoy on mornings such as these. Two seconds later, the phone started to buzz again. Tutting in annoyance Anna rolled over and grabbed the phone, rubbing the sleep from her eyes in an attempt to focus on the caller ID.

It was Tanya. She ignored it and pushed the phone underneath Freddie's pillow, where she was sure she would no longer hear the vibrations. Focusing on the remnants of the fabulous dream she had woken from, Anna drifted off into a peaceful sleep. Barely five minutes later, the key sounded in the front door. The sound pulled Anna back into the day and she groaned pitifully, pulling the pillow over her face.

She knew it was Tanya, even before she heard the tapping of stilettos coming up the hallway on the wooden floor. The bedroom door flew open and in Tanya swept, a vision of bouncy red curls and fully made-up smile. She jumped up onto the bed without ceremony and leaped forward onto Anna, hugging her through the covers.

'Happy birthday, old woman!' She laughed loudly as Anna mumbled protests and tried half-heartedly to push her off.

'Oh, Tan, you're squashing me. God, honestly, you're like a bloody kid. A kid who likes mornings far too much,' she moaned. Wriggling out of her friend's grasp, she pulled herself up on the pillows into a half-sitting position. She pushed her mess of dark hair back off her face and gave her tired eyes one last rub. 'What are you doing here anyway?'

Tanya rolled her eyes, her enthusiasm not dampened in the slightest by her friend's mood.

'It's your birthday, you twat. Now get your lazy arse out of bed – I bought breakfast. Where's Freddie?' Tanya looked around expecting to see him standing somewhere, looking as unimpressed as Anna seemed to be.

'I don't know – he didn't come home last night.'

'Oh. OK.' Tanya sobered up her face and nodded seriously. 'Well, it's understandable… you are getting on a bit now, aren't you?'

'Oh shut up!' Anna hit her on the arm, her expression jumping to one of amused offence. Tanya laughed and moved back out of swiping distance. Anna's eyes narrowed, but a grin crept up her face. 'You know he's not like that.'

'Yeah, I'm just messing.' Tanya smiled fondly at her dishevelled friend. She kept it to herself that Freddie used to be exactly like that, back in the days before Anna came along. She had been burned by the old Freddie herself, years before. But to his credit, with Anna he was different. No other woman had ever achieved the level of respect and care that Freddie showed Anna. The whole of London knew that Freddie was straight as a die, as far as she was concerned.

'Seriously, though, get up. We have things to do. It's your birthday, and I really do have breakfast sitting in the hall. It'll be colder than a nun's snatch if you don't get a move on.'

'Oh, right. OK.' Anna shuffled forward and slid off the bed. She grabbed her dressing gown and made her way out to the kitchen, resentfully resigning herself to the fact that her lie-in just wasn't going to happen. She sat at the breakfast bar as Tanya unpacked the big greasy breakfast onto plates and gratefully accepted the large coffee that came with it.

Tanya looked her up and down. 'You look like shit.'

'Oh, alright Tanya, thank you!' Anna complained. She glanced at the mirror in the hallway. Her hair was everywhere, bits stuck up over her head like some exotic bird. Her face was pale and drawn, and she had bags under her eyes big enough to do a week's shopping. Her dressing gown hung off her shoulder, showing the rumpled, baggy white T-shirt of Freddie's that she'd slept in. Tanya was right. She did look like shit. She nodded her acceptance grudgingly and carried on sipping the coffee. 'Some of us didn't get to bed until three, Tan. We can't all roll out of bed looking as glamorous as you.'

'Well, even I don't roll out of bed looking as glamorous as me. It takes detailed work, as you well know,' Tanya responded light-heartedly. 'And actually I didn't get to bed until about three either, but for much more fun reasons than you!' She giggled, biting into some toast. 'Eugh, this shit's cold.'

Anna rolled her eyes and stood up to make some fresh toast. Only Tanya would get a breakfast takeaway from a café and expect toast to stay warm.

'I'll do that – sit down,' Tanya bossed.

Anna did as she was told, not having the energy to argue. Her phone buzzed again and she looked down. 'Oh,' she exclaimed in surprise.

'That Freddie then?'

'No, sadly not. It's an old friend from uni – Amanda. She texted to wish me happy birthday, asking if we can catch up soon. I haven't seen her in years.'

'Ah, that's nice,' Tanya replied, pulling the hot toast out of the toaster. 'Why don't you invite her tonight?'

'No, it's OK. She's got kids and lives outside the city. I'd have to plan something properly, in advance.'

'Oh, she's one of those. A "breeder".' Tanya pulled a funny face. Anna laughed. 'Come on.' Tanya grinned. 'You need to eat this, get dressed and then we have to go. It's your party tonight, and you need to look hot. So we're going shopping.' She clapped her hands excitedly. 'We are going to get you the best dress ever. Tonight, my girl, is going to be a party to remember.'

*

Michael leaned back on his car and stared down the street. Freddie was supposed to meet him here an hour ago and still hadn't made an appearance. He was sure Paul had said he would be about this morning too, but so far he hadn't been able to get hold of either of them. Freddie's phone was going straight to voicemail and Paul's was just ringing out. Something was off. He scratched the back of his head and deliberated over what to do. He pulled his phone out again and dialled another number. It was picked up on the second ring.

'Anna, hi, it's Michael. Is Freddie with you?' He bit at a fingernail. 'No? OK, no worries… What? Yeah, it's all fine. I just couldn't remember if he was working this morning or not… I've actually just got a text come through, that'll most likely be him now… Yeah, gotta go, I'll see you later at the party. Bye.' He clicked off the call and bit his lip. He hadn't received a text – he just didn't want to alarm Anna.

He tried both Freddie and Paul again with no luck.

'Fuck sake, Freddie,' he muttered. With one more look in both directions, Michael got back in his car. He had things to do anyway; he would just wait for Freddie to get in touch. Turning the music up, he revved the engine and screeched off, leaving nothing but dust behind him.

# CHAPTER ELEVEN

Freddie started to come to and tried to open his eyes. He immediately closed them. The banging inside his head was intense. Like the worst hangover he had ever had and then some. He could feel the pain pulsating from the point on his skull where he'd been knocked out. It felt like they'd done some actual damage, the bastards. Whoever they were, they were dead men when he got out of here. They didn't want him dead, that much he knew. They would have already killed him if they had, and he couldn't think of anything he'd done that would warrant a good torture session, so hopefully that was out of the question.

He squinted an eye open again. They had some sort of cloth bag over his head. He couldn't see anything through it, but he could just make out that there was a light over to his right.

Careful not to move too much and draw attention from whoever was around him, Freddie checked his situation over. He was seated on a hard chair, his ankles tied to the legs, his torso bound tightly to the chair back and his wrists cuffed behind. Cuffed? He touched the cold metal thoughtfully. Not many people used cuffs. It was smarter to use tape or rope, something that could be burned. No evidence that way. These people were either total rookies or far too confident of not being caught.

Freddie tried to lick his lips and realised that they had been taped. He breathed heavily through his nose in annoyance. He heard someone shift their weight nearby and realised that he had given himself away. *Might as well get on with it*, he thought. It wasn't like he was going anywhere fast, tied up like this. There was a shuffling sound as though someone was leaning back and possibly pulling something out of their pocket. He figured it was a phone. He was right.

'Hiya. He's awake.' The voice was deep and hoarse. He had the accent of a Londoner who had picked it up over time but hadn't been born here. Freddie listened, trying to gather as much information as he could from what little was available to him. 'Yeah, OK. If you're sure… I guess.' The guy sounded awkward. He didn't want to be here. Freddie smiled. He might be able to work that to his advantage.

The bag was lifted off his head and the man stepped back. Freddie blinked, his eyes adjusting to the sudden light. The pain seared through his head again, but he ignored it. He wasn't surprised it hurt. They had done a thorough job of making sure he was unconscious. He tried to judge how long he had been out. From the stiffness in his body, it had been a fairly long time.

Freddie was surprised at his surroundings. He had expected a warehouse or some dilapidated building that had been totally forgotten about over the years. The room he found himself in now was unusually large and opulently decorated. It was a little old-fashioned, but it worked. The floor-to-ceiling drapes hung over the long windows, antique furniture and delicately patterned wallpaper contrasted starkly against the large, flatscreen TV on the wall and fire-escape maps were framed next to the door. He was in a hotel room.

The man in front of him was desperately trying to keep a poker face, but Freddie could see the worry behind his eyes. Freddie watched him and began to methodically work out who this man could be. The lines on his face and the naturally tight way he held himself indicated a very stressful life. The clothes he wore were practical, plain and inexpensive. Not someone who wanted to be noticed; no ambition. A wedding ring sat on a pudgy finger, and his hands were soft and clean. He was nothing more than a family man with a stressful day job and no real balls. So what was he doing here? Freddie dismissed the idea that he could be part of another firm. He just wasn't the type. But who else would have the balls and the need to kidnap an East End baron like him off the street in broad daylight?

'Um… I'm going to take the tape off now,' the man said, his tone nervous. 'Don't bother making any noise – we have the whole floor. No one will hear you.' He stepped forward and gingerly picked at the corner of the tape until he had it in his grasp. With one swift movement, he yanked it off. Freddie let out a small, tight breath and then narrowed his eyes.

'Why on earth would I shout out?' he asked, rolling his eyes. 'If I was somehow saved by some do-gooder down the hall, there would be the question as to why I had been taken in the first place. And as much as I am currently unaware myself as to why that is, I don't want the fucking filth on my doorstep any more than you do, mate.'

The man's puffy face turned a deep shade of red, and he cast his eyes down to the ground.

Freddie frowned. 'Or maybe you do want the filth to find you… is that it? Why would you want that, after you've just kidnapped someone? Do you even know who I am?'

'Yes. You're Freddie Tyler, the gangster,' he answered seriously.

Freddie laughed, totally confused by the man he was faced with.

'Who was that you called?' He was met with silence. 'Who's your boss?' More silence. Freddie frowned, trying to work out a way to draw the man into further conversation.

The door swung open, and the man's face flooded with relief. 'Can I go now?' he addressed the tall, severe-looking woman who walked in. She nodded curtly at him, and he made a hasty exit. Freddie made a strange sound, half laughing, half groaning as he realised who she was. He threw his head back and looked to the heavens for a moment as everything began to click.

'DCI Riley, now this actually is a surprise. I thought you piggies were too clean to be going around kidnapping people? If I'd thought you had a dark side I would have put you on my payroll ages ago,' he taunted, an amused smile on his face. 'Guess that explains the cuffs. You've been gagging to cuff me for a while, haven't you?'

He watched her cross the room towards him. He was beginning to connect the dots, now that he had seen Riley had a hand in it, but he needed confirmation. He tried to wind her up in the hope she would snap straight to the point. 'I know you want me, Sarah, but I'm pretty sure kidnapping me and tying me up is a step too far. Or is your lust for me just too strong for you to care?'

'Shut up, Tyler. I wouldn't touch you with a bargepole.'

He smiled lazily and cocked one eyebrow in disbelief. Her face immediately coloured, and she looked away at the window angrily. Freddie laughed under his breath. He knew she found him attractive, and he also knew she hated herself for it. She despised Freddie as a person and couldn't forgive herself for being so weak.

'So why am I here then, if not for your own personal amusement? You can't arrest me. Aside from the fact you have nothing on me, I'm tied to a chair... so I think you know any case you tried would be thrown out the second I sue you for mistreatment.'

'Mistreatment?' Sarah sneered.

'Yes, mistreatment, Miss Riley. I'm a very delicate soul, me.' He nodded soberly.

Sarah stared at Freddie hatefully, her arms folded across her chest. Suddenly she smiled, broadly and relaxed, sitting down at the table. Freddie blinked, not expecting the change. She crossed her legs and reached for the glass bottle of water standing next to two clean tumblers.

'Well, I wouldn't worry about that, flower. You aren't here for anything above board. Should suit you to the ground actually. Oh' – she looked at the water and then back at Freddie – 'did you want some? You must be very thirty after your ordeal.'

'Yeah, that would be good,' Freddie answered carefully, not knowing where she was going with all of this. He waited as she poured a glassful and drank deeply from it. His mouth felt dryer than ever. There was a strange, bitter taste too. He suspected they might have used something on him, laudanum or some other drug, to keep him knocked out while they moved him.

She looked over and he raised an eyebrow, still waiting.

'Oh, I asked if you wanted some. I didn't say you could actually have it.' Her smile spread across her whole face as his eyes narrowed. He closed his mouth and looked away, nodding. He wasn't going to give her the satisfaction of rising to it. He shut his eyes briefly as a wave of dizziness washed over him. He felt totally drained.

'What time is it?'

'Just coming up for ten.'

'What?' Freddie frowned at the window. It was still bright daylight outside. 'It can't be, it's still… Jesus! Do you mean in the morning? Have I been here all night?' Freddie strained against the binds holding him. 'Get me out of here, Sarah, *now*. This isn't funny.'

She had begun to laugh at him as he jolted the chair back and forth, trying to loosen the rope around his legs.

'Untie me now!' he roared in frustration as she totally ignored his pleas. He couldn't get out himself; he was tied too well. He took some deep breaths, trying to calm down. His anger just seemed to be fuelling her amusement. It wasn't going to get him anywhere. He pushed down the urge to lose it again with difficulty. 'Fuck,' he breathed.

It was Anna's birthday today. She would have woken up alone. Hopefully she would forgive him for that. She was pretty good about that sort of thing, understanding that his work kept him away some nights. But he needed to get back to her today of all days. On top of that, he had his work cut out for him. He had missed a whole night and most of the morning. There were things that needed doing. How dare that jumped-up bitch take him like this?

'Why have you even taken me? What do you want? Bit over the top, don't you think?'

Sarah smirked, enjoying his discomfort. 'I told you that you wouldn't get away with it, that shit you pulled down the docks. I told you I'd get you back.'

'What and risk me making a formal complaint? You realise you've given me the ammo I need to make sure you're never allowed near me again?'

'Oh, I wouldn't be too sure about that.'

'What's that supposed to mean?' Freddie demanded.

'It means that you won't be telling anyone about this little encounter, however badly you want to use it against me.' Her expression was confident.

'Why?'

'You can't touch me, not with who I work for. There are some people even you can't mess with. You'll be meeting him this evening.'

'What do you mean "this evening"?' Freddie began to raise his voice again in alarm. 'Sarah, I need to be somewhere. This little game, whatever it is, needs to stop. Now. Tell me what he wants and be done with it.'

'You aren't going anywhere today, Freddie. He wants to speak to you himself. I have my orders and that's that. Maybe if you hadn't been such a dick I could have asked a little bit nicer. But you were. So I decided to make sure you were here early.' She smiled at him sweetly, her eyes full of glee at the sight of Freddie Tyler so helpless.

'You bitch,' Freddie spat, anger and frustration boiling through his veins. He tried to focus on the situation rather than her. 'What could he possibly want with me, behind closed doors? And who was that snivelling no-mark in here earlier? What's he got to do with anything?'

'Like I said, you'll see later tonight. Your appointment is after work hours. Some of us actually put hard graft in each day, you know. Not like you.'

'You have no idea what I do every day and the work I had to put in to get where I am today, DCI Riley.' Freddie spoke her name as though there was a bad taste in his mouth. 'You also have no idea the advantages I have and what I can do to people who cross me.' He looked her in the eyes – hard. 'But you will. When whatever this is is over, you will.'

'Wrong. Like I said, you can't touch me. I have protection. You'll get over it eventually,' she replied smugly. 'Now I suggest we don't speak anymore, otherwise I might just replace that tape. You've got a long day ahead of you. Don't worry, I'll have some food bought in.'

She picked up the remote and switched on the TV. 'There you go. I've even thrown in some entertainment.'

She walked across the room and made herself comfortable on the bed, turning her attention to her phone. She kicked off her low-heeled black court shoes and let them fall to the floor.

Freddie stared out of the window. There was no point asking more questions – she clearly wasn't going to answer him. She would just take pleasure in his frustration, and he didn't fancy giving her an excuse to tape his mouth shut again. This was the worst possible timing. He squeezed his eyes shut and silently balled his hands into fists. Breathing deeply, he began thinking up ways of destroying Riley later, when he was back in the game. This, Freddie thought darkly, was the final nail in DCI Riley's professional coffin.

# CHAPTER TWELVE

Anna checked her phone for the hundredth time that day as the taxi pulled up outside Mollie's house. Just like all the other times, there were no messages and no missed calls. Sighing disappointedly, she put it back into her small clutch bag. Next to her, Tanya paid the driver and opened the door.

'Come on, love. I'm sure there's a very good reason for him not contacting you. There best be anyway. If there ain't, I'll lynch the bugger!'

Anna forced a smile. She knew Tanya was right. It just wasn't like Freddie to disappear like this, especially not on her birthday. She was starting to get really worried about him. Maybe something bad had happened.

'Maybe I should call the hospitals again.'

'You already did that. He ain't there. Come on, just come and enjoy your birthday, yeah? Whatever he's doing and whatever the reason, he's arranged all this, and you know he wants you to go in there and enjoy yourself with all your family and friends.' Tanya put her arm round her and guided her up the path.

'Yes, OK,' Anna replied. She would go in there and smile. She knew Tanya was trying to help. Tanya just didn't understand that the most important family member and friend in her life was Freddie himself. How could she fully enjoy a birthday with friends and family if he wasn't there?

She took a deep breath and walked through the door into the party, which sounded as though it was already in full swing.

There was a loud cheer throughout the room as Anna walked in, and streamers were set off each side of her, raining ribbons and sparkles down over her head. In spite of herself, Anna laughed. Thea was right at the front, taking photos of her grand entrance. Anna covered her face.

'Thea, you know I hate my photo being taken!' she said with a laugh.

'Sorry, Freddie's orders! Where is he anyway?'

'I don't actually—'

'Anna! Anna, over here! Happy birthday!' It was Amy, a good friend of hers and wife to Bill Hanlon, one of Freddie's associates. She waved excitedly across the room and Bill smiled a warm greeting. She grinned and waved back before being caught in a hug by her mother.

'Darling! Here you are! We wondered when you were going to get here. Happy birthday! Have you had a nice day?'

'Er, yes, thanks, Mum.' Anna untangled herself from her mother's arms and planted a kiss on her father's cheek. 'Hi, Dad. When did you guys get here? Are you—'

'Happy birthday, love! Come on in. Let's get you inside away from the door, that's it.' Mollie guided her forward into the crowd of people all waiting to wish her a happy birthday. 'Here she is, everyone! Anna, what do you want to drink? Come outside and have a look. There's a cocktail man who can make you whatever you fancy.'

'What?' Anna asked, feeling overwhelmed by how many people there were and how much detail had gone into the decorations that seemed to completely cover the house.

'Ooh, he's very good. I've had four already. And I feel absolutely fine. I don't think there's any alcohol in them meself. Four.' Mollie held up three fingers in Anna's face and nodded, her slightly glazed eyes wide.

'Right. Well. That's good then.' Anna watched Mollie bustle off and made her way out to the garden, saying hello to everyone on the way. By the time she had politely greeted everyone that she passed and reached the garden doors, Tanya had already skipped ahead and was back with a brightly coloured cocktail in each hand. She passed a fluorescent orange one to Anna and sipped at her own blue concoction.

'Cor, she's right, you know. These are bloody good. Mm.'

Anna looked outside. Her eyebrows shot up and she looked at Tanya.

'Did you know about all of this?'

'Some of it. It's pretty alright, ain't it?'

Anna shook her head in disbelief. The whole garden was lit up professionally, and ornate tables and chairs littered the edges. In the middle there was a black-and-white-chequered dance floor with a DJ behind, currently mixing chilled beats. The cocktail bar was off to one side and on the other was a hog roast, the pig crackling and spitting away as it turned on the spike. Around that were tables laden with enough food to feed a small army. At the back of the garden was a cordoned-off area and a man Anna didn't know, who seemed to be guarding it.

'What's that?' She pointed.

'I think that's fireworks. For later. Mm, I'm going to have to get another one of these. They're bloody good.' Tanya walked off, and Anna took a deep drink from her own glass. *Not bad*, she thought. Looking around she smiled at everything Freddie had arranged. He had gone overboard as usual, but it did look amazing.

The chilled house music washed over her and mixed with the sounds of easy conversation and laughter. She felt a sharp pang of longing for Freddie. She wished he was here to enjoy the party by her side. If he'd gone to all of this trouble, why would he miss it himself? Anna was seriously worried.

*

Inside the house, Michael paced the room, biting his lip. He still hadn't heard from Freddie, and now he was beginning to panic. He had finally reached Paul an hour before. Paul had sounded irritated for some reason and had just told him to wait until he got there. Michael had been watching the door ever since. Finally it opened and Paul stepped in. At once he flew towards the door, and before Paul had a chance to close it, Michael had dragged him back out the front so that they could talk alone.

'Paul, where have you been?' he asked, desperation in his voice.

'What's up with you?' Paul frowned, annoyed. 'I've been busy today. I told Freddie I wouldn't be around, that I had personal things to do. What's wrong?'

'So you haven't seen Freddie?' Michael questioned.

'No, I told you I hadn't.' Paul shifted his weight awkwardly and looked back towards the front door. 'I had some things to do.'

'What things?' Michael asked.

'Fuck sake, Michael, what is this, twenty questions?' Paul snapped. 'That's my own business, thank you – go mind yours. Does a man not have a right to his own life anymore? Jesus!'

'Alright, only asking!' Michael put his hands up in defence. 'It's just that Freddie's been on the missing list too; thought you might have been together.'

'What do you mean?'

'I mean, he didn't turn up to meet me this morning, and I haven't been able to get hold of him since. Neither has Anna by the looks of things. He ain't even here and it's his big party for her.' Michael pulled the packet of cigarettes from his jacket pocket and lit one. He took a deep drag and blew out the smoke, agitated, before smoothing down the front of his jacket. He hated appearing even slightly rumpled, at any time.

'Well… I don't know what to say to that. Where is he then?' Paul scratched his head and looked up the road as if Freddie might just appear there.

'I don't know – that's my point.' Michael internally rolled his eyes, waiting for his older brother to catch up. He didn't know what to do or where to go at this point. 'Sammy's in there, so is Bill and neither of them has heard from him either; I already checked.'

'Have you called through to CoCo?'

'No, but I figured if he was there he would have replied to one of my messages.'

Paul took out his phone and clicked one of the speed-dial numbers. He took the cigarette from Michael with his one free hand and took a deep drag on it as he began to pace up and down the pavement. Michael lit himself a new cigarette and waited.

'Aisha, it's Paul. Is Freddie in…? Has he been in today? No… OK, if he does turn up can you tell him we're looking for him. Thanks, love.' He clicked off and the brothers looked at each other in grave silence for a long minute.

'We can't all go or Mum will know something's up,' Paul said eventually. 'You know how Freddie feels about that. I'll go. No one really saw me arrive yet anyway. I'll take Sammy with me. Do me a favour and send him out. I'll be in my car. Stay here' – he took one last long drag and threw the butt into the bushes – 'keep everything under control and make excuses. I'll let you know when I find out what's going on.'

Paul sighed heavily and made his way back to his car. Michael walked back to the house with purpose. He wished he could go too, but what Paul said made sense. They had to keep things under wraps until they knew what was going on.

# CHAPTER THIRTEEN

Freddie stretched and worked each muscle again, as much as he could. The straight, hard-backed chair was incredibly uncomfortable, and his muscles ached from the strain of the position he was in. Every so often he worked them. It was to keep them ready, more than anything. There still might be an opportunity for escape – he just had to stay alert and hope they had a moment of slipped concentration.

Sarah Riley had come and gone throughout the day, leaving him with two burly minders. He had tried to engage with them, but they ignored him. He could tell they were in the force, most likely under Riley's command. He focused in on one of the plod's watches until he could make out the time. It was just after seven. People would be arriving now, ready for Anna to arrive at eight. He was glad that he'd roped Tanya into the plans. At least Anna would actually make it to her party, if nothing else. He always had a back-up plan in place, just in case. They came in handy at times like these.

'Oi, you – fatty,' he called out to one of them again, hoping maybe continuous annoyance would rile them into giving something away. 'What's the dinner plans then, eh? Do I get my hands this time or are you going to feed me another sandwich? Not very manly, is it, mate, feeding another man while he's tied up like a twat? That what you signed up to the force for, is it?'

The bulky man huffed slightly and turned the page of the paper he was reading. Other than that, there was no response.

'Nah, you signed up for the adventure, didn't you? Thought you'd be out there catching criminals, keeping the streets clean… modern-day hero, right? Yeah, you're the type. How's that working out for ya?'

The next page was turned again, not a flicker crossing his face. 'How is it that two big strong men like you are too pussy to even undo my hands? Are you that unsure of yourselves?'

The one he was addressing started to colour slightly. It was working – he was getting pissed off. Freddie's tone turned cold. 'Or is it just that you know exactly who I am and know that I'd fucking crush you, given the chance?'

Finally the man looked over, anger burning in his narrowed eyes. *Bingo*, thought Freddie.

'Charles,' the second man murmured from across the room. He shook his head at his companion. Charles gave Freddie one last hard look, then turned his attention back to the paper. He shifted his weight in the chair so that his body was turned away. Freddie rolled his eyes.

The sound of the door being opened caught his attention and Freddie waited with bated breath. Sarah Riley came in first, followed by three men. Two bodyguards by the looks of them and the man who had orchestrated this whole thing.

Tall, slim and attractive for his fifty-odd years, Ben Hargreaves walked across the room and sat down on one of the comfortable chairs around the coffee table. His dark hair was speckled with grey, and deep lines were etched into his forehead. He undid the button on his grey suit jacket and took off his tie, then ran his hands through his hair and over his face. He looked exhausted. His eyes were sunken into his face as though he hadn't slept in a month. His expression was haunted. None of these details surprised Freddie, knowing what he knew.

The two men in black suits stood behind Ben, one either side, and Ben frowned when he finally focused on Freddie, trussed up like a chicken in the chair.

'Untie him now.' Ben gave Freddie a cold, unapologetic stare.

Sarah stepped forward and took off his restraints. She was purposefully rough, making sure to drag the binds across the raw skin on his ankles. Freddie didn't give her the satisfaction of a reaction.

Standing stiffly, Freddie stretched his legs and back and rubbed at his wrists. He cracked his neck to each side and then sat on the small sofa opposite Ben Hargreaves, leaning back and placing his arms nonchalantly along the top of the sofa's low back.

'I can't say it's been the most polite invite I've ever received.'

Ben bent forward, his arms leaning on his knees, taking all of his upper body weight.

'Do you know who I am?'

'I wouldn't be very well informed if I didn't, Mr Secretary. And I'm assuming by the fact that you've gone to such lengths to get me here under cloak and dagger that you know exactly who I am too.'

'I do indeed,' he answered tightly.

'What I'm not entirely sure of is why. I understand the connection, but I don't see how I can help you any more than I already have through the normal channels. Unless it isn't help you're looking for but some kind of misplaced vengeance?' He lifted an eyebrow, questioning.

Ben shook his head and rubbed his eyes again, his expression irate. 'No, not vengeance. Not quite. Sarah, can you go get some coffee for us all please?'

Freddie waited quietly. He knew exactly who Ben was. He would be a fool not to. Ben Hargreaves was the Secretary of State for Justice. He was the head of the police force, the one who made all the big decisions, the face of the force on TV. He was the man who waged war on the royals of the underground, on men like Freddie. More importantly, though, at this particular moment in time, he was also the father of Katherine Hargreaves, the woman who had disappeared from Freddie's club.

'I require your help,' Ben stated bluntly.

Freddie shook his head immediately. 'I've given everything I have to the police already. I'm not withholding anything; I want this off my doorstep as quick as possible. Let's be blunt here, Hargreaves – do you really think I want a spotlight on my club, considering who I am?'

'I'm not talking about watching your CCTV tapes, Freddie. I want you to find my daughter.' Ben stared at him intensely. 'I have the entire police force at my disposal. I've had them working on this since she disappeared and nothing has come up. Nothing.' His voice shook with frustration. 'I know you don't have kids, Freddie. But imagine how you would feel if this was your sister, or your partner. What wouldn't you do to get them back?'

Ben took a deep breath to steady his exhausted emotions. He looked like a man on the brink of a breakdown, Freddie thought.

'I will do anything to get my little girl back home, safe and sound. And if… if…' He squeezed his eyes shut and clenched his fists. His breathing shuddered, but he forced the words out. 'If the worst has happened, if she can't come home… I want to know why. I want to know who and how, and I want justice. Do you understand?'

Freddie studied the haggard man in front of him. He was barely holding it together. As a rule, Freddie didn't work with people who were emotionally involved. It never worked out when emotion and business collided. But this was a very different situation to normal. If he did help the minister, he would have something over him to use if he ever needed help at a later date. That being said, this was a man who could destroy him in an instant if he chose to. His was a radar Freddie would rather not be on at all.

'What makes you think I can help you where the police force can't?' he asked.

'Let's not bullshit, Freddie. You might be good at hiding it on paper, but we all know who you are here. You're a piece of shit from the gutters of the East End who parades around taking what he wants and flouting the laws that uphold the society he lives in. You peddle drugs to kids, flesh to perverts; you lie, cheat and steal. You are the epitome of everything that is wrong in this world... But because of this, you don't have your hands tied in the way that the rest of us do. I want you to use all the contacts and the methods you have available to find my daughter. I don't have time to sit behind all the red tape. Whoever has her isn't painting her nails and playing chess – they are hurting her. I need her home, and I don't care what you do to make that happen.'

Freddie sighed heavily. 'I'll think about it,' he said.

'No. I don't think I'm making myself clear.' Ben's face turned hard, and his eyes bored into Freddie's, a strangely dead look to them. 'This isn't a request. You are to drop everything and start immediately. If you don't do as I say, I've had some evidence fabricated that can put you away for years. I'll have it planted and your premises raided like *that*.' Ben snapped his fingers. 'And if that isn't incentive enough for you, I'm going to make you a promise. If you don't do your job here, I'll also make sure that the same happens to your girlfriend. Oh, I know!' Ben put his hand up to calm a now-seething Freddie. 'I know she's clean. Crystal clean, actually, isn't she? That surprised me. Not sure what a girl like that is doing with a criminal like you, but there we go. She *is* with you. And so to make sure that there is no... confusion on your part, I'm going to pull her into it too. And to make sure you understand just how serious I am, I'm going to make you one further promise.'

Ben's gaze burned into Freddie, the determination clear behind his steel-grey eyes. 'If you don't get me what I want, after I've made sure that you're both banged up for many years, I will have one of my guards visit Anna's cell one night, hours after lights out. I will have her throat cut, as she lies there trying to scream. And I will make sure that she knows that it's all happening because of you.'

He sat back, watching the horror and fury build up in Freddie's expression. 'I am a desperate man right now, Freddie, and I no longer care what lines I have to cross to get my daughter back.'

Freddie fought hard to suppress the urge to launch himself across the room and rip the other man's face off. How dare he threaten Anna? How dare he even cast his thoughts that way? She was a civilian, off limits to those in their world. But then Ben wasn't from their world. He flaunted their rules with the same disrespect that Freddie showed for his. That realisation didn't stop him wanting to break Ben's jaw though. It took every ounce of his self-discipline not to eliminate the threat to his and Anna's lives right there and then. There were some people that even Freddie couldn't touch. And Ben was at the top of the list. He seethed – he had no choice but to do what Hargreaves wanted.

Sarah entered the room with the coffees and Ben took one from her. She placed one on the table in front of Freddie, then sat to the side of the room with the two men who had been watching Freddie when he was tied up. Freddie ignored the hot drink and stared at Ben, his eyes glinting with cold fury.

'Well, you've certainly stepped up your game, haven't you, Minister?' he said levelly. 'You don't exactly leave me much choice. Right, well… my brothers and I—'

'No. Just you, Freddie. I don't trust anyone right now. Especially those in your line of work. I know it wasn't you – as you pointed out, you have nothing to gain. But it could be anyone else. It could have been one of your men. That's why it must be only you who investigates.'

Freddie frowned and leaned forward. 'How do you expect me to find her without actually asking around and letting people know I'm looking?' he said scornfully. 'Think about it.'

Freddie watched as Ben's deep mistrust and common sense warred with each other behind his eyes.

'Fine. I'll leave your methods up to you, but just keep in mind, Freddie, it's you I'm holding accountable. If you fail, or if it ever comes to light that we have had dealings, Anna will die scared and alone in her six-by-four cell, and you will rot in yours for the rest of your life. Just so we're clear.'

'Can I go now?' Freddie asked curtly.

'Yes. Go. Get started. Here are my contact details.' He handed a piece of paper over as Freddie stood up. 'Sarah has your personal effects.'

Freddie walked over and took his phone, wallet and car keys from her. She was silent for once, but he didn't miss the smug smile on her face. Bitch.

'Remember, Freddie, knowledge of this meeting is on a need-to-know basis. There will be consequences if this gets out.'

'Yeah, I got that bit,' Freddie replied caustically. He walked purposefully out the door before he was unable to stop himself ripping Ben's throat out. He didn't look back.

# CHAPTER FOURTEEN

Freddie walked into Mollie's house while the party was still in full swing. Michael immediately sidled up and looked at him questioningly. Freddie had sent a text to both him and Paul, letting them know that he was OK and on his way over. They had been waiting to find out what had happened.

'Where you been?' Michael asked under his breath.

'Not now.' Freddie's reply was curt. 'Where's Anna?'

'Out the back with Tanya and Amy.'

Freddie stepped away from his younger brother and, smiling politely at everyone he passed, made a beeline for the garden. Anna was seated at one of the wrought-iron garden tables to the side of the open-air dance floor. Amy and Tanya were talking animatedly either side of her. She had a fixed smile on her face, but Freddie could tell that she wasn't listening. Her eyes were unfocused, and she was holding her body tensely. She was unhappy. A fresh wave of anger swept over Freddie. He was going to make Riley pay for keeping him away from Anna on her birthday. She must have known. It would have been the icing on the cake for her.

He crossed the lawn and stepped into her line of sight. Her eyes widened in surprise, then a real smile crossed her face. She stood up, and he gathered her in a big bear hug.

'Are you OK?' she whispered in his ear, worried.

'I'm fine. I'm sorry I couldn't be here.' He stepped back so that he could look her in the eyes. She saw his sincerity, but something else was there as well. She frowned.

'That's OK. But really, what's wrong?'

Freddie worked things over in his head. He couldn't tell her. The less people who knew the better. He didn't need any distractions; he just needed to get this sorted. Then he would have Hargreaves off his back and the threat to his freedom and Anna's life would go away. He gave her a tight smile.

'Nothing, Anna,' he said firmly. 'Now come on, let's enjoy this party.'

She tensed and tilted her head to one side. 'No, there's something not quite...'

Sammy came up behind them, holding two drinks. 'You made it, Fred. Here, you have some catching up to do.' He handed him one of the glasses and chinked it with the other. Freddie turned on the party charm and turned to address the guests.

'Better late than never, eh?' A few of them laughed. 'Now how about we show the neighbours what a good old knees-up really is?' He turned to the fences either side. 'And if any of you listening want to join us, come on over – the door's open!'

He put his arm around Anna's waist and kissed her forehead. Pulling her forward, he manoeuvred her onto the dance floor, where he swung her around and twirled her until she laughed aloud. He knew how to liven up a room when the need arose. He checked out her expression. She wasn't totally buying it, but he had managed to get her to ignore the issue for now at least. Distraction was often the best play.

\*

Hours later a happy but exhausted Anna collapsed backward on her bed.

'That was a genuinely fabulous party, Freddie. I have to admit, you have a gift. You may have missed your calling in life.'

'What, as a party planner?' He laughed, leaning over her and kissing her full lips. 'I don't think it would pay quite as well,' he joked. She laughed and pulled him in by the open collar of his shirt for a deeper kiss.

'I missed you this morning,' she murmured through the kisses. She pulled him closer, but Freddie pushed her arms back down and withdrew.

'I know.' He studied her face, a sadly serious expression on his own. He kissed her lightly once more, then stood up. 'I have to go out.'

'Now?' Anna hoisted herself up on her elbows. She was disappointed. She had assumed after being away for so long that his diary might have at least been clear just for tonight. She wanted to cuddle up to his warm body and fall asleep knowing that he was next to her. 'Can it not wait? For an hour at least?' She smiled coyly and tried to wrap her legs around his, but he stepped out of the way before she could get a good hold.

'Not tonight, sorry. This can't wait.'

Anna stood up and pulled his hands up to her face. She kissed them and was about to say something when she paused. Her eyes rested on his wrists. They were bruised from the cuffs. Anna's expression darkened. Freddie groaned inwardly, watching the expression on her face. She was trying to work out what had happened before she spoke. Anna's intelligence was one of the things he loved about her, but at times it really didn't do him any favours. She was too sharp to hide anything from. He shrugged out of her grasp and pulled his sleeves down over the bruises.

'Look, Anna, I can't talk about it right now, OK? Everything is fine. I have a bit of a delicate job on at the moment, one that… it's just going to take up a lot of time for a bit.' He shrugged his jacket back on, irritated. He was annoyed that he couldn't just tell her. But it was better this way. He needed to think with a clean head.

Her jaw dropped and her frown deepened. 'Are you serious? What the hell happened to your wrists?' she asked helplessly.

'Nothing,' Freddie snapped, much more harshly than he had meant to. 'Leave it.' There was a long silence.

'Right. Well. That's that then, isn't it,' she said flatly. 'Perhaps next time you turn your phone off for over twenty-four hours you could just send me a courtesy text beforehand. It would save me the hassle of ringing around the hospitals again like a complete idiot.' Her sarcastic tone couldn't hide the hurt that wobbled in her words. 'And I'm sure those bruises were just from walking into a door, right?' She shot him a tight, humourless smile and walked out of the room into the study next door.

She slumped into a big Sherlock armchair and folded her arms. She was shocked and upset and thoroughly pissed off at how Freddie was acting. She heard him walk through the hallway and hesitate by the study door. She held her breath, hoping he would come in but still too annoyed to make the next move herself. After a few seconds his steps carried on down the hall and out of the front door. It closed with a small thud and Anna was alone.

She squeezed her arms closer to her chest. Mentally she kicked herself for her outburst. It wasn't something she would usually do, but then again, Freddie didn't usually give her reason to. She took a deep breath and laid her head back on the chair. She knew she had to trust Freddie. The life he led was dangerous, but that was something she had known from the start. She had accepted life with him knowing that at times it would be hard and that there was always a chance he wouldn't come home. It was who he was, and he was good at staying on top.

Usually she didn't talk business with Freddie. The day-to-day stuff, the running of his various operations, she left well alone. That way, if ever it came up she could honestly say she knew nothing. But she knew the general gist of it. Some things he did talk about at length. They discussed the clubs; something she understood well, running a successful one herself. She knew that most of Freddie's money was laundered through the clubs.

Freddie respected the distance Anna kept from the details, but he had never kept anything from her if she outright asked. Especially if she asked about an injury. Freddie did sometimes come home showing evidence of some sort of struggle, but it was rare, and each time he'd told her what happened to put her mind at rest. That didn't worry her. It was part and parcel of his life, and she knew he was always one step ahead of the game. What worried her was that this time he was trying to hide what had happened. That had to be a bad sign.

Anna sighed and looked over to the bottle of whisky and the tumbler on the side table next to her. She picked them up and studied the tumbler for a moment, moving it so that the facets sparkled in the light from the corner lamps that illuminated the room. A gift from a business associate of Freddie's. She traced her fingers down the sharper edges, where it had been cut to the design. An expensive, empty gift. Opening the bottle of whisky, she poured a large measure and took a sip. The amber liquid burned her throat as she swallowed it down.

She blew out a long breath before taking the next sip; this was not what she usually drank. It was Freddie's poison. But right now she wanted to take the edge off and calm her head down. There was no way she would sleep now. She was in for a long night.

to hear one more word from you, unless it's actually useful.' He sat down heavily and took a deep breath. He didn't need this shit. Not from his own brother. Paul held his stare, his expression serious. After a tense minute, he broke the silence.

'I'll go scout about, see if anyone has heard anything. I'll start with the local estates. They won't have spoken to the police. Someone might have seen something. Call me if you need me somewhere.' He picked up his Barbour jacket and walked out of the room.

Sammy stood up and yawned. 'If she was picked up for trafficking, Viktor Morina should know something about it. He'll be in one of his dens now, but I can sort out a visit tomorrow,' Sammy offered.

Viktor was one of the more prominent Albanian faces in South London. A dangerous man at the best of times, he was known to have a very volatile nature. He could be laughing with you one minute and smash a bottle over your head the next, especially if he'd been drinking. At this time of night it was practically suicide to try to meet up with him. He would be heavily drunk, surrounded by a small army of followers in one of his brothels. The best time of day to try to speak to him would be late morning, when he would be almost fully recovered from the night before and ready to conduct business with anyone he needed to.

Freddie curled his lip. He disliked Viktor; didn't agree with the way he ran his business. But it wasn't his concern. The Albanians stuck to their own territories and Freddie ignored them. Freddie had no qualms about Viktor running whorehouses. He owned some himself. What he did have a problem with was how Viktor got his girls.

In Freddie's own houses, the girls were hired properly. They came of their own free will. They were looked after, protected and could leave at any time. It might be illegal, but no one was suffering. It was just business. Viktor on the other hand abducted his girls, got them addicted to heroin and forced them to work in poor conditions. They were mistreated, malnourished and were unwilling victims. Freddie had always turned a blind eye. They weren't on his turf, and he wasn't out to save the world. But he didn't like it either.

Sammy was right though. If anyone had taken her for use or sale of her body, Viktor would know about it. As well as his whorehouses here, his firm was linked to a chain of them across Europe, and he was also known to sell women directly to wealthy Arabs.

'We'll go together. Pick me up at ten.'

Sammy nodded and picked his phone up off the coffee table. 'See you then. Later, Mickey.'

Michael narrowed his eyes. He hated being called Mickey. 'Michael,' he corrected curtly.

'Sorry, mate, I've known you so long I forget sometimes. Night, guys.'

He left the two of them there. Freddie laughed at his younger brother's seething expression.

'He don't mean it, come on. We called you Mickey for years – it's a slip of the tongue.'

'Well, I don't like it,' Michael's tone was icy. A cold, strange look flashed across his face. Freddie caught it and paused.

'Alright,' he said carefully, watching Michael intently. 'No need to get your knickers in a twist.'

Michael blinked and sniffed. He looked away and puffed out his chest. Freddie hid a smile. He knew Michael had a big chip on his shoulder at being the youngest. He wanted to feel older. Harder.

'What do you want me on anyway?' Michael asked, changing the subject.

'I'm not sure to be honest,' Freddie answered. 'It's a bit of a dead ender at the moment. If you could just keep your ear to the ground, see if you can think of anything for the time being. I'm going to need more help with the day-to-day stuff. This is going to keep me busy.'

'Sure, no problem. Keep me posted then. I'll do the rounds in the morning and give you a shout after.'

'Great. Off you go then. Get some sleep. '

'Alright. See ya, Freddie.' Michael pushed up off the chair with both arms. He straightened the sleeves of his jacket, then, giving Freddie a nod and a smile, he set off. The door closed and Freddie slumped back into his chair. He stared blankly at the black-and-white photo print mounted on the wall opposite. It was one of Thea's. He sighed tiredly and rubbed his head. He felt like he had the weight of the world on his shoulders. All he wanted to do was sleep. He hadn't stopped, and his body ached for a shower.

Sitting up straight, he pushed those thoughts to the side. Sleep could wait. Katherine Hargreaves couldn't.

# CHAPTER SIXTEEN

The torchlight jerked Katherine awake. She opened her eyes and immediately squeezed them shut, the bright light causing her pain. She shuffled back on the mattress awkwardly, trying to half sit up and move as far away from her captor as possible at the same time. What time was it? Was it even night? She had no clue anymore. He must have come in while she was in a deep sleep. She hadn't heard him arrive. The torchlight backed off as her captor sat in the chair a few feet away. She tried to get her bearings. The room swam, and she groaned weakly. A harsh, hacking cough made its way out of her lungs and her whole body convulsed.

Katherine wiped the sweat out of her eye with her forearm. It had been so hot these last couple of days. Or at least she thought it was a couple of days. She was unsure how often she was drifting in and out of this uneasy sleep now. She was very ill, this much she was sure of. Her skin was burning up and everything ached. She was sure it was something to do with the festering wounds across her ankles. The binds had been too tight for too long. Cutting through the flesh, they seemed to almost immediately breed infection there. The pain was intense and inescapable.

Finally adjusting to the light coming from the torch, her eyes rested on the rusting bucket just to the side of the bed. It had been put there for her to relieve herself in, but he only took it out when it was practically full. The putrid stench coming from it made her want to vomit, but she forced her stomach to relax.

She couldn't afford to waste what small amount of food she was thrown each day. Her lungs spasmed, and her body curled as her coughs reverberated harshly around the small space. The involuntary motion caused her legs to strain against the binds again, and they pressed cruelly into her open wounds. Pus seeped out of one side. Katherine cried out, unable to contain the agony as what felt like hot spears shot up her shins.

'Please,' she begged shakily, 'please untie my legs. I can't move anywhere – it will make no difference to you. Please…' she trailed off, dizziness washing over her again. She lay back, her limp, greasy hair falling off her face. There was no answer, and he made no move to do as she had requested.

'Why?' she questioned weakly, hot tears of despair rolling back and disappearing into her hairline.

The silence continued.

She licked her dry lips, very aware of how furry her tongue was and how rancid her own breath smelled. She kept trying. 'Could you at least bring me some drugs? Some penicillin if you can get hold of some, or some paracetamol at least, to bring the fever down? I'm no use to you dead. And if I keep getting worse, chances are I will die.'

Her body shuddered again and Katherine fought to control it. 'You would have to… dispose of me if I die. And nothing stays gone forever. They always find bodies. There is always some evidence.'

He snorted, amused.

The torch moved closer and Katherine flinched. She never knew what to expect. The light focused down on her ankles.

Katherine narrowed her gaze, trying to make out any of the man's features. He was always behind the light, but while it was pointed at her feet she could just make out a side profile. She peered forward trying to see, but as she did the light swung back around and glared in her face.

'Argh!' She fell back, squeezing her eyes shut.

'Ah-ah-ah – naughty, naughty,' he tutted as he backed away again. Katherine blinked in surprise. The garbled sound that came out of his mouth made her realise he was using something to mask his voice. He sounded like some sort of broken robot. Her quick brain processed this. Voice changers weren't hard to get hold of. Any toy store held them in stock for children to play with. But the fact he was using one must mean he was someone she knew, otherwise why would he need to go to such lengths?

'No peeking, Katherine,' the deep, gravelly voice continued. 'I don't want you seeing my beautiful face and falling in love with me now.'

Katherine's veins filled with hot rage at his words and, forgetting her fear for a moment, she bit back at him. 'I could never feel anything for a monster like you,' she spat, furious. 'You aren't a man – a real man doesn't treat women this way. Doesn't treat *any* person this way.'

She caught herself and bit her lip, suddenly realising who she was speaking to. She tensed, ready to be beaten – or worse.

After a heavy pause, her captor laughed. 'So there is a personality in there after all. People never stop surprising you.' He chuckled. 'So, you don't think I'm a real man, no?'

'No, I don't. I think you are sick and have no idea how to be a man or anything else worth being.'

'I'm sick?'

'Yes, sick. Whoever you are, you aren't right in the head. It doesn't take a rocket scientist to see that you are clearly fucked in the head, and you know what? Whatever you do to me, they will find out. Because whatever else you are, you aren't smart enough to get away with it. They'll figure out it was you.'

Spitting this out with as much venom as her depleted energy would allow, Katherine finished off with a violent coughing fit before curling back up in the foetal position. She shook in terror as the torch came forward again. This time it pressed against her forehead as he uttered just one last word.

'Good.'

# CHAPTER SEVENTEEN

Freddie and Sammy stood before a rundown bar in one of the grottier parts of South London. Freddie looked unimpressed, his hands in his trouser pockets and one eyebrow raised. Sammy grimaced and waited. He knew Freddie didn't want to have to go in there and ask this low-life rat for information. But it was what it was.

What looked like it had once been black paint had peeled off the rotten wood of the front door. The wooden window frames were equally as neglected. The brick was pockmarked and adorned with graffiti.

'Would you have that as your main gaff for business?' Freddie asked Sammy, turning his nose up at the state of the building. 'I mean… really?' He gestured towards it with one arm, turning his palm upwards in question.

The pair looked totally out of place. Freddie was wearing his customary dark grey suit and white shirt, pressed to perfection. Sammy had forgone his suit today but still looked smart in beige chinos and a dark polo shirt. As ever, the polo shirt only enhanced how buff and fit he was. Freddie always joked that Sammy was really a Swedish bodybuilder in disguise, with his physique and pale blond hair. Now here they were, two sore thumbs in the wrong part of London. Freddie sighed heavily.

'Right, fuck it. Come on then.'

As they reached the door it creaked open and a greasy, rodent-like man gestured towards the back. 'Viktor says to come. He waits in back for you.'

Freddie and Sammy followed him through the dank pub, ignoring the pungent smell of stale beer mixed with BO and cigar smoke. The dark green carpet was clearly decades old, covered in stains with holes worn right through to the brick tiles underneath. Around them, seated at the tables, were clusters of men all staring at the newcomers with deep mistrust and dislike. Freddie pointedly ignored them and straightened his jacket. At the other end of the bar another door was opened, and they were led through a corridor to a large room at the back of the building. Freddie and Sammy entered and looked about them.

A round table sat in the middle of the dark, cluttered room. Shelves and side tables were covered in boxes and paperwork, and one small window let a few slivers of natural light in. Curls of smoke played in the light and hung in the air, where they were unable to escape. Sitting at the table facing them was Viktor.

Viktor stared at Freddie with an amused, cocky smile, and Freddie fought to keep his lip from curling in angry disgust. Gesturing with a scarred hand to the seats around the table, he nodded. 'Please, sit. It must have been long, stressful journey from all the way up there on your golden throne, Freddie Tyler.'

Viktor's thick Albanian accent came out in a mocking tone. The men around him laughed, and Viktor's cat-like smile grew, showing a set of uneven, tobacco-stained teeth framed with thin, chapped lips. His face was weathered and pockmarked, his skin sunken around the eyes and under his cheekbones. Freddie noted this quietly. It was a clear sign of how malnourished he must have been as a child. Freddie had seen it before, in some of the neglected junkies' kids in the council estates of the East End.

Wild, untamed eyebrows contrasted starkly with the greasy slicked-back hair that had been combed and gelled within an inch of its life. Each bony finger on his scarred hands was adorned with a chunky gold ring. Freddie wondered what had caused such extensive scarring but kept his curiosity to himself.

Viktor looked scruffy in a white vest, shell suit and trainers. Matching thick gold chains hung around his neck. Freddie sat down in one of the chairs. Sammy stayed standing but moved closer to Freddie. He hovered just behind him in a protective stance, wary of the weaponry that he could see the men around them were packing.

'You're right, it has been a long journey all the way down to this end of the food chain.' Freddie raised an eyebrow and smiled at Viktor coldly.

Viktor's smile disappeared and a flash of annoyance crossed his face. He had meant to unnerve Freddie and it had not worked. He barked an order to one of the men standing by.

'Go and bring us vodka. I believe Mr Freddie Tyler here has business he wish to discuss with me.'

The man scooted off quickly.

'We don't have time for vodka today, Viktor. I just have a couple of questions I was hoping you could answer.' Freddie pulled a picture of Katherine out of his inner jacket pocket and slid it across the table with his index finger. 'This girl, she disappeared from one of my clubs last weekend. I need to find her. Is she one of yours?'

Viktor didn't look at the picture. 'Why you care about one girl?' He held his arms out wide in question, then picked up the lit cigarette from the nearly full ashtray in front of him. 'Girls, they go missing. There are a lot that disappear.' He shrugged. 'She is not relation of yours. I know – I keep tab. It would be bad for business to take relation of someone like you.'

'No, she ain't a relation, but she's been taken from the front door of one of my busiest clubs.' Freddie's tone was clipped. He tried to stay polite, aware that he was in Viktor's territory here. 'The police are all over me like flies on shit. Specials, not the pigs I can control. I can't do anything until this is gone.'

'Why specials?' Viktor frowned, suddenly more alert.

'She's the Secretary of State for Justice's daughter. So it ain't gonna be dropped until she's found. I want to find her quietly and get this sorted, before it goes any further.'

'I see.' Viktor's tone was more serious now, and he pulled the picture closer to study. After a few seconds he flicked the photo back across the table to Freddie. 'No. She is not one of mine. All special orders are overseen by me. She is not a face I have passed on inspection. And she is too high class to be taken for the houses. None of my men would risk a take like that for common house girl.'

'OK. Could anyone else in your line of work have taken her? Is that something you could find out?'

'Possibly.' Viktor sat back, the corners of his mouth curling upwards. 'But what can you do for me in return?'

Freddie ground his teeth but made sure to keep his expression neutral. 'What do you want, Viktor?'

'I want space on your secure shipments over to Europe, once a month. I will pay you.'

'What for?'

'My special orders, of course.'

'No.' Freddie's reply was swift and automatic.

Viktor scowled at him. 'Why not? My money is as good as from anybody else.'

'I don't sell women.'

'Nobody is asking you to. That is my job.'

'I won't take part in it. Any other requests instead?'

'I do not need anything else. What I need is secure passage.'

'Then I can't help you.'

'I see.' Viktor strummed his fingers on the table and pursed his lips. 'You are the only player with decent access right now. You know you hold the monopoly?'

'I do.'

'You know... I didn't get here by luck. I came to England as a boy, as an immigrant. In my country my family were poor; we had nothing. I decided to change that. And I did. Not through being polite, not through taking "no" as an answer and not through caring about other people. I changed our position through making hard decisions, doing things that were not good and through climbing over the backs of other people.'

'That much I can believe,' Freddie answered.

Viktor gave him a humourless smile. 'I still live that way. If people get in my way, I will climb them like a ladder to get what I need.'

Freddie stood up abruptly and straightened his jacket. 'We're done here. Thank you for your help, Viktor. Goodbye. Come on, Sammy.'

Freddie turned and walked back out the way he had come in. Viktor's voice carried through after them.

'Oh, we are far from done, Freddie Tyler. But that can wait for now.'

Sammy followed Freddie out, walking at a swift pace. No one got in their way, and they were back out on the street in seconds. Freddie unlocked the car. They jumped in and Freddie started it up. Sammy looked back towards the pub as Freddie pulled away. No one had come out after them. He let out the breath he'd been holding.

'Good timing,' he said.

'Yep. He was getting ready to board the crazy train. Power-hungry ingrates like that are all the fucking same.'

'Still, he's a power-hungry ingrate with a pretty big business. We should keep half an eye on that. Make sure he stays in his box.'

'Mm.' Freddie nodded in agreement. 'Still, at least we can cross him off the list. Katherine isn't on the market. Sure, there are other players, but they're a network. He'd know by now if she was on there after all the publicity she's had. You saw his face – he hadn't considered it anything to do with him before today. It was new information.'

'True. So what do we do now?'

Freddie suddenly pulled over to the side of the road and stopped outside a flower shop. The shopfront was bright and colourful with all different bouquets displayed ready to be picked up and taken home to loved ones.

'Well, right now I have a different sort of fire to put out. And then I'm going to get some sleep and a shower. Cause I ain't slept in two days and I'm knackered. But after that we'll sit and work out what our next move is.'

Freddie got out of the car and slammed the door. Sammy watched him pick out the largest bunch of bright pink roses that he could find, then disappear into the shop. He chuckled to himself. His whole life was on the line and still he found time to think about Anna.

'Soppy twat,' he mumbled to himself, shaking his head fondly. He stared at the busy street and his face slowly turned sober again. They had a difficult journey ahead of them. He prayed that they made it through this one.

# CHAPTER EIGHTEEN

Late that night after a busy evening with the club, Tanya stepped out of the small newsagent's at the corner of her road and walked towards the front door of her building. Her bag contained half a watermelon and a litre of vodka. She had seen a video about frozen vodka melon balls and wanted to try it out at home. If it went well she would invite everyone over for dinner and serve them up as a fun dessert. Maybe she could invite Anna and Freddie over one night that Daniel was free. She had been looking for a way to introduce them to her new boyfriend; that could be the time to do it.

A strange noise sounded behind her, and as she turned to see what it was, a shadow disappeared down the side alley between two of the buildings she'd just passed. Tanya knew that there was nothing down there except a dead end. There should be no reason for anyone to go down there. She took a deep breath as she paused and watched the space for a moment. It was dark, and she didn't relish going to find out who, or what, it was. With one last wary look, she turned and carried on towards her door. The last few metres of empty pavement suddenly felt like a mile, and she hurried forward as fast as her Louboutins would carry her. The sharp taps of the stiletto heels sounded very loud as she strained her ears for any other sounds behind.

Holding her head high, she pursed her lips and wrapped her fingers around the keys in her pocket, placing one between each finger, knowing she could use them as a weapon if she needed to. She flicked her hair back and dismissed the stab of worry in her gut. She was a hard East End warrior, for Christ's sake. No one scared Tanya Smith.

Reaching the front door of the building she opened it and stepped inside. Taking a moment to scout the road with her eyes she nodded, satisfied that no one was there. She took a long breath and shook it off. As she took the lift up to her flat she wondered about the shadow. It wasn't the first time she had seen something odd. Twice in the last week she thought she'd seen someone tailing her, but each time they'd disappeared from view when she'd tried to look. Both times it had been dark and not sensible to check things out. She might be able to look after herself, but she wasn't a mug; she wasn't about to go looking for trouble.

Tanya entered her flat and walked into the living room. It was huge compared to the little place she and Anna used to live in together. Not that she had minded their cramped little home. It was the first place she had really felt at home in, and she and Anna had created many happy memories there. She had made some good memories in her new place too, though. It was a home she was truly proud of. The first property she had ever owned and where she had enough money to decorate and kit it out in proper style. She smiled happily, dropping the keys in the pretty metal bowl on the side unit. Something stirred at the end of the big cream couch and a small, fluffy white cat ran over to rub itself against her legs.

'Ah, Princess, 'ave you missed me?' She leaned over and stroked the purring animal. 'I have a treat for you in the cupboard. A whole tin of tuna, how about that, eh? Proper spoilt, you are, ain't ya? Come on then.'

Through in the long galley kitchen, Tanya emptied the fish into Princess's bowl and then walked back into the lounge. Kicking her high, black patent shoes off to one side, Tanya flicked the telly on to the news for some background noise. She liked having it on quietly, now that she was on her own. The white noise relaxed her.

Her phone beeped and she opened the message expectantly. She assumed it was Anna at this time of night. Her brow furrowed as she read the message and then read it again. It wasn't Anna. It was from a number she didn't recognise.

*Karma is coming for you.*

'What the actual fuck!' she shouted, shocked and confused. Her mouth hung open as she paused where she stood, trying to work out what it meant. The memory of the noise down the alley crept up on her again uneasily. Darting to the window she pulled the curtain to one side and stared down at the dark mouth of the alley. It was too black to make much out, but she was sure she caught a ripple of movement as though someone was turning away.

Tanya shivered. She felt cold suddenly. Paranoid, Tanya made a thorough check of her flat. There was no one there – of course there wasn't. She shook her head.

'You're goin' mad, mate,' she chastised herself under her breath.

After making sure the door was double-locked, she closed the curtains and sat down on the sofa with a blanket wrapped around her. She gnawed at a long red fingernail absentmindedly, staring at the text. Frowning angrily, she texted back.

*Who is this and what the fuck is that supposed to mean?*

Not used to feeling scared, Tanya rode her anger headfirst into battle. She waited several minutes, but there was no response. Clicking on the number, she tried calling it. It immediately went to a pre-recorded network message, informing her that the phone was switched off. There was no voicemail.

'Fuck sake,' Tanya huffed, irritated by this intrusion on what she had hoped would be a relaxed night in. Scrolling down her contacts, she tried Daniel. That went through to voicemail.

She clicked off, not wanting to bother him while he was working. Going to her speed dial, she pressed the first one. Anna picked up.

'Hey, what's up?'

'Not much, just have a quick question.'

'Shoot.' Anna sounded busy. Tanya could hear people trying to get her attention in the background.

'Can Freddie still track numbers to people?'

'If they're registered, yes. Why?'

'Would you ask him to find a name out for me, if I give you the number?'

'Yes, of course. Are you OK?'

'Yeah, it's just…' Tanya paused. She didn't want to worry Anna. It was just a stupid text. 'It's just someone joking around, sending naughty messages. Won't tell me who he is, the pervert. Probably someone I never called back after a first date or something. Just want to find out who, so I can give them what for.'

'Oh! Only you, Tan!' Anna laughed. 'Sure, text it over and I'll ask him to run the number.'

'Thanks, mate. You're a diamond.'

'No worries. See you tomorrow.'

'Yep, bye.' Tanya ended the call and threw her phone to the other end of the sofa. She folded her arms across her chest. Bastard. Whoever it was, she hoped they tripped into an open pothole.

She picked up the remote and checked to see what films were on. She didn't feel like making vodka melon balls tonight after all.

# CHAPTER NINETEEN

Anna tapped her fingers on the bar, her mind elsewhere. It was a slow night; Mondays always were. She hadn't really needed to come in today – Carl was on – but she was feeling restless at home. Freddie was out again, and whereas usually she would just get on with her own life without thinking about what he was up to, right now she couldn't seem to shake a nagging worry that things weren't right.

Freddie had come home yesterday morning after their unusual argument with a huge bunch of roses. They hadn't discussed the previous night's events, and Anna had pretended to accept it, as she knew he was hoping she would.

She pushed her thick, dark hair back over her shoulder, out of her face. It was styled immaculately tonight. Anna always liked to make an effort with her appearance, but she made more effort than usual whenever she felt uneasy. It made her feel more in control. Blood-red lips and perfectly winged eyeliner stood out in her pale face. She sat up straighter in her bar stool and signalled Carl to come over. She handed him the empty glass in front of her.

'Can I have another please?'

'Of course.' Carl took the glass and set about getting Anna another large vodka, lime and soda. He watched her out of the corner of his eye. She looked beautiful this evening, perfectly made-up and dressed to kill. But she also looked sad. The corners of her mouth were downturned, and her eyes had lost their happy, confident twinkle. She sat straight, her chin a little higher than normal – defiant.

Carl wondered what had made her so unhappy. It was unusual for Anna. *Well, these days anyway*, he thought. He pursed his lips, his eyes sympathetic. He cared about Anna – deeply. He cared about Tanya too. He was a lot older than they were. A terminal bachelor fast approaching fifty, the club was his second home, and his staff were like family to him. His two vivacious employers were almost like the daughters he never had. Not that he ever said it out loud. He was careful not to overstep the mark, but he made sure he was always there for them when they needed someone to talk to. Tanya was usually the one pouring her heart out over the bar, seeking advice. Anna always closed up when things went wrong.

He put a cheery smile back on his face and took Anna's drink over to her.

'Thanks. These seem to be going down a little too well. I should probably stop after this otherwise the accounts will make no sense at all.'

Carl picked up his polishing rag and started rubbing the champagne glasses up to a clear shine. He watched the act on stage as he replied in a carefully casual voice. 'You don't need to do the accounts tonight – it's Monday. You'd only have yesterday's to do.'

'Well…' Anna tailed off, not having an answer for that. She didn't want to admit that she was searching for reasons not to go home. She sipped her drink and turned to watch the act too. It was one of the twin acts. Both girls twisted and turned in the hoops that hung from the ceiling. They moved in perfect unison to the music.

Carl glanced sideways at her. 'I don't like having idle hands either. Freddie not about tonight?'

Anna tensed in her chair and picked her drink up. She sipped it then placed it back on the bar. Her chin rose slightly higher and she sniffed. 'No, he's busy.'

'Yes, of course, he would be. I imagine he's under it at the moment, what with that missing girl so hot on the news. Must be a nightmare. It would have to be outside his club of all places, eh?'

'Yes, I guess so.' Anna's lips closed tightly. Carl nodded to himself and dropped it. He knew when not to push.

'Oh, what you doin' here then? You ain't supposed to be in tonight.' Tanya swept in like a breath of fresh air and joined them at the bar.

'You aren't either,' replied Anna, giving her best friend a welcoming hug.

'Yeah, well, I was getting bored at home on me tod, thought I'd come have a few drinks with Carl here. I did text you to see if you was about,' she said accusingly.

'Oh, sorry.' Anna shook her head and reached into her bag, pulling out her phone. Three messages lit up on the screen. The first was from her mother, asking if she'd had a good time at her party, and the second was from Tanya asking if she was free for drinks. The third was from Freddie letting her know he would be late home again. The message preview faded off screen midway through a suggestion of dinner out the following evening. Anna's finger hovered above the message for a second, about to open and reply, but then she changed her mind. She clicked the screen off and put the phone away. If he was busy that was fine. So was she.

Tanya slid into the chair next to her and crossed her slim legs, facing her friend with a happy smile on her face.

'Glad you're here anyway. What you drinking? Why you all dressed up? You off out?'

'No, no plans. Same as you, actually, was a bit bored, fancied a drink.'

'Oh well, that's nice, ain't it?' Tanya's voice rose a few octaves. 'I didn't get no text asking to join you, did I!' She pushed Anna playfully.

'Sorry, just sort of headed here. Wasn't really planning anything in particular.'

Tanya's smile faded slightly as she studied Anna's expression. Her tone turned to one of concern.

'Mate, what's wrong?'

Anna didn't reply, just winked and half smiled as if to indicate that she was OK.

Tanya turned to Carl. 'I think we need cocktails. What do you reckon, Carl, want to whip us up something special and outrageous, eh? Girls' night out?'

'Definitely. I'll whip up one of my new recipes. Give me a few minutes.' Carl took the subtle hint and moved to the other end of the bar to make the drinks, giving them some space.

Tanya rubbed Anna's arm gently. 'Come on, what's going on?' she asked, quietly.

Anna leaned forward, placing her elbows on the bar and resting her forehead on her hands.

'I don't really know, Tan. That's the problem.'

'What? I need a bit more than that.'

'Freddie. He's acting really weird. That whole thing with my birthday, he still hasn't explained any of it. He's been out late each night since and just acting really distracted.'

Tanya chewed her lip and answered slowly. 'Well… I mean, that's not really out of the ordinary, is it? It's, you know… well that's just Freddie, ain't it?' She shrugged apologetically. 'You aren't describing anything new. He's always been like that, and you've always been OK with it.'

'Yeah, but…' Anna turned her body towards Tanya and tried to find a way to explain what she meant. 'It isn't like usual, you know? Like… when I say distracted, I don't mean how he usually is. It's different – something is different. But I can't work it out, because he won't talk to me. Usually, if I outright ask something, he always answers. But he won't tell me what's going on this time; he's actively keeping secrets. That's not like him.'

'Well, maybe it's for your own good then. You know Freddie. You know he loves the bones of you. He wouldn't do something to piss you off unless he had to.'

'Maybe.' Anna stared into the distance. 'Or maybe he's doing something he shouldn't.'

'Well, he does a lot of things he shouldn't. That's his job.' Tanya laughed.

'Yes. Unless it's something he shouldn't do in respect of our relationship.' Anna's voice shook a little as she said it out loud.

Tanya's laughter stopped abruptly. 'No. Don't even go there. He ain't like that, not with you.'

'Not with me?' Anna picked up on the end of Tanya's sentence. Tanya kicked herself. She hadn't meant to say that bit out loud. Anna didn't know much of what Freddie had been like before her, romantically. Which was a good job, really – he had been a bit of a wildling. She was the woman who'd finally tamed him.

'Well, yeah, you know... just, he ain't like that.' Tanya tried to recover and bluff it out.

'No, you said not with me. Which implies he has been like that with other people. So tell me?' She stared Tanya out.

Tanya felt herself growing red. She was no good at lying to Anna. Anna knew her better than anyone.

'Oh, Anna, that was donkey's years ago. He was young and hot-blooded. He ain't like that these days.' Still, she felt a flicker of doubt enter her mind. Was he still like that, deep down? She pushed the thought away firmly. Freddie loved Anna. 'Anna, you're just being paranoid. He might have been a bit of a Jack the Lad when he was wet behind the ears, but that makes no difference to how he is with you now. He worships you, and what's more, he actually respects you. He wouldn't mess things up. You're his family, and you know what family means to him.'

Anna mulled Tanya's words over for a moment. 'I hope so.' She sighed heavily. 'But there's definitely something going on, and I need to find out what it is. Because something just doesn't feel right.'

Carl returned with two large, overly decorated cocktails and a bowl of sweets.

'Here you go, girls. Get these down you. I call them Carl's Sherbet Lemons. I have a whole load of new ones actually. I was going to show you them soon, see if we can work some of them onto the new menu. Tonight is as good a time as any.' He pushed them towards Anna and Tanya and they both tried the mixture.

'Oh, that's lush,' said Tanya. 'Might wake up diabetic tomorrow, the amount of sugar in there, but it does taste good.'

'Mm, it does taste exactly like a sherbet lemon. That is interesting.' Anna was pleasantly surprised. 'What other ones have you got?'

'OK, so I have the Palma Violet, the Toffee Apple…' Carl began to reel off his extensive list of cocktails. Anna listened with great interest, finally distracted from her woes. Tanya pretended to listen and studied Anna quietly. Anna really was worried. She made a mental note to collar Freddie the next time she saw him and find out what he was up to. Whatever it was, he needed to put a stop to it. Anna was very black and white, a no-nonsense kind of girl. The reason she and Freddie worked so well was because he was so open. She needed that. After all she had been through before, Anna couldn't bear not to feel in control. If he wasn't careful, he could really mess that up. She really hoped he didn't, for both of their sakes.

# CHAPTER TWENTY

Freddie walked quickly into the large warehouse, Paul marching along by his side. It looked abandoned from the outside and was surrounded by tall wire fences topped with barbed wire. Danger signs hung from the locked gate. These were, of course, fabricated; the site was perfectly safe and far from abandoned.

The pair passed room after room, empty other than the old bits of broken-down equipment and battered furniture that the previous owners had left behind. A hum of general activity sounded from ahead and they slowed down. This must be it.

Freddie paused outside one of the occupied rooms as they passed. The door was closed, but he could see through the window. Tilting his head to the side he watched as several workers in gloves, face masks and hairnets went about their work. He followed the woman nearest to him with his eyes. She picked up one of the thick bricks of cocaine and split it in a tray. Measuring out a specific amount of bicarbonate of soda from a large box, she added that to the cocaine and mixed it in. When she seemed satisfied that it was evenly mixed, she balled the cocaine back up using its natural stickiness and sealed it into a bag.

Opening the door, Freddie stuck his head in and addressed her as she passed to grab another brick.

'Hello.' He grinned charismatically. 'What's the ratio of the bicarb you're putting into the coke?' He pointed at her work station. Her eyes widened, unused to such bold intrusion by someone she didn't know.

'Sorry?' she asked, her voice quiet and unsure.

'No need to be,' Freddie joked, winking. 'What's the ratio again?' He raised his eyebrow expectantly and waited.

'Er, twenty-five per cent bicarb, same as always,' she replied.

'Great, thanks.' Freddie nodded goodbye and shut the door. His smile dropped, replaced by a grim look.

They continued down the hallway until they reached the end, where it opened up into a large space with dusty windows all around. The room was bare except for a smart-looking, dark-brown sofa, two matching armchairs and a coffee table in the middle. A beige patterned rug lay underneath the strange lounge area, giving it a cosy feel. A middle-aged, darkly tanned man stood up when he saw the brothers walk through the door. He smiled, and bright white veneers shone out against his weathered skin. He stepped forward to welcome them in.

'Freddie, Paul, how wonderful it is to see you again.' A deep Spanish accent curled around his words as he spoke.

'Marco, good to see you too.' Freddie shook his hand and took the seat offered to him. Paul followed suit. There was a tray with biscuits and fresh coffee on the table in front of them, and Marco poured them each a cup.

'This is Spanish coffee, from back home. Not many people know this but we have a special way of roasting the beans back in my home town.' He handed Freddie and Paul two coffees and went about making his own. 'Back in the twenties, they began to add sugar during the roasting process. It would create a glaze on the bean and preserve it for longer. People realised that not only did it do a good job of preservation, it also added something special to the taste and the aroma.' Marco talked with passion. 'Please, try it – tell me what you think.'

Freddie took a sip and nodded, enjoying the subtly sweet smoky flavour. 'It's good. What's it called?' he asked with genuine interest. He enjoyed decent coffee and liked the idea of adding this to his selection at home.

'This process is called *torrefacto*. You cannot get these beans in a shop, but there are other fabulous Spanish beans which go through the same process.'

'OK.' Freddie nodded and made a mental note. He looked around at the strange, empty warehouse with the lounge in the middle.

'How long you been running things from here?'

'Oh, about two years, give or take a little. It has been a good location. No one comes this way, and it is well protected. It has been my favourite base since leaving my operations in Spain. I did have a wonderful set-up in Spain, but' – he shrugged – 'London has a much bigger need for my services. I cannot sit in my small town and ignore that call.'

Freddie studied Marco as he continued talking about his home town. He didn't know Marco very well; they had only met a short time ago, through Bill. He dressed smartly and his rather flamboyant blue suit was made from quality material. His watch and the ring on his finger were expensive. He clearly had a lucrative operation. Was this because he was the best or was it because he was skimming off the weight of the product he was selling to unknowing clients?

'… and they sell the most beautiful, ripe tomatoes in the local markets. Nothing like you see here. So flavoursome, so pure.' He kissed his balled fingers in a show of appreciation.

Freddie smiled tightly. 'Pure, indeed… and what about your product? Is that pure? I'd like to test some, if you could bring some over.'

'Of course.' Marco clicked his fingers at one of the men standing by the door and he disappeared.

It was standard practice to test the product before committing to anything in their business, so Marco took no offence. Within a minute Marco's man was back with a small silver serving tray. On it was a mound of fluffy, white powder.

Paul pulled a small testing kit out of his pocket and laid it out on the table. Using a tiny plastic spoon he picked up a small amount of the product. He carefully levelled the spoon so that there wasn't too much and tipped it into a test tube. Opening a small plastic bottle, he squeezed a clear liquid into the tube, swirling it around to mix with the cocaine. Almost immediately the liquid turned a deep reddish brown. Paul nodded to Freddie and held up the vial for him to see.

'High purity,' Freddie confirmed. Leaning forward he dabbed at the powder, picking some of it up with his finger. He rubbed it into his top gum and ran his tongue around the area. It went completely numb, and there wasn't too much of a sharp tang to the taste. He nodded. 'Not bad.'

He sat back in the chair and stared levelly at Marco, twisting his mouth to one side. It was top-quality product, the shit on the tray, but was it what they were actually going to get?

'Question, Marco… what form does it come to me in? How will it be packaged? If I make a large order, I need to size it up for storage.' He asked the question lightly. He exchanged a look with Paul. His brother knew what he was asking and sat forward, also interested in Marco's response.

'Well' – Marco met Freddie's gaze – 'for you it will come in one-kilo bricks. For Freddie Tyler I would not consider anything else.' He nodded graciously. 'It will come to you as it is now, on this tray.'

Freddie nodded slowly. 'How would it come for other clients?' he asked.

Marco shifted uncomfortably. 'That depends entirely on the client,' he replied, before pursing his mouth.

'Right.' Freddie looked at Paul. 'Good. That's the right answer. I'll take five bricks now, and if everything is up to scratch we can talk about a higher amount and an ongoing contract.'

'Perfect. I can have them in a bag ready to go in five minutes. Diego.' He clicked at the man by the door again. Diego nodded, having heard the conversation, and disappeared to get the product.

Marco turned back to Freddie and clapped his hands together. 'Now, that will be three hundred thousand dollars. How will you be paying?'

'I'll pay you two hundred and *fifty* thousand, same as I pay all my suppliers. Fifty grand a brick, American dollars, non-negotiable. Where am I transferring to?'

'Fifty thousand… this is—'

'Marco' – Freddie's tone was sharp – 'I don't negotiate, and that's a fair price. You either want my business or you don't. They're your two options. Choose.'

Marco breathed heavily as he considered Freddie's words. He wanted Freddie's business badly. Freddie and his firm ran Central London, and if he played his cards right, he could end up being their biggest supplier. But Freddie's offer was ten grand less per kilo than he liked to charge, which would eat into his profits considerably. He warred with himself. He was a man who had expensive tastes, but on the other hand the profit would still be fairly good, and the scale of Freddie's future orders would hopefully be very high. He eyed the younger man and noted the unwavering, steely look in his eye. Freddie Tyler would not be moved on his decision, this much was very clear.

'OK, fifty thousand per kilo it is. You kill me, Freddie Tyler. Another dollar less and I starve,' he added dramatically, waving his arms as though he had been defeated, 'but I feel we have a good, long working relationship ahead of us, so I give you that price with my blessing.'

'Good. Let's move forward then. Where do you want the money?'

'I have a consultancy company set up in South America.'

'Columbia?'

'No, Peru. Better value, not so many beheadings.' He shrugged casually as though he was discussing the weather. Paul hid a grin.

He liked the eccentric Marco. He found him very amusing. He couldn't let on though; Freddie liked them to keep the upper hand with suppliers with a hard-fronted poker face. It kept them from getting too comfortable.

'OK, get me the details and I'll get that sent over now.'

'Perfect. Well, Freddie Tyler, I am excited about our future.'

Freddie took Marco's proffered hand and shook it. 'Me too, Marco. Me too.'

\*

Anna walked into the little coffee shop and smiled at the woman waving her hands at her excitedly. She wove through the busy tables until she reached her, then sat down, leaning over and hugging her friend in greeting.

'Hello, how are you?' she asked, her voice happy. It had been years since she had seen Amanda, though they messaged from time to time. The pair had been friends at university.

'I'm OK, thank you. How are you? I can't believe it's been so long. You don't look a day older than the last time we met,' Amanda replied sunnily. 'I took the liberty of ordering you a skinny vanilla latte,' she continued. 'I don't know if you still drink them, but I remember that's all you used to drink when we were younger.'

Anna laughed heartily. 'Oh my God, I can't believe you remember that! I do still drink those, yes. Thank you.' She settled in and shrugged off the thin cardigan she was wearing over her dress. 'It's so hot in here.'

'Yes, it is a bit. Sorry, I should have picked somewhere better.'

'No, no, this is fine,' Anna quickly reassured her friend. 'It's just lovely to see you. I have to admit it was a surprise hearing from you out of the blue. A great surprise, of course.'

'Yes, well… I have a bit of business I had to attend to in the city, so thought I would kill two birds with one stone,' Amanda answered.

'Ah, I see. Are you working again now? I think the last time we spoke you had just had your second and had decided to stay home with the kids?' Anna tried to remember the details. It was hard to keep up with Amanda sometimes. She was one of those rare people who wasn't on social media. Not that Anna was particularly fond of it herself, but she did like that it made it easier to stay in touch with people.

'No, I'm not working. I'm still at home with the kids.' Amanda's voice faltered and she looked away. 'This was more something of a, er, personal nature.' She took a sip of her coffee.

'Oh, OK.' Anna didn't know how to respond to that. She frowned as she saw the worry lines form on Amanda's brow. She suddenly realised that her friend looked incredibly tired. Thin, too – her pretty blue top was too big for her small frame. She looked as though she had lost a lot of weight recently.

'Is everything OK, Amanda? You don't seem yourself.'

'Um.' Amanda sighed heavily and gave a sheepish smile. 'No, not really. Honestly, things have been a bit crap lately and I just really needed some quality time with a friend.'

'Oh, hun, I'm so sorry to hear that.' Anna reached out and squeezed Amanda's arm, feeling a wave of concern for her. 'What's going on?'

'Oh God, I really didn't want to just turn up after all this time and start moaning about my problems,' Amanda said, reluctance in her voice.

'Don't be silly!' Anna exclaimed. 'It doesn't matter how long it's been – I'm your friend. You can tell me anything. A problem shared is a problem halved,' Anna repeated one of her mother's favourite quotes. 'Come on. Spill,' she ordered.

Amanda's shoulders sunk as she gave in. 'Things just aren't good with my husband at the moment. He…' She took a deep breath. 'I found out he's having an affair. He doesn't know that I know.'

'Oh no.' Anna's heart felt heavy as she watched Amanda crumple.

'I've known for a while that he played away.' A tear fell and Amanda quickly wiped it away, embarrassed to be crying in public. 'At first he just started coming home late and seemed preoccupied. He said it was work, and I believed him. Then he started not coming home at all some nights, and his excuses didn't seem to quite add up. I still ignored it though. He was my husband – I trusted him. But then I found his secret phone and saw the messages…' She sighed. 'I hid my feelings for a while, turned a blind eye, hoping that maybe it would stop once he got it out of his system. That was the first time. This one is the third. And lately something has been different. This girl isn't just a casual fling – he's seeing her regularly. I think he has real feelings for her.'

'Amanda, I'm so sorry.' Anna didn't know what to say. She had never met Amanda's husband, but she had always thought that they were happy together. Then again, she had always thought that she and Freddie were happy together too. She felt a sinking sensation in her stomach as the conversation reminded her of her own worries.

'It's OK, really.' Amanda wiped her face and sat straighter as she regained her composure. 'I'm used to it. I shouldn't keep getting so upset.'

'No, Amanda, you shouldn't be used to it!' Anna replied, feeling angry. 'You shouldn't have to put up with that. He shouldn't be doing that to you – to you and your family. Why haven't you confronted him? Or left? Amanda, you are worth so much more than this treatment.'

'I know that, Anna. Of course I do. But I can't just think about me; I have to think about the children too. They come first. If this all came to a head and we split up, it would destroy them. They are so young still. They need stability. And honestly, I wouldn't be able to provide them with the same sort of life they have now. I would have nothing if I left. And I've been out of work for so long that even if I didn't have small children to look after, no one would hire me on the sort of salary I'd need to be able to provide for them.'

Anna sat back and sipped her coffee. She understood her friend's thought process. But it wasn't fair. Why should Amanda have to be so unhappy? She wished there was a way for her to help her, but she couldn't think of one just yet.

Why did some men think it was OK to treat the women in their life with such disrespect and cruelty? she wondered. She thought back to her own unhappy past with her ex, Tony. He had been an evil bastard, rotten to the core. He had beaten her, mentally tortured her and trapped her in a lonely, unhappy life. It had been hell, even after she found the courage to leave him. Her nightmare had only ended when Freddie had finally killed him. Though that hadn't just been because of how ill Tony had treated her. Tony had incidentally gone up against Freddie professionally, not knowing of their connection. He had planned to take Freddie out and claim Central London for himself. Luckily Freddie had been one step ahead, as he always was, and had nipped the issue in the bud.

'Anyway, that's enough about me,' Amanda said. 'I want to hear about you. How are things going? Tell me about your club – I've heard amazing things.'

'The club is doing really well. You know, you should come for a night out sometime. Take your mind off things – let your hair down. We could have a girls' night. I can introduce you to my business partner, Tanya. She's a real character.' Anna smiled as she thought of her vivacious best friend.

'Yes. I think I might take you up on that,' Amanda said, her expression suddenly determined. 'That actually sounds like it's exactly what I need.'

# CHAPTER TWENTY-ONE

Michael waited in the dark, the only light coming from the end of his lit cigarette. His eyes had adjusted, so he could make out the dark shapes moving silently across the water as they made their way out and back from the large container ship sitting out at sea. One of the ships they used to smuggle goods in had been stopped earlier in the evening, before it was able to come up river. No one knew why, but one of their men on board had managed to get a message out to Freddie. This was very unusual, so Freddie had sent Michael and Paul to clear out their goods before anything else happened.

They had picked up a group of dockhands and two vans, and had driven over to the coastline, nearest to where the ship sat out at sea. Upon arrival, they had cut the bolts on three small motorboats nearby and were currently using them to shift the cargo from the container ship to the shore. Their men on deck were doing a clean job, and so far they had managed to stay out of the way of the coast guard. They didn't dare put lights on and only used the motors out of hearing distance of the main ship.

Still, Michael felt incredibly tense. This hadn't been properly planned – there were no back-up routes. If one thing went wrong, they would be totally screwed.

The sea breeze caressed his face and neck, and he breathed in deeply. Taking one more drag on his cigarette he flicked it away and the cherry end went out in the darkness. Pulling a pair of leather gloves out of his pocket he put them on, securing each finger in thoroughly. As the next boat pulled up Michael stepped forward into the lapping waves on the pebble beach and grabbed one of the sides of the wooden front. Paul picked up the other side, and the two of them hauled it up onto the beach until it was secure enough not to be pulled back by the waves. Two men jumped out and, without a word, all four of them began moving the wooden boxes from the bottom of the small craft to the open back of the van.

'How much more?' Michael asked quietly. It was a deserted beach, but sound carried further here, and you never knew who might be about.

'The other two have got the rest; they're right behind us. The ship's clean.'

'Good.' The boxes all packed up, they turned towards the shore to watch the next two boats come in. Thick clouds filled the sky, blocking the excess light from the moon. The sea was calm, the waves breaking lazily as they hit the shore. It would have been a nice night to be there, had it not been for the threat of being caught and arrested, Michael thought.

'Shit,' Paul swore under his breath.

'What?'

'Look – over there.' He pointed to a speck of light in the distance. It was moving steadily towards the container ship. It was the coast guard. They were still far away, but that didn't mean they were safe. The coast guard's light shone far and they still had two boats in the water. Michael's stomach tightened and his dark blue eyes watched intently, all his senses alert.

The second boat reached the shore and they ran forward to pull it up. This time six pairs of hands moved the cargo, making light work of it. One box, two, three; they continued until there were none. The glass bottles inside chinked together as they were jostled about. Paul stretched his arms out, his muscles beginning to complain at the heaviness of the boxes.

In just seconds they were waiting again in the dark with bated breath. Time moved slowly, and after what seemed an age, the third boat glided quietly in over the black water, its bow crunching up on the gravelly shore. They pulled it in and the last two men joined them on the beach. They formed a human chain from the boat to the back of the second van, passing each box along from one to the other like a production line.

Suddenly a short, sharp siren blast cracked through the air. The brothers glanced at each other and then out to sea, where the coast guard had changed direction. They were headed straight for them. A long beam of light shone over, its power luckily very weak over such an expanse of water.

'Get the last boxes in – quickly!' Paul shouted. Michael estimated what they'd be able to see in such weak light. Not much, he reckoned. Not enough anyway, if they were careful to leave nothing else.

'Open that box,' he ordered the nearest dockhand.

'What? This ain't the time for a fucking drink, Mickey!' Paul said, his voice rising in disbelief.

'Michael,' he growled. 'Just give me a bottle.' He took one and walked towards the first boat. The coast guard called out through a megaphone, the muffled voice authoritative.

'This is the coast guard. Stop what you're doing and put your hands up.'

'Fuck that for a laugh,' Michael said. He opened the top of the bottle and poured it out all over the first boat, shaking it around to cover as much surface area as possible. He threw the empty bottle into the back of the van and then, returning to the boat, picked out a small zipped pouch from under the front seat. 'Cover the other two, one bottle each. Do it now. Keep the empties,' he ordered.

He was quickly obeyed, two of the dockhands hurriedly emptying bottles in the same manner they had seen Michael do.

'This is the coast guard. I repeat, put your hands up and stay where you are.'

Michael waded into the water and pushed the boat out so that the current began to pull it away. Opening the zip of the pouch in his hand, he pulled out a flare gun. Without hesitation he loaded it, pointed it into the middle of the boat and took a shot. Immediately there was a huge flash of light and smoke began to fill the air. As the flare thrashed around, the alcohol took hold and fire burst to life. The flames licked across the hull and quickly engulfed the small vessel.

'Holy fuck!' Paul laughed. 'Alright then.'

Michael pushed the other two boats off into the sea one by one, setting them alight in the same manner.

'Get that van out of here,' Paul ordered one of his men, pointing to the first vehicle. The dark van pulled off swiftly and disappeared into the distance up the road.

Michael waded out of the water, the three boats now all sporting raging fires as the wood and oxygen-rich air fuelled them. The coast guard was speeding towards the shore now, too close for comfort.

'Come on, let's get out of here,' Paul urged, pulling his brother forward with urgency. Michael turned to see the flaming boats. His eyes twinkled with humour and his mouth curled up in an entranced smile. Paul pushed him roughly along and opened the van door. 'Get in, you fucking nutter!'

Michael pulled himself into the front seat and closed the door as Paul ran round to the driver's door. He watched the scene they were leaving out of the window. The coast guard had almost reached the beach but had no choice but to stop behind the three floating firestorms.

'Stop right there!' they screeched over the megaphone in pure frustration.

'Go, go, go!' Michael laughed as Paul slammed his foot down on the accelerator. He sped out as fast as he could, leaving the lights off so that they couldn't read the number plate or make out which road he was taking. They bounced along the rural road faster than they usually would. They could hear bottles breaking in the back, but Paul didn't slow down. A few broken bottles wasn't the worst outcome in the grand scheme of things.

They travelled in tense silence for nearly half an hour before Paul slowed to a more reasonable pace. He had turned the lights on, not wanting to draw police attention. Checking the mirrors one last time, he blew out a loud breath of relief.

'Well, that was certainly a close one, boys,' he said jovially. There was a murmur of agreement from the back. Michael still had a wide grin on his face.

'They must have been so pissed off with those boats.' He shook his head, amused.

'It was a good distraction, that's for sure,' Paul replied.

'Well, it was more to get rid of any lingering DNA from this lot. Some of them weren't wearing gloves.'

'Oh, good spot.'

'But yeah, it worked out nicely all round.'

'Mm. Except not for the owners. They ain't half gonna be raging tomorrow.'

'That's what insurance is for,' Michael replied. 'Plus, they're probably owned by a bunch of posh fucks who use them to go out to Daddy's yacht.' Michael's lip curled. 'They could use a taste of reality for a change.'

Paul glanced at his younger brother. Ever since Michael had suffered at the hands of bullies at private school years before, he'd had a chip on his shoulder where the upper class were concerned. He hated them with a passion. Paul had been subjected to Michael's heated rants on the subject on more than one occasion. He hoped this wasn't going to be one of those times.

'Yeah… wonder why the ship was stopped?' Paul pulled the conversation back round to the events of the evening.

'Beats me. Whatever the reason, it don't matter now.'

'Call Freddie, will ya? He'll be waiting.'

Michael pressed one of the speed dials on his phone and waited for his brother to answer. He smiled to himself again as he remembered the three little boats.

'Michael, how'd it go?'

'All clean. Where are we headed?'

'Go meet Alan – he'll sort a place out for now.'

'Gotcha.' Michael clicked off the call. 'Head for the docks.'

'OK.'

The two men fell into silence for the rest of the journey, each lost in their own thoughts.

# CHAPTER TWENTY-TWO

Freddie's phone rang shrilly in the early-morning silence, vibrating on the wooden bedside table. Coming round slowly from the comfortable nothingness of a deep sleep, Freddie tried to ignore it. He was warm in the cocoon of the large bed, the puffy duvet wrapped up around his naked body and Anna draped over him where she had fallen asleep on his chest. He wrapped his muscular arms around her and snuggled in closer as the phone rang off. Sleep began to overcome him again, clawing him back into its dark security.

The peace-shattering ring sounded again and Anna tapped his arm. She murmured sleepily through the curtain of dark hair that had curled over her face.

'Freddie, get it. It's not stopping.'

Freddie groaned and moved into a half-sitting position as Anna slid off him and curled up deeper under the covers. He rubbed his eyes and tried to blink away the sleep that wasn't quite done with him. Squinting at the digital clock next to his phone, he frowned. It wasn't even 6 a.m.

He picked the phone up and answered the withheld number. 'What is it?' he asked, groggily annoyed. It had better be good for someone to call him at this hour.

'Freddie, my friend, how are you?' The thick Albanian accent dripped sarcasm down the line.

Freddie sat upright, his frown deepening. 'Viktor?' he asked, confused.

'Yes, that's right. How are you this morning, Freddie Tyler?'

'What?' Freddie looked back at the clock to make sure he was reading it correctly. 'Why the fuck are you calling me at this hour? And how did you get my number?'

'Now, now, Mr Tyler, that is no way to speak to a friend.'

'Are you having a laugh? It's barely even light outside. This isn't OK. What do you want?'

'You're right. First light. Which means that a certain ship currently sitting out at sea is about to be raided by border control.'

Freddie sat up straight abruptly. His attention was now sharp, and he quickly pieced together Viktor's plan. He shook his head. He had known something wasn't right.

'You are not the only one with friends in strange places, Freddie Tyler. I have friends too, and as we speak they are boarding that boat. When they find your latest shipment, and they will, they will be looking to me for confirmation of what to do next.'

Freddie could hear the widening of Viktor's smile in his voice. He curled his lip in cold fury. He reached for his boxers and slipped into them.

'What to do, what to do. Now, perhaps if you were to rethink your decision on allowing me to buy some of your shipment space... perhaps there is something I can do about this little problem.'

Freddie stood up and shrugged on the thin cotton dressing gown hanging on the back of the bedroom door as he passed it. He walked down the hall, his shoulders tensed in a boxer's stance, the dressing gown flapping behind him, still undone.

'You are very quiet, Freddie. You are working out what you have on there, yes?'

Freddie reached his office and made his way behind the dark, heavy desk. He opened up his cigarette packet and lit one, breathing in the thick smoke deeply. He exhaled and put the phone on the desk in front of him, pressing the speakerphone button.

'I have nothing on that ship, Viktor.'

'No? This is not what I have heard.'

'I'm sure it's not. However, like I said, I have nothing on that ship anymore, Viktor. You see' – Freddie leaned forward, placing his elbows on the desk – 'I had my men pull everything out last night. That ship is as clean as a whistle. The only thing your friends are going to find of mine is a half-empty container with a bunch of value-price baked-bean tins. I am and will always be one step ahead of you. Do you know why?' Freddie's eyes burned and his face turned hard.

'Why?' Viktor asked, his voice less confident.

'Because I'm Freddie fucking Tyler.' He ended the call and sat back in the large leather swivel chair. Staring angrily at the wall, he smoked his cigarette in silence. The rage and disbelief built up in him more and more as he processed everything. The fact that he'd had to put his brothers and men on such a risky job in the first place already bothered him. To find out that this jumped-up low-life had tried to do him over and hold a gun to his head filled him with fury.

He picked his phone back up and scrolled through the contacts. He pressed dial and waited. The phone was finally answered with a groggy greeting.

'Dean. I need you to pay Viktor Morina a visit. He needs a lesson in who not to mess with. Take a small crew, use the back room in the drug-storage unit. Bag his head – don't want him knowing where that is. A broken arm should do it. Then dump him back with a final warning. There are rules in this life. He needs to learn that you stick to them or deal with the consequences.'

'Gotcha. I'll sort it today.'

'Good man.'

The line clicked off. Freddie stubbed out his cigarette and rubbed his eyes tiredly. Dean was his best breaker. He seemed to have it down to a real art.

Satisfied that this was being dealt with, he phoned Paul. Paul didn't answer; the line rang through to answerphone. Freddie frowned. Paul was getting harder to get hold of lately, which was unusual. In their line of work time was sensitive – urgent issues came up constantly. No matter where they were, if Freddie rang, they answered. Not this time though. Freddie waited for the beep.

'It's me. Listen, we've got a leak on the ship. Or if not on, someone dockside. Viktor set us up with border control; he knew which ship and what to look for. We need to find out who it is – quickly. Until we've dealt with it I'm putting a hold on next week's load. Call me when you get this.'

Ending the call, Freddie caught a movement out of the corner of his eye. He looked up to find Anna leaning around the doorway. He could see half of her smooth, naked body pressing against the doorframe; the rest was hidden from view behind the wall. She leaned her head against the frame, smiling tiredly at him. His eyes roamed over her body. Even three years in, she was still the most beautiful, alluring thing he had ever seen.

'Come here,' he demanded, his voice husky.

She shook her head, her eyes bright under a fringe of dark lashes. The early-morning darkness seemed to add to her allure, her pale, creamy skin standing out from the shadows.

He cleared his throat. 'Please?' he asked, his voice softer. He needed her. He wanted her.

Anna's expression was sombre, and she held his stare for a moment. He could see the sadness behind her eyes. He could see the weight of the secrets he was holding between them.

With a small smile that did not reach her eyes she turned and went back to bed. Freddie sighed heavily and closed his eyes. He prayed to God that Katherine turned up soon. Because if she didn't, one way or another, Freddie wasn't sure their relationship would survive.

# CHAPTER TWENTY-THREE

'Thea, you pair up with Dominic. Email your project outline back to me by the end of the day tomorrow and then crack on. See you all next week.'

Thea smiled at the hesitant young man she had been paired with as he came over to join her at her table. He was about average height and build, with wavy brown hair and a nice smile. She guessed that he was around her own age, which was a bonus. The age span was vast on the photography course she had joined. She didn't fancy running around the city with an over-eager eighteen-year-old any more than she wanted to snap the local wildflowers with the retired hobbyists.

'Hi, I'm Dominic.' He held his hand out and Thea shook it.

'Thea. Nice to meet you properly. Don't think we've spoken before, have we?'

'No, no. I usually just sit by myself over there.' He trailed off awkwardly, his cheeks turning pink. Thea smiled broadly at him. He was adorable. She wasn't used to meeting men who were so shy.

'So, do you have any ideas what you would like to do for our project?'

'No, not really. I haven't given it much thought yet.' The project they had been given was 'life in the city'. It was purposely broad so that they could interpret it however they wanted. 'What about you? Do you have any ideas?'

'Actually I do.' Thea nodded eagerly. 'Well… It was sort of something I was going to do already anyway, but I think it would work pretty well for this too. Two birds with one stone and all that.' She shifted her chair to face her body towards him. 'Only if it's OK with you though. I'm happy to do something else and just do this in me spare time.'

'What is it?'

'Well, my brothers are all… businessmen in the city. They run a few different businesses, and so they move around and walk the city a lot. I had the idea that I would collect photos of them on their different routes through London, over time and through the summer right up to winter. Natural ones, not posed. Same people, different streets, weather and expressions. Show them their connection to the city they love so much. Then I want to put it all together into an album. I was going to give it to them for Christmas. I think it would be ideal to use it for this too, especially as this is a long-term project. What do you think?'

Thea waited as he thought it over. She was careful not to mention what business her brothers were into. It didn't worry her, bringing another person into her project. She had already decided that she would only follow her brothers and snap them on the main streets, never at or too close to their areas of work. There would be nothing for anyone to see except three men going about their day, lost in travel and thought. Perfectly safe. She had been in this family for long enough to know how to protect their secrets.

'Hmm.' He nodded sombrely. 'That sounds perfect actually. Will you tell them that you're doing it?'

'No. They'll be too guarded in their expressions if they know.'

'OK. Well, let's do it then.'

'Great! So why don't we meet for coffee tomorrow and we can put together a game plan? What time are you free?'

'I'm free any time. I work for myself, so pretty flexible.'

Thea nodded and smiled politely but didn't ask for any further details. Although she was curious as to what he did, she didn't want to invite the same questions back. She worked for Freddie, keeping the books. It was a legal-enough answer – if she didn't mention the second set of books and all the money laundering – but the less probing from strangers the better.

'Let's say lunchtime then. One o'clock at the Starbucks on the corner?'

'OK, I'll see you there then. Catch you later.' Dominic grinned and waved his goodbye, before heading on his way.

Thea was pleased that he was on board with her idea. It saved her having to run two projects at the same time.

She checked the time and her eyebrows shot up. Time to go. She had things to do.

*

Freddie stared at his hands, which were wrapped around a full, hot mug of tea. He could see the cuffs restraining his wrists in his mind's eye. He could see the cuffs around Anna's wrists too, leading her away to the cell in which she would later be murdered. The burden of what might happen to her because of who he was weighed on him heavily. And it was becoming a bigger possibility as the days went on. They had found nothing, not one single possible trail on the missing girl. It was as though she had disappeared into thin air.

Ben Hargreaves had phoned Freddie again that morning, the voice coming down the line that of a desperate man. He had reiterated his threats, sounding close to breaking down into insanity. The desperation worried Freddie even more than the threats. Desperate men were dangerous creatures, volatile and unpredictable.

The door of the small, greasy café opened and Sammy walked in. He took the seat opposite Freddie and signalled the short, round woman at the counter. She bustled over with her pad and pen and waited expectantly.

'Tea please, love, and… what have you ordered, Fred?'

'Nothing, mate.'

'Two full English with extra toast.'

'I'm alright—'

'You need to eat, Fred. You got a long day ahead.' He winked and nodded at the old woman, and she disappeared to give the cook the order.

Sammy sat back and examined his friend. Freddie looked about ten years older today, the stress lines in his forehead deepened under his heavy, serious expression.

Freddie ran his hand down his face and off his chin. 'Anna's going to be dragged off to prison, Sammy, for no reason other than the fact she's with me, and then they're gonna kill her.'

'No, she ain't—'

'Yes, she is, Sam. And there's nothing I can do about it. Nothing.' He stared his friend in the eye. 'I can't find this girl. She ain't nowhere to be found. I've talked to all the firms we deal with and all the informants we know on the street. I've had scouts out everywhere and nothing's come back. There's no blackmailer to barter with. She's not been taken for sale. There's no body washed up on the riverside. She ain't run away and been picked up on any cameras. She's just gone. Disappeared into thin air. I've got nothing to go on. Nothing. And Hargreaves wants blood. He's going to bury us behind bars, and then he's going to slit Anna's throat just to spite me more, and there's nothing I can do to stop him. He's possibly the one person in the world I can't buy or manipulate. I can't even kill him.' Freddie stared off into the distance.

'Alright, that's enough.' Sammy's voice was stern. 'Stop it. We will get through this, just like we do everything. Alright? Sitting here maudlin' won't help no one. You need to snap out of it.'

Freddie was silent for a few moments, his eyes glazing over as he stared out of the window. Then his head snapped round and he focused in on his worried friend. He straightened himself up in his chair and pulled his jacket back into place.

'Well,' he said finally, his voice light. 'You're getting mouthy these days, ain't ya, you big Swedish lout.'

Sammy chuckled deeply, his broad, muscular body bobbing up and down as he did so.

'I figure I've earned that right over the years, mate. Don't matter who you are, if you can't accept straight talk from your closest friends, you ain't going to get very far.'

'That's true. But seriously, I've totally run out of ideas. Unless something comes up, short of searching the city inch by inch, there's no more I can do.'

The waitress came over with their breakfasts, and they leaned back so that she could place the heavily laden plates down in front of them.

'Here you go lads. Enjoy.' She nodded and left them to it, wiping greasy hands on her apron where some of the juices had spilled over.

Freddie took a slow breath as he stared at the steaming plate with disinterest. He couldn't take any pleasure in food these days. His appetite seemed to decrease every time he thought about the noose that was slowly tightening around Anna's neck. He took a bite to appease Sammy and chewed the food without really tasting it.

Something needed to come up soon. Time was running out.

# CHAPTER TWENTY-FOUR

Anna walked along the South Bank warming her hands around the takeaway coffee she was nursing. Usually this place was full of tourists, but not at this time of day. It was barely seven in the morning. Only the locals making their way to work were hurrying along. It was a fairly warm summer this year, but the morning chill still had its hold as the sun sat low in the sky. She pulled the thin tan jacket she wore closer to her chest.

Westminster stood proud and tall in the weak morning sun, the river glistening in between it and her. Big red buses made their way over Westminster Bridge, back and forth. Underneath, small cargo boats sailed slowly and determinedly up the river.

Turning her back on that bridge, she walked along the riverside to the Golden Jubilee Bridge. She mounted the steps, keeping out of the way of the businessmen and -women rushing to get to their desks on time. The breeze flowed through her thick, dark hair, lifting it off her neck, and she breathed in the fresher air by the river deeply. Her shoulders relaxed in what seemed like the first time in a week. Walking to the centre of the bridge, she stopped and turned to face the view again. She leaned forward, resting her forearms on the railings of the bridge, and drank some more of her coffee.

She loved coming here. It was where she came to think and reflect. Standing on the middle of the bridge, watching the world go by felt like standing in the eye of a storm; a perfectly calm centre, while the world swirled on around her. Big Ben chimed, signalling that it was now quarter past seven. So early, Anna thought. Freddie would still be asleep; he wouldn't stir for an hour or two yet. She had been restless all night, finally giving up trying to sleep at around six. She had thrown some clothes on and slipped out into the breaking dawn, too irritated to lie there any longer.

Anna's eyes dropped tiredly to the surface of the murky brown water. The waves chopped and churned in the wake of one of the boats, throwing up frothy peaks. She wondered as she always did what was hidden under the dark surface. How many engagement rings lay in the mud at the bottom, thrown by the broken-hearted victims of uncovered liars and cheats? How many other tokens of love lay there; keys and wishes dropped by hopeful lovers, excited by their unknown future?

Her thoughts wandered to the darker corners of her mind. How many bodies lay rotting underneath the layers of rubbish and rusting trolleys, weighed down by chains and cement? Was Tony down there? Had Freddie disposed of her psychotic ex in this very river, after he killed him three years ago? He had to be somewhere. It wasn't as though they could have sent him back home for a funeral with a bullet in his brain. She had never asked Freddie what they'd done with his body. She didn't want to know. She didn't really care. Perhaps she should, but she couldn't find it in herself. Not after everything he had done to her. The world and every single person in it were better off without him. No one had mourned his death.

She pushed these thoughts from her mind. It was easier to push them away now. They no longer haunted her the way they used to. The trauma she experienced with Tony had forever changed her – that she couldn't get away from. But it no longer upset her to think about it.

Her thoughts returned to Freddie. She wished for the hundredth time that she could get him to open up about whatever was worrying him so much. He was barely eating, and tossed and turned for hours each night. He was constantly distracted, and she had never seen him so tense. It made her feel uneasy. Something was very wrong – she knew it was. But this time he had frozen her out, and there was nothing she could do about it. She was starting to wonder whether they were as strong a couple as she had thought they were.

The one and only unsettling conclusion that she kept coming back to was that it must be another woman. Even the thought made her feel sick, but what else could there possibly be?

She closed her eyes and took a deep breath, trying to hold herself together. If things didn't become clear soon, she was going to have to do something she really didn't want to do. As much as she loved Freddie, if this continued, she wouldn't put up with it – she'd leave him. Even though it would kill her to do it. After all she'd been through, Anna had too much self-respect to stay with anyone who lost her trust. Even more so after meeting up with Amanda and hearing her tale.

Amanda's predicament had sharply reminded Anna how awful an existence it could be, being trapped in a relationship without trust or happiness. She had been there before, but unlike Amanda she didn't have children to think of. She wasn't trapped this time. She only had herself to worry about. Her heart ached at the thought of leaving. But it was a possibility that she needed to consider. That was why she had come here, to think things through with a clear mind.

'Anna?' A soft, tentative voice broke through her thoughts, and she swung round at the unexpected intrusion. 'I thought that was you.' A tall, slender young woman smiled at her from a few steps away.

'Sophie!' Anna exclaimed, surprised. 'What are you doing here?'

'I'm on my way to breakfast. There's a really nice vegan place around the corner which does amazing food.'

'Ah, that's nice,' Anna said warmly. 'Are you meeting your boyfriend?'

'No, I'm still single. Haven't met the right guy yet.' She laughed awkwardly, her voice wistful. 'I'm just meeting a friend. What about you? It's really early.' Sophie smiled.

'Oh, I just…' Anna motioned back towards the river helplessly, trying to think up a good reason that didn't sound odd. 'I come here sometimes,' she said, smiling awkwardly, 'to walk and stuff.' She nodded, aware of how vague she sounded.

Sophie was one of their aerial dancers at the club. She was one of their best acts, extremely talented. She made swinging in hoops and across the room by ropes look effortless. From a drunken attempt one night after closing, Anna knew that it was actually very far from effortless. A kind, free-spirited soul, Sophie was also someone that Anna liked personally too. She often stayed behind for drinks after closing with herself and Tanya.

Sophie pushed a stray strand of her naturally light-blonde hair behind her ear and nodded easily in response.

'If you fancy some food, you're more than welcome to join us?' she offered. The corners of her big blue eyes crinkled prettily as she smiled.

Anna smiled warmly back. 'Thank you, but I've got to head back soon. Maybe next time.'

'OK, well I'll see you tonight then. Are you on or is Tanya?'

'Er, I'm not sure yet.'

'OK. If you change your mind about breakfast just give me a call. See you later.'

'See you later.' Anna waved her off and Sophie carried on her way to meet her friend. She turned back to look at the water again, rubbing her forehead tiredly. She wouldn't find any answers in the water today. The mucky, dense river looked about as clear as her relationship was right now.

She straightened up and pulled her jacket around tighter. Her shoulders pulled back and her body tensed up again. Anna strode back the way she came with her head held high, leaving her thoughts behind her. There was no more time today for self-pity and brooding thoughts. She had things to do. Life went on.

# CHAPTER TWENTY-FIVE

Katherine breathed in hoarsely. Everything hurt. She was certain now that she had an infection from the festering wounds around her ankles. They just wouldn't heal. Every time she coughed, her legs jerked involuntarily and any thin layers of scabbing that had started to form would rip back open. The pain was so bad she would scream in agony, but no sound came out anymore. The coughing and screaming and damp conditions had all but got rid of her voice.

The door opened, the torch shone over and she closed her eyes to the harsh, bright intrusion. She waited for him to sit on the chair he usually favoured, but this time he walked straight over to the bed. Her eyes flew open as she tried to get some small glimpse of him, but as the light moved, allowing her to see, she clocked the ski mask that covered his face. Her hopes dropped. He stopped by her feet and suddenly pulled up her calves.

She screamed an almost silent scream, the agony almost making her pass out. She felt the ropes being moved off her ankles. She heard the tear of her skin as some of it pulled away with the rope where it had become half attached. Her eyes filled with tears as the pain intensified. The rope was pulled away totally, releasing a putrid stench from the rotting flesh.

Unable to contain herself anymore, she heaved over to the side and retched onto the floor, the meagre contents of her stomach spilling out next to the bed. Her body kept convulsing even after there was nothing left. Hot tears fell down her face, one after the other, making track lines in the deep layers of dirt.

She heard the clunking of the chain being picked back up from the floor and winced in renewed terror as he came to the top of the bed.

'Please, no,' she breathed, gulping in quick bursts of air as she began to go into shock. He grabbed at her bound wrists. She half-heartedly tried to pull away, her lack of strength evident. He tutted.

'Stop it,' he ordered curtly, his words sounding deep and guttural through the voice changer. 'I'm just moving it to your wrists.'

He attached one end of the chain to the ropes around her wrists and the other end onto the bedframe, then pulled hard to make sure that they were secure. Katherine watched as he carefully placed the putrid ropes he had taken off her ankles inside a plastic food bag and sealed it. With his gloved hand he put that bag inside another coloured plastic bag, hiding them from view.

Wiping the dirty tears off her face, Katherine lay her aching head back on the pillow. He had listened to her after all. She had begged him to remove the ropes and finally he had. He was still a psycho, but perhaps there was a small sliver of humanity in there somewhere. She tried to reach out to it.

'Thank you,' she said quietly, her voice gravelly.

There was a pause. 'This was not for your comfort. If anything I need you to suffer. That is the only way this will work.'

Katherine couldn't answer, frozen at his words. It felt like there was a rock sitting heavily in the pit of her stomach where the last few strands of hope had been.

He walked away with the bagged-up ropes, shut the door and left her there alone again. It was only after he went that she sinkingly realised he hadn't left her any food this time.

# CHAPTER TWENTY-SIX

Sarah Riley stared up at the swinging sign above the door of The Black Bear pub. She had heard of this place but had never had cause to visit it. It wasn't exactly somewhere she was keen to be entering either, but in this instance she had no choice. Freddie Tyler was currently inside, and she had to speak to him urgently. There was no time to set up a meeting or wait until he was somewhere she was more comfortable with. Taking a deep breath, she strode forward and through the front door.

The décor of the place was traditional. The mahogany bar was polished to a shine, and the brass beer pumps were complemented by the warm tones on the walls. Small round tables were dotted around the room surrounded by sturdy wooden chairs, and comfortable booths lined one of the walls. If this place wasn't one of the most notorious hubs for organised crime gangs in London, she would have quite liked it.

The chatter in the room slowed to a stop as the people drinking at the tables registered Sarah. Eyes looked her up and down, and expressions turned hostile. One of the men in the corner snorted in surprised amusement. Not all of them knew who she was personally, but they could tell she was filth. The way she dressed, walked, held herself all gave it away. She wasn't stupid; she knew this was the case. But then again, she wasn't trying to hide who she was.

Lifting her chin in forced confidence, Sarah slowly walked forward through the long room. Out of the corner of her eye she saw two of the men who had been seated at the end of the bar get up and fall in line behind her, closing off her route to the door. Her heart began to race, but she held her outward composure. It wouldn't do to let the bastards think they were scaring her. The only sound came from a radio somewhere behind the bar.

She moved slowly, to appear casual, checking round the high backs of each booth, looking for Freddie. As she reached the far end, she heard the hum of a quiet conversation, which had continued regardless of her presence, coming from the end booth. She sped up her pace a little, and as the inside of the booth came into view, she almost felt a small wave of relief. He was here.

Freddie paused mid-sentence and blinked at her, frowning. 'And what the fuck are you doing here?'

He leaned out and looked back down towards the busier end of the bar. 'I wondered why you'd all gone quiet. What's the matter, no one fancy pork for dinner?'

There was a wave of laughter, and he grinned at them before sitting back straight. He looked up at her and raised one eyebrow in disdain. The two men behind her stood together, clearly awaiting instruction from Freddie.

Sarah had gone red at his comment but stayed silent, well aware of the vulnerable position she was in. Police were far from welcome in this pub. She was beginning to question whether she had made the right choice. If Freddie decided to throw her to the wolves here, anything could happen. But what she had to say couldn't have waited.

'I asked you a question,' Freddie said to her. He stubbed out the cigarette he was smoking in the ashtray in front of him. Yet another middle finger to the law, she noted. But of course that was nothing of importance to a man like him. She cleared her throat.

'I need to talk to you and it can't wait,' she answered simply.

He stared her out, the dislike clear in his face. Eventually he looked behind her and gave the nod to the two men with a wink.

She felt them move away and heard them take their places back at the bar. She breathed out and relaxed her stance slightly.

Freddie turned to the two men he was sitting with, who were watching the exchange with open interest.

'Excuse us for a minute, will you?'

'Sure. No problem, Freddie.' They stood up and went to refill their glasses at the other end of the bar.

Freddie motioned towards the empty bench. 'Sit.'

'I'm not a dog, Mr Tyler,' Sarah snapped, her eyes narrowed.

Freddie raised his eyebrows and screwed his mouth to one side as if in disagreement. Sarah fought the urge to rip into him but reminded herself where she was. She let it go grudgingly.

'Do you actually know where you are?' he asked, genuinely curious.

'I'm well aware.'

'Then have you got a death wish?' His eyes glinted wickedly as she squirmed in her seat. 'You realise that if anyone in here decided to do anything to you due to your, er, life choices, shall we say, then there ain't one person in this room that wouldn't back them up. Your kind ain't welcome in here. Most of these men have either gone away or had someone they care for taken away by one of you.'

'Well then, maybe they should—'

'I'd be very careful what you say right now,' Freddie interrupted her with a slow, deliberate tone that brooked no nonsense. Sarah felt a chill run through her as his eyes pierced into her intently. 'These men take an even bigger dislike to coppers who play both sides of the law and still have the gall to look down on them. And let's face it, you're more bent than Elton John.'

'I most certainly am not.' Sarah's tone was indignant.

'Oh, save me the production,' Freddie scorned. 'You think you hide it well, but you don't – not to the people who look closely. Your watch for example. You don't see many plods with TAG Heuers on their wrists. Or driving top-of-the-range Mercs either.'

Sarah held his stare. 'My finances are nothing to do with you, nor do they make me bent,' she spat.

'No. But when a little birdy tells me that you don't come from money and live a sad, single life alone with your cat, it makes me wonder.'

Sarah took a deep breath and refocused the conversation on what had brought her here in the first place.

'Listen' – she dropped her voice – 'something was left on Hargreaves' back step this morning. It's from the kidnapper.'

'Not here,' Freddie barked, silencing her. The last thing he needed was to look like he was working with the police, especially here.

'Where then?' she asked.

'My cabin at the docks. One hour.'

'Fine.' She turned and glanced warily at the sea of unfriendly eyes between her and the door. As she looked back at Freddie she could see the amusement in his face. He was enjoying her unease. Lifting her chin, she walked swiftly back out the way she came.

As she neared the door one of the men watching her jumped forward and barked near her ear. She nearly jumped out of her skin, and the crowd around her burst into cruel, raucous laughter. She straightened herself and marched out of the front door.

Freddie chuckled under his breath as his companions once again took their seats. The older of the two men smiled at Freddie curiously.

'Ain't that the pig that's been sniffing round about that missing girl? Surely they don't think you had anything to do with it.'

'Nah, they know I haven't.' Freddie stared at the doorway Sarah had just left through, hiding his annoyance. 'She's just taken a little fancy to me. Likes the idea of a man the wrong side of the tracks and don't seem to understand the feeling ain't mutual.'

'Ha!' He banged his hand on the table and shook his head. 'Bloody hell, Fred. That ain't the attention you need. And what is she like, walking in here like that? That desperate cow needs to go find someone in her own world to give her a good seeing to. Jesus.' His gravelly voice held a melodic Irish accent.

'Now that I agree with!' Freddie laughed. 'And hopefully that's exactly what she will do.'

He downed the last of his drink and stood up. 'I have to get off. So have your guy meet Robbie at the gym ring tomorrow and we'll see how it goes. Hopefully he has what it takes.'

'Will do, Freddie. Thanks again.'

'No problem at all.' Freddie patted the older man on the shoulder respectfully as he passed. As he reached the man who had barked at Sarah, he grinned and chuckled again with him, then left to head to the docks.

# CHAPTER TWENTY-SEVEN

Freddie walked down the cobbled path towards his office in the bright sunshine and breathed in the breeze that flowed off the river. He loved London in the summer. Everyone else seemed to prefer the country or the beach, but not Freddie. Here was the place to be. London. The centre of the universe.

He frowned as he heard raised voices coloured with anger. The path curved round and the Portakabin came into view. Alan stood with his back to the front door, his stance stubborn and his arms crossed. Sarah Riley was right in front of him, her hand on her hips as she argued. She leaned forward and stretched up to her full height so that she towered over him. Alan did not move and determinedly stuck his chin out further. Freddie growled under his breath. Who the fuck did she think she was, trying to intimidate one of his men like that? He quickened his pace and approached the scene.

'Hey, what are you doing?' He pushed past her and then walked back into her personal space, forcing her away from Alan. Sarah stepped back and took a deep breath, straightening the front of her jacket.

'You just told me to meet you here,' she snapped.

'Yeah, meet me here, not go ahead and let yourself in. Alan works for me, and as we've discussed before, I don't take kindly to one of mine being treated disrespectfully.'

Sarah pursed her lips and narrowed her eyes. The reminder of their last 'conversation' was enough to keep her from commenting further.

Alan let out a heavy breath and stepped away from the door, more relaxed now that there was no banshee trying to force her way into places she wasn't allowed. He righted his flat cap on his head and acknowledged Freddie with an upward tip of the head. 'Alright, Freddie?'

'Good, mate. You?'

'Yeah. I'll see ya later.'

'OK. Thanks, Alan.'

Opening the door, Freddie walked in and motioned with his hand for Sarah to follow. He took his seat behind the desk, crossed his fingers in front of him and waited. After a moment's hesitation Sarah closed the door and walked over to the desk. She unbuttoned her jacket and pulled an evidence bag out of her inner pocket. She dropped it onto the desk in front of Freddie. Freddie picked it up and began studying the contents through the plastic.

'It arrived this morning in an empty cake box on the back step. I took it to forensics and they confirmed that it definitely is Katherine's blood. There's infection too; she's not in a good condition. There are other particles but nothing that directly gives away the location. Some soot and other common London grime suggests that this comes from somewhere still in the city. No DNA on there from anyone else.'

Freddie turned the ropes over in his hands. 'What about the cake box?'

'Nothing of any use. Some vanilla icing smudged on the inside. It's a basic, cheap white box that half the bakeries in London use. No prints or DNA on that either.'

'And I'm guessing you're going to tell me that there are no cameras on the back of the house either, right?'

'Correct. They don't have cameras at all.'

'Can you get the tapes from the local traffic cameras?'

'I've got someone working on that at the moment.'

'Get them over to me as soon as possible.'

Sarah frowned then raised one eyebrow. 'I don't answer to you, Tyler. I'm only passing this on because I've been directly ordered to by Hargreaves. Don't think for a second that we're working together.'

Freddie sat forward and frowned back at her. 'Just get me the tapes. I don't know what you've got stuck up your arse, but whatever it is, pull it out, get off your high horse and get on with your job. I want this stupid girl found. I don't give a flying fuck what you do or don't like here, that is the only objective.'

'You know what, I'll tell you something now, sunshine: you might be the high and mighty here in your seedy little underworld, but you are nothing in my world. When this is over I'm going to be watching you like a hawk. I'm going to have you followed wherever you go. I'm going to make it my mission' – she leaned forward over the desk – 'to bring you in for every tiny little misdemeanour. I'm going to wait for that one mistake you make that trips you up and gives me everything I need to lock you away for a very long time. And when that day comes' – she stood back up and smiled coldly – 'I'm going to relish it.'

Freddie's mouth curled slowly into a smile as he watched her, and after she had finished talking he burst out laughing. His deep, rumbling laughter filled the small space, and after a minute he shook his head at her, not able to stop. Sarah blinked, not expecting this response. Her body filled with frustrated anger at his mocking laugh. Without another word, she turned and swept back out of the Portakabin, slamming the door behind her.

As soon as he was sure she was gone, Freddie stopped laughing, and his grin turned down to a wry smile. He pulled out his cigarettes from his pocket and lit one. DCI Sarah Riley wouldn't be putting him or anyone else away once this was all over. After all this had been dealt with, he would make sure that she never worked in the force again.

Freddie picked the bag up again. Still no blackmail, no demands – nothing. What was this person thinking? What was going on inside their head? If Freddie didn't work it out soon, he'd lose everything.

# CHAPTER TWENTY-EIGHT

Tanya put her arm through Daniel's as they left Club Anya and waved goodbye to the bouncers. She smiled happily as they walked down the road on their way out of Soho. The streets were busy with merry-makers as was usual for 11.30 p.m. on a Friday. Tanya had been working her shift at the club when Daniel had turned up to surprise her. Carl had immediately offered to close up, insisting that she go enjoy herself, when she'd introduced her new boyfriend to him.

*Boyfriend*, Tanya giggled internally. It sounded so strange. She had never really had a proper boyfriend before. She had casually seen people in the past for a little while, but nothing serious. Mainly she just dated and things never really worked out. Not that she was fussed – she had plenty in her life and didn't need a boyfriend to be happy. But it was a nice change to have someone she could talk to and share things with in that way that couples do. It was certainly something she could get used to. She wrapped the long, polished fingers of her free hand around his arm and smiled up at him warmly.

'I still can't believe you're here. What with your work and mine, it's near impossible to get you to myself on a Friday night.' She said it lightly, no accusation behind her words.

'I know. But it turns out that I have this entire weekend totally work free. The client I was working with had to go away at short notice,' Daniel replied enthusiastically. 'Which means that I actually have some prime, quality time with my best girl.' He stepped in front of her and grasped her to him, lifting her slightly off the ground with a big grin on his face. Tanya shrieked and laughed at him, wrapping her arms around his neck. 'That is, if you think you can manage to free up your schedule too?' He leaned forward and kissed the tip of her nose.

Two lads smoking outside a nearby bar gave a whistle. 'Oi, oi, get a room, you two.'

'Not a bad idea. What do you think, Tanya?'

She laughed again, amused at his open display. She pushed him back gently and freed herself from his arms. Placing her hand in his, she pulled him along further down the street.

'Come on, let's go back to mine. I can't cook you breakfast in bed in a hotel room, can I?' She raised one perfectly arched eyebrow, playfully.

'You make a good case, Miss Smith.' He pretended to consider his options. 'Let's go.'

'Sorted. And yeah, I should be able to free up the weekend. Anna's on tomorrow night anyway. I was supposed to go through some stuff about the acts in the afternoon with her, but she probably won't mind postponing till Sunday night.'

'Or you could still go, bring me along and I can finally meet her?' Daniel offered.

'Oh! Yeah, that's actually a pretty pukka idea,' Tanya replied gleefully. 'I'm sure they think I'm making you up, you know.'

'Really? How could anyone possibly make up such an amazing character as me? What with my charisma and charm and utter godliness in be—ahh!' Daniel darted out of the way as Tanya poked him in the sides.

'What, and your girly ticklishness, eh?' she teased. Her phone beeped in her pocket and she pulled it out to check who had messaged her. 'Saved by the bell.'

'Whatever, I'm not ticklish. Just thought I'd seen a crack in the pavement – didn't want to risk falling into it, you know? Had to move.'

'Sure you did,' Tanya cackled, 'you're a modern day—' Her voice trailed off and her smile disappeared. She stopped walking and swung round, looking back down the street.

'What's wrong? Tanya?'

A lump settled in the pit of her stomach as she frantically searched the crowded street with her eyes. It could be anyone, any of these people. Even if not, the sender could be hiding in a number of places. There were alleys and side streets all around them. Parked cars with dark windows, flats above bars with wide viewpoints. She took a deep breath and tried to focus on acting normally. She wasn't going to let whoever it was know that they had rattled her cage.

'It's nothing. Just thought I heard someone call my name, that's all. Must've heard wrong.' She forced herself to smile and turn back to face the way they were walking. Daniel didn't notice the strain in her face or that her wide smile didn't quite reach her eyes.

'Oh right. I get that all the time. With such a common name, there's always someone shouting it out.'

'Well, there had to be something common about you, posh boy,' Tanya joked. She ran her hand through her hair and used the movement to mask another quick glance back.

'Right, wait here – I'll get us a cab.' Daniel touched her arm briefly then walked out into the road. He focused on the oncoming traffic, looking for a taxi with its light on.

Checking that he was still occupied, Tanya pulled the phone back out of her pocket and read the message again.

*I'm watching you, whore.*

Pursing her lips, she clicked off the screen. She shivered, despite the warmth of the summer evening. She needed to ask Anna if Freddie had had time to check this number. Battling the urge to send a reply, she slipped the phone back into her pocket.

There was no point. Her last text had received no response. Until she knew what she was dealing with, she would maintain silence. There was no point starting a fight with a ghost.

'Tanya? Come on, let's go.' Daniel opened the door to the taxi and ushered her inside before joining her.

Tanya snuggled up to him in the chair and pushed the text to the back of her mind. Whoever this keyboard warrior was, they could wait until tomorrow. They did not get to ruin her Friday night.

# CHAPTER TWENTY-NINE

Michael walked into Ruby Ten and headed straight for the end of the bar where he could see Dean already waiting for him. He sat down on the bar stool that Dean had kept empty and greeted the other man warmly.

'Deano, how are ya, mate? What's 'appening?'

'Michael, I'm good; I'm good. What you drinking?'

Michael lifted up his hand to get the barmaid's attention. She immediately stopped serving the waiting crowd of customers to their loud dismay and took herself over to Michael.

'What can I get you, Michael?' she asked brightly.

'Whisky and Coke – the good stuff – and whatever Dean wants.'

'I'll have the same, cheers.'

She went off to get their order, and Michael turned back to Dean, unbuttoning his suit jacket now that he had sat down.

'So how did things go with Viktor?'

'Fine. For me anyway. Picked him up easy enough. Those men of his don't pay very close attention to their jobs. Sloppy, the lot of them.' Dean shook his head in disgust. 'I took Viktor for a little chat. He broke quickly. No balls under the bullshit after all. Did his arm in, dropped him back last night where we found him. Shouldn't be any more trouble.'

'Great. That's perfect, mate.' Michael patted him on the arm, then reached into his inner pocket and pulled out a thick envelope. 'Freddie says thanks.' He slipped it across the bar and Dean took it, putting it straight into his own pocket. He wouldn't count it in front of Michael – that would be an insult. Plus, he knew it would all be there anyway. Freddie was a good businessman and a fair boss. He never shorted anyone.

The barmaid returned with their drinks and disappeared back to the waiting punters. Before Michael had taken a sip, his phone beeped. It was a message from Paul.

*Not going to make drinks tonight. Crack on, I'll see you tomorrow.*

Michael tutted in annoyance and shoved the phone back in his pocket. His face clouded over into a dark expression. This was the third time in as many weeks that Paul had cancelled on him. The three brothers had busy, highly stressed lives. Winding down with drinks together whenever they could was something they did to help themselves transition from work mode to personal life. Michael in particular counted on this after a heavy day. Unlike Freddie, he didn't have a partner to unburden to, and he didn't have his brother Paul's easy-going ability to shake things off.

'You OK, mate?' Dean asked.

'Yeah, fine.' He didn't offer any more, and Dean didn't ask. If Michael wanted to talk, he would.

'OK. Well, I'd best be off. Catch you later, yeah?' Dean downed the last of his drink and headed through the throng of people on the dance floor towards the exit.

Michael sighed and indicated to the barmaid that he wanted a refill. Scanning the crowd while he waited, he observed all the groups of people dancing and having fun. His gaze paused on a group of young men at the VIP table. He could hear their laughter over the music as one of them made a joke. The floppy hair and subtle designer clothing, along with their haughty looks, showed them for what they were. Posh wankers splashing cash that they didn't earn, in order to gain respect they didn't deserve, from people who knew no better. Michael narrowed his eyes. People like them only came here to stroke their own egos and look down on the normal people they saw as beneath them. His fist tightened and he clenched his jaw.

Michael earned everything he had; he earned the respect he was accorded and the money that paid for his lifestyle. The memory of the boys who made his life hell at school flashed through his mind. No one would ever make him feel like that again.

Looking away, Michael noticed a familiar bunch of girls on the dance floor, and he recognised one of them immediately. It was Carla from the massage parlour in Soho. He studied her, interested in how she was here in her natural form. She smiled and laughed easily, enjoying the music. She rocked her body back and forth. Her eyes closed, she pulled her hair up and away from her neck. She looked happy, relaxed.

Shifting round to face her fully he settled in to watch. She would be a good distraction. Carla's silky golden hair slid through her fingers, back onto her shoulders again. He liked her hair. It was always shiny and smelled fresh.

The song changed and Carla opened her eyes. Her mouth curled into a smile as she swayed from side to side. Obviously one she liked a lot. The next one was clearly not a favourite, as she stopped dancing and moved to pick up her drink. She turned and leaned back on the table, sipping through her straw and watching her friends. Her eyes wandered and eventually met Michael's. A millisecond passed, recognition dawned and a warm grin spread across her face. She immediately tottered over to him.

'Well, fancy seeing you 'ere!' She greeted him with a hug and a flirty kiss on the cheek. ''Aving a good night?'

'I am now,' he answered with a smile, putting his arm around her waist. She giggled and pushed up against him.

'What about you? Having fun?' He motioned towards her group of friends.

She glanced back at them. 'Yeah, it's been a good laugh. Not seen you in here before.'

'I'm usually pretty busy this time of night.'

'Yeah I bet.' She bit her lip. 'So, you busy now then?'

'No, not particularly. Last-minute cancellation.'

'Well' – Carla tilted her head to the side alluringly – 'maybe I could help fill up your time. If you fancied it.' She winked with a full set of perfectly positioned false eyelashes.

Michael pondered on the offer for a moment. He was interested. He had only really been with Carla in the massage parlour before. It could be fun to have her to himself for a little while, and he was free tonight. He didn't have to meet Freddie until the next day.

'You want to come with me?' he questioned her, making sure he was reading her words correctly. He didn't fancy staying here and joining her group of friends.

'Yeah,' she replied.

'Alright. Go tell your friends you're leaving,' Michael said.

He waited while she gave her friends a quick explanation and picked up her small clutch bag. As soon as she returned he steered her towards the door and out of the building to grab a cab.

# CHAPTER THIRTY

The cab pulled up outside a high-rise building in Shadwell, and Michael and Carla stepped out. Michael paid the cabby and tapped in the entrance code to the door. The buzzer sounded and the door clicked open.

'Not many people know that I have this place. Only Freddie and Paul and my sister.' He walked into the lift and pressed the button for the top floor. Carla looked around with interest. 'So this is to stay between us.'

Carla nodded her understanding. He knew she would do as he asked. She knew the score.

'I bought this flat ages ago. But... me old mum never took very well to my brothers moving out, so I still spend at least half my nights at hers, and she don't know about here. She thinks I live there with her, and I still get a decent amount of time in my own space. So it's a win-win situation. Saves the aggro.'

Carla laughed. 'Well, I think that's really nice actually. You're sweet.'

'Mm.' Michael tensed and gave her a sideways look. 'So are poisoned apples.' His voice was loaded.

'Oh.' Carla's smile faltered. 'What a funny thing to say.'

'So is calling me sweet. Don't mistake me for something I ain't. I'm a Tyler.'

The lift filled with tension as Michael's eyes bored into her. Carla wasn't sure what to say. Calling him sweet was clearly a big mistake.

Suddenly a loud ping sounded, making Carla jump, and the door opened onto the top floor. The tension evaporated as quickly as it had gathered. Michael walked out of the lift and fumbled in his pocket for the keys. Carla swallowed and followed him to the front door of his flat, shaking off the strange feeling.

Opening the door, Michael walked in and stepped to the side to allow her to enter. They walked into a large, open room – clearly the main room. The walls and carpet were light grey with the occasional black-and-white abstract painting hung on the walls. There was a black leather sofa and two matching chairs surrounding a glass coffee table. It reminded her of something you might find in a plush office; it didn't look comfortable to her at all. There were no cushions and no ornaments on the coffee table. It looked like a very cold, clean showroom.

Behind the lounge area there was a glass dining table and six high-backed chairs. Michael hung his jacket on the back of one of these. Aware of Michael's finicky OCD ways, Carla followed suit and hung hers on the chair next to the one he had chosen.

'Want the grand tour?' Michael asked, his easy smile back in place.

Carla relaxed. 'Yeah, go on then.'

'Kitchen's this way.' Michael took her round to the right, almost back on themselves, and she noticed that the room was bigger than she had originally thought. The kitchen was recessed much further than the front door. It was all open-plan. The stainless-steel pots and pans that hung above the pristine cooker looked as though they had never been used. They probably never had, she reasoned. There was a breakfast bar with stools, and on the worktop was a large fruit bowl with some spare keys and a couple of apples in it. She was glad to see this tiny smidgen of evidence that there was life in this flat after all. It seemed so barren otherwise.

'That room over there is my office. That's out of bounds – you're to stay out of there.' Michael pointed towards a closed door and moved swiftly on. 'This is the bedroom.' He opened this door and she peeked inside. The masculine grey, white and black theme seemed to run throughout the whole flat. Still, the bed looked large and comfortable. A grin crept up on her face, and she turned her body towards Michael. Running her hands up his torso she began to unbutton his shirt.

'Well, I can think of a few things we can do in that room.'

Michael stopped her hands with his own as she reached for the third button.

'Later. First come in here.' He opened another door to the bathroom and pushed her gently into it. 'Get undressed,' he ordered.

Stumbling backward into the room, Carla steadied herself, and, turning towards the sink, began to do as he had asked. She slid the skimpy dress off her body, shimmying her bottom from side to side as she pulled her thong down with it. They fell to the ground, and she stepped out of the small pile of clothes, her stiletto heels click-clacking on the marble floor tiles. Using one finger, she pulled the slim back straps of her shoes down and stepped out of those too. Now she was fully naked. She took a quick peek in the mirror in front of her at Michael. He was turning the taps on in the large walk-in rainforest shower.

Carla bent down and picked up her clothes and shoes. Dumping the shoes next to the sink she hurriedly folded the dress and thong, making sure to do it neatly. She placed them on the edge of the sink unit and then propped the shoes on top. Dropping her arms to her sides, she leaned against the towel rail and waited for Michael. She wasn't sure what mood he was in tonight. Something about him seemed agitated and unpredictable. It made her feel slightly uneasy, but there was nothing she could do about that now. It wasn't like she could walk out on a Tyler.

She had thought this would be a bit of fun when she'd first seen him in the club. She'd had a lot to drink tonight for her friend Tina's birthday. She'd downed far too many tequila shots, that was for sure. *Bloody Tina*, she thought. She'd let her guard down; her instincts weren't quite as sharp as usual. When she saw Michael all that came to mind initially was how fit he was. Fit and rich and powerful; a heady combination. She fancied having a bit of him just for fun, for once. It was only in the lift, however, that she had been sharply reminded what a control freak he was and of his odd ways. She felt fully sober now and had her work head firmly back on her shoulders. Tonight would still be a freebie – that was fair enough. She had started things, after all. But she would make sure to keep him happy and leave him satisfied above feeding her own pleasure. Maybe it would still be enjoyable after all, even if he was a bit of a strange one.

Michael walked over to Carla and let her undress him, like she did in the parlour sometimes. She folded each item perfectly and he began to relax a little. When she finished he took her hands before she could touch his body.

'Get in the shower. You've been dancing and sweating in the club. I like you clean. Go on, get in,' he ordered, his tone brooking no argument.

Carla looked slightly surprised but got in without a word. Michael picked up a hard sponge loofah and covered it with soap. Turning Carla away from him he grabbed the back of her shoulder and pushed her forward directly under the water flow. She gasped at the sudden hot water but steadied herself. She trembled slightly. This felt strange. Michael wasn't full of lust and focused on getting his cock off, like most of her punters would be at this point. He seemed cold – detached and mechanical somehow.

He grasped the loofah tightly with his other hand and with clear purpose pushed it down on her back, scrubbing across her skin as hard as he could.

Carla let out a small exclamation of pain and then bit hard into her lip to silence herself. The loofah scraped harshly across, again and again, feeling like it was shredding the skin from her very body.

Michael watched the raw, red patch spread across her skin where he scrubbed. It made him feel good. He felt the tension trickle away out of his body as he methodically disposed of every single germ and microscopic piece of dirt on Carla's body.

Silent tears began to fall from Carla's face and blend into the shower water, as she began to seriously regret her decision to leave the club with Michael Tyler.


Sunlight crept through a chink in the curtains, waking Carla. She blinked away the sleep in her eyes and looked around, trying to get her bearings. She hadn't meant to stay the night, but she must have fallen asleep. After scrubbing her raw, Michael had led her to the bedroom where they had stayed up for many passionate hours. To Carla's surprise, she had actually really enjoyed herself too. It seemed that once Michael had got his frantic need to clean her out of his system, he had relaxed back into a more normal person. Perhaps she had been wrong about him, after all. She smiled lazily, recalling their activities.

Getting up out of the bed, she pulled a sheet around her and padded softly through to the main room, looking for Michael. The bathroom door was closed, and she could hear the shower running. He was getting ready for the day. Carla wandered around as she waited for him, looking more closely at Michael's home. She wondered if he ever really relaxed.

Her gaze paused on the open door to his office. He must have left it open by mistake. Glancing at the bathroom door to check he was still busy, she hurried over and peered inside. She grinned to herself, knowing she was being cheeky. He had told her it was off limits, and she knew why. He was a Tyler. The details of his business were shady at best – he wouldn't want anyone seeing. He wouldn't want to risk exposure. But she wasn't going to tell anyone; he had no need to worry about her. She knew the score.

Stepping inside she looked around. It was as stark as the rest of the house. There was a sofa and a bookshelf on one side, and a large desk with a computer on the other. The computer was switched on, both of the wide screens on the desk shining with life in the small room. Carla stepped closer to look at what Michael was working on, curiosity getting the better of her. Frowning, she leaned forward onto the desk, staring at the screen to her left.

The back of her neck prickled and Carla swung round, suddenly aware that she wasn't alone. Michael stood in the doorway, a towel around his waist, still dripping from the shower he had just vacated. His face was as dark as thunder, and Carla cowered backward. Michael stepped forward. His voice was heavy with anger as he spoke.

'You really should have listened…'

# CHAPTER THIRTY-ONE

Paul smiled crookedly in greeting as he entered Freddie's home office. Sammy was already there, and he acknowledged him with a nod.

'Alright,' he said. Checking his phone screen briefly, he slipped it into his pocket and sat down in one of the comfortable stuffed leather chairs next to Sammy.

'Alright, mate,' Freddie said. 'We've got the footage from the local cameras. Got dropped off at the office this morning.'

'Nice one. Where's Michael?'

'Running some errands for me – I'm behind. Which reminds me, where've you been hiding? Things have been really busy here.'

'I've been busy too – had some things to take care of. I'm here now though. What do you want me to do?'

Freddie frowned and looked at his younger brother. 'What stuff?'

'Fuck sake, Freddie, stuff! I 'ave got a personal life too, you know. Jesus!' Paul raised his voice, flustered. His face turned crimson. He didn't like being the centre of attention at the best of times.

'Alright, mate – keep your hair on. I was only asking.' Freddie put his hands up in surrender and Paul settled back down, his face moody.

Freddie pursed his lips. Paul had been acting really weirdly lately – super cagey. They used to be so much closer, but it seemed like Paul was putting more and more distance between them these days. He looked at Sammy, who gave him a subtle shake of the head, indicating that he had no idea what was up with Paul either.

Closing the door on this issue for now, Freddie turned back towards the computer screen and turned it so that all three of them could see.

'I had a look through this earlier and I think I might have found something. This runs from ten in the evening through to seven the next morning, right? At ten there's still some activity – not much but some. I figured that probably ain't them though. Whoever it is is a ghost. My guess is they wouldn't risk being seen. Same in the morning – it starts getting busy around six. So I fast-forwarded through most of the night and there are only two people that show up at odd times. This one.' Freddie pressed the play button and they both leaned in to see. 'He's just a neighbour stepping out for a cigarette. He goes back in after a minute. Then later on at 2.24 a.m. this comes up.' Freddie forwarded to the time he had stated and moved back so that the others could crowd in to watch.

Initially nothing moved. There was nothing on the screen but the view down a quiet road lit up by street lamps. Then out of the bottom right-hand corner a man appeared, his back turned to the camera. He wore a dark jacket and hat, clearly for the purposes of hiding, as it wasn't cold enough to warrant that much outerwear. He walked quickly down the street, his hands in his pockets until the camera could barely pick him up in the distance. Sammy squeezed his eyes at the screen and moved nearer. Just before he disappeared into the dark completely, the man took a right turn down a side street. Freddie paused the footage and they all sat back.

'He was going east, away from Hargreaves' house here, and the camera didn't pick him up on his way in, so he would have arrived from another direction. There was another tape from one of the other roads near the house, but he wasn't on there either.'

'How many blind roads are there leading in?' Sammy asked.

'Two more fully blind, and the road the other camera was on is partial. There are side streets meeting it all the way along, and the camera only starts halfway down.'

Sammy sighed heavily and rubbed his face in frustration. Paul scratched his head.

'It's not a lot to go on,' Freddie admitted, 'but it does give us something.'

'What?' Paul asked, frowning at the screen.

'Well, we know it's a well-built bloke. He ain't that old, the pace he's bouncing down the road at. And although it's a very thin connection, I'm guessing he lives east somewhere. He ain't parked around that corner, because no lights or cars appear on the screen after that.'

'He could have gone the other way,' Paul chipped in.

Freddie shook his head. 'Dead-end street, but there's an alleyway that runs up towards some bus stops.'

'Well then, he could be going either way, Fred,' Sammy said.

'I thought that,' Freddie replied, 'but I checked the routes out this afternoon. Hargreaves' house is in the middle of two stops. If he was going west, he would have walked to the one in the other direction. This is of course on the thin presumption that he went to catch one of those buses. You know what this city is like – it's a maze. There are so many options, but if I was to go with my gut, I'd say he took a bus east.'

'You missed your calling in life, Fred.' Sammy grinned. 'You should have been a detective.'

'Fuck that,' Freddie shot back, laughing. 'Not enough pay for me, mate. Plus, I'd hate to be the one to put hard-working people like us out of business. There's criminals, and there's *criminals*. We might sit on the wrong side of the law, but at the end of the day we're just businessmen. The likes of politicians, however, now that's where they really should be looking. The men who shaft the people.'

Sammy nodded with a grin. Freddie got particularly het up over dirty politicians. He hated them with a passion. Whatever wrong he did – and he did commit many wrong deeds – Freddie was always fair and looked after those around him. He felt obliged to help the people who got a rough ride and never took undue advantage just to line his own pocket.

'Anyway,' Freddie continued, 'I don't have time to talk about that. I'm not sure how to proceed from here. Any ideas?'

A silence fell over the room as they each mulled this over. The only sound was the quiet ticking of Freddie's office clock. Eventually Sammy sat forward.

'If we're assuming at the moment that he did leave by bus, then he would probably have arrived by bus, right? And if he was coming from the other direction, he probably would have got off at the other bus stop. It's a long shot, but if he gets away with leaving something on the doorstep he might come round again.'

'I doubt it. If he's clever he'll realise there'll be pigs watching the house at night now. Hargreaves ain't Joe Bloggs – he's the Secretary of State for Justice. He has an army of flatfoots at his disposal.'

'Yeah, but… he likes to play with fire, though, don't he? He wouldn't have left the ropes on the doorstep if he didn't.'

'True… It's a long shot, but we've got nothing else at the moment. Paul, can you get a man at the bus stop, onwards from tonight. Don't tell him anything, just the spec of what to look for and follow.'

'Sure, no problem.'

'Sammy, check out the back routes coming in to that stop. See if there's anywhere you'd hide a kidnapped girl near any of the stops.'

Sammy whistled. That was going to be a long list. There were a lot of stops and far too many places where this was possible in London.

'I know,' Freddie said, seeing his face. 'But it's all we have, mate.' He slapped him on the back. 'We're going to have to do this the hard way. And I'll tell you something for nothing.' His face clouded over. 'When I get my hands on this fucker, after the threat he's placed over my head… he's going to wish he had never been born.'

# CHAPTER THIRTY-TWO

Katherine barely moved as her captor entered the room. She didn't care why he was here. Her spirit was all but broken, her mind wandering in despairing circles. Dark all the time, nothing to look at, nothing to hear, she felt like she was starting to go mad. She could feel sores all over her body from where she had lain too long in this foetid bed. They hurt her constantly, but this was something she was getting used to. Her ankles stung, her bones ached with the cold and her head pounded from malnourishment. Even her teeth hurt now, for some reason. A few sores just added to the fun.

The light shone in her face, and she closed her eyes against it tiredly.

'You don't look so hot,' came the deep computerised tone. She wished she could hear his real voice, just for a second. Maybe she could work out who he was.

'Hah.' She managed a weak laugh. There was a silence.

'I've bought you something. I need you to hold still.'

The light shone onto a syringe half full with some sort of cloudy white liquid. Katherine jumped in shock and screamed, her voice so hoarse that it barely came out as more than a whisper.

'No, no, no!' Katherine shook her head and dragged herself as far back as she could. 'No, please. Please not that – not drugs. Just kill me, please!' Tears streamed down her gaunt, filthy face, making lines in the dirt on her skin. Her whole body shook in terror. Her captor tutted impatiently.

'It's penicillin. It's to make you better. I need you alive.'

Katherine stared at the needle in horror still, not sure whether to believe him.

He continued. 'I brought you a blanket too and a jumper. Should keep you warm enough.' To prove his point, he threw a carrier bag on the bed with the mentioned items inside. 'If you make this difficult, I'll ensure you regret it,' he warned. 'Understand?'

Katherine nodded through her tears, wishing she was anywhere but here.

'Now hold still. This is going in your arm.'

His leather gloves came into view and grabbed her bound wrists. Katherine winced and sobbed, but she let him take her hands without quarrel. He wiped the skin above her most visible vein with a small, square wet wipe. Katherine could smell the alcohol on it. The hypocrisy of cleaning the needle site, while keeping her festering in all this dirt would have made her laugh if it had been any other situation.

He held her arm tight, pressed the sharp tip of the needle against her skin and without hesitation smoothly slid it into the vein. Katherine cried out, in fear more than anything else, as she felt the cold liquid enter her bloodstream.

'There, all done. Not long to go now,' he said, matter-of-factly. His hand was still on her arm, his thumb pressing down on the open needle site to stop the blood. 'Put your thumb where mine is and keep the pressure on for a couple of minutes,' he ordered.

Katherine shivered and pulled her arm back. She awkwardly twisted her hand so that she could replace his thumb with hers. Her captor pulled something out of his pocket and held it forward for her to see. She frowned in confusion. It was a small rectangular object with buttons on it, wrapped in cling film.

'You're wondering what this is.' It wasn't a question – it was a statement. 'This is a voice recorder.' Katherine's heart grew cold as she heard an evil smile curl into his strange, robotic voice, 'I have a little message that you're going to read out for me.'

# CHAPTER THIRTY-THREE

Tanya laughed and threw a pillow at Anna. They were curled up together on the sofa in Anna's comfortable lounge, drinking wine and chilling out after a busy week with the club.

'I would pay good money to see you dance on the tables in our club,' Tanya said. Tears of laughter streamed from Anna's eyes, and she clamped her hand over her mouth as she rocked with mirth. Her face turned red, and she waved her hands at Tanya.

'Stop! I can't laugh anymore!'

'Oh come on, are you telling me that you aren't the slightest bit tempted? Come on, I reckon you'd be really good! Throwing your stuff about. I mean, well… you'd have to actually learn to dance though. I've seen you after a couple of tequilas – you ain't exactly winning any competitions…' Tanya pursed her lips and shook her hips from side to side with exaggerated awkwardness. Anna shrieked with laughter again and bent her head over, trying to gain control of herself.

'Stop it! I really can't take any more!'

Tanya laughed along with her. 'Yeah, on second thoughts, we can't afford to lose the business – don't ever get up on those tables.'

Anna wiped the tears from her eyes. 'God, you do make me laugh, Tanya Smith. It's what I love about you. Talking of making people laugh, I was hoping we could get a date in the diary for a girls' night out soon. Just in the club, with my friend Amanda. Up for it?'

'Yeah, sure. That the one with the dog-on-heat husband?'

'That's the one,' Anna replied. 'She looked so sad when I met her. Defeated almost. I want to cheer her up, make her smile again. Even if it is just for one night.'

'Sure – sounds good. I'm always up for a good night out, you know me.'

'I do indeed,' Anna said, chuckling. She reached over to grab her glass and found it was empty. The bottle of Pinot Grigio was too.

'OK, we're out. Wait here. I've got another in the fridge; I'll go grab it.'

'Grab my phone, will ya? I think I left it on the breakfast bar.'

Anna's bare feet padded across the shiny tiles towards the recycling. Dumping the empty bottle inside, she opened the fridge and grasped the neck of the full bottle she had chilling in the rack. She flicked her long, dark hair back over her shoulder where it had fallen forward and looked around the kitchen for Tanya's phone. As she reached it, the phone beeped and a message came up on the screen. Anna didn't mean to look, but the light drew her gaze instinctively to the screen. Her mouth formed a wide circle of shock, and her brow furrowed.

'Tanya!' She marched through to the lounge, absently clutching the bottle.

'What?' Tanya held her hands up in mock surrender at the sight of her friend's face. 'What've I done?' She giggled tipsily.

'You haven't done anything, but who the hell is sending you this?' Anna asked. She sounded surprised and annoyed. Tanya reached forward and took the phone. She scanned the message, and her face clouded over. Suddenly she felt rather sober. She opened it and read it properly.

*I know what you're doing, bitch.*

Tanya sighed and clicked the phone screen off. Anna spread her arms out in question.

'What the hell?' she asked, concerned for her friend. 'Who is that? What's that about?'

Tanya reached out and took the wine bottle out of Anna's hand and screwed off the cap. She poured them both a glass and handed Anna hers as she sat down next to her on the sofa again.

'I don't actually know. I've had a couple of weird messages from that number, but if I reply I don't get an answer, and when I call it, it's always off.' She shrugged. 'It's probably just a wrong number, some random having a pop at someone who's pissed them off.' She didn't mention all the times she had been followed. There was no reason to worry Anna further; she looked worried enough as it was.

'Why didn't you tell me about it before?' Anna drank some of her wine and settled back into the corner of the sofa.

'Well, I sorta did. You know that number I asked if Freddie could trace? That was this number.'

Anna's eyebrows shot up, and her eyes narrowed accusingly. 'You told me that was some pervert you'd dated sending rude texts!'

'Well, you never know, it could be. Just… a different type of rude.' Tanya drank deeply from her glass, avoiding eye contact. Anna shook her head and sighed loudly.

There was a sound in the hallway behind them, and the front door opened and closed. Two male voices floated towards them, deep in conversation. Anna turned her head to greet Freddie.

'Hey, you. Hi, Paul. How's it going?'

'Yeah, alright, Anna. You?' Paul answered politely.

Freddie bent and kissed Anna's cheek. He smiled at Tanya. 'Alright, Tan?'

'Freddie,' she answered with a nod. 'Paul.' She turned her attention towards him. 'How you been? Ain't seen you in ages.'

'All good,' Paul answered shortly. He seemed distracted, Anna thought.

'What you girls been up to then?' Freddie grinned at them both charmingly. Anna couldn't help but smile back; his mood was always so infectious. Her smile was tight though. She couldn't shake off the tension between them, no matter how much she wanted to.

Tanya grinned and pointed to the wine bottle. 'Enjoying your local shop's finest cheap plonk and talking about you, ya dirty bastard.' She winked to let him know she was joking.

'Oh yeah, anything juicy?' he replied mischievously.

'Yeah, loads.'

'Freddie?' Anna interjected. 'Did anything come of that number I gave you to check for Tanya?'

'Nah, sorry – meant to say. It was a burner, not registered.'

'What's that?' Paul asked Freddie.

'Tanya had a few dodgy texts, wanted the number tracked. Nothing came of it though. Still getting them?' he asked her.

'Yeah, nothing serious though, just some dirty twat who clearly needs a shag.' She shot Anna a glance, warning her not to say anything. Anna ignored it.

'Actually, Freddie, it's someone sending cryptic hate messages, but as usual Tanya thinks she can handle everything on her own without telling anyone. I only know because I saw one just come through.'

'What?' Freddie held his hand out for Tanya's phone. 'Let me see.'

Tanya huffed but passed it over. Freddie read them and handed it back, his expression full of disgust.

'That's fucked up. Who is it? Do you have any idea?'

'No, I don't. I'm sure I've pissed many people off in my time, but nothing too serious and nothing that stands out.' She shrugged. 'Ain't bothering me. It's probably a wrong number.'

Freddie looked concerned. 'Do you want me to put someone with you for a bit, just in case?'

'No, I bloody well don't!' Tanya replied indignantly. 'Jesus, I'm a big girl who's dealt with plenty of saddos and nut jobs in my time. A couple of texts ain't nothing to worry about.'

'Yes, but you don't know who this one is, Tanya,' Anna tried to reason.

'I'm not talking about it anymore. It's done; I'm fine.' Tanya's jaw set in a firm line, and she eyed them all hard.

Anna sighed and shook her head at Freddie. There was no point trying to push her – she was a stubborn mare when she wanted to be.

'Come on then or we'll be late to meet Irish Craig.' Freddie turned to Anna and paused awkwardly. 'Only popped home to grab a package on my way. I'll see you later. Paul?' Paul was looking at Tanya and chewing his lip, his expression unreadable. 'Paul?' Freddie repeated.

'Yep. Bye, Anna. Tanya.' He followed Freddie from the house and the girls found themselves alone once more.

Tanya watched Anna's expression grow heavier again. 'Things still not right between you two?' she asked.

'No. Not at all.' Anna answered sadly.

Tanya squeezed Anna's shoulder. 'I'm sorry, mate. I'm sure it's nothing though. Or at least not what you're thinking.'

'That's the thing though, Tan. I don't even know what to think anymore.'

They sat in silence for a few minutes until Anna took a deep breath and picked up the bottle of wine. She forced a smile.

'Right, well. Let's get back to having some us time, shall we? Lord knows we both need it!'

'Indeed.' Tanya smiled back warmly as she held out her glass to be refilled. Behind the smile though, her stomach began to twist in worry. The fact it was a burner phone meant that whoever was following her had thought this through. They didn't want to be discovered. Things were beginning to seem more serious than she had originally thought.

# CHAPTER THIRTY-FOUR

Michael stepped out of the tall terraced house he had just been negotiating in and began walking down the street. He couldn't get a parking space when he arrived, so his car was a few minutes away. He called Freddie to give him an update.

'Hey, yeah, just got out.' Throwing a cursory look over his shoulder, Michael mentally noted a young man in a hoody a few metres behind him. He was always careful to check no one was listening when he was discussing business, just like Freddie had taught him.

'Nah, they wanted the higher margin but less stuff. I've told them they get both or neither.' Checking both ways, he crossed the road.

The man in the hoody crossed the road behind him.

'Yes, I told them that too. Gave them till five to confirm which it will be.' Michael glanced sideways at the reflection in the windows of the cars he passed as he walked. The hoody was catching up. He frowned. Something looked off about the way he was walking.

'I've gotta go, catch you later.'

Michael kept his eye on the reflections as he walked and trained his ears onto the soft thudding sounds of the other man's footsteps. The hoody had his hands deep in his pockets, and his shoulders were locked up – tense.

A short gap came up between two cars and Michael quickened his pace to the next one, losing sight of his follower. As he came up to the next car, the reflection came back into view, and just in time. Michael's eyes widened and he dived sideways and watched the reflection of a blade plunge down towards his back.

He got out of the way just in time. The knife sliced down through the air just inches from his body. He turned to face the man who had just tried to stab him. His furious gaze locked onto the other man's startled expression, and he leaped forward before the hoody had time to recover from his hesitation.

Grasping his attacker's wrists, he tried to force him to drop the knife, but he held on with determination. They silently struggled against each other, fairly evenly matched for strength. Michael made a sound of frustration. He wasn't getting anywhere like this. He rocked back and then bought his knee up into his attacker's side as hard as he could, throwing all of his body weight into it. It worked. The man doubled over, winded.

Michael took the knife and twisting his attacker's arm behind his back, held it against his ribs. He took a couple of deep breaths, his heart beating fast and swiftly checked up and down the street. There was no one around; no one had seen the short struggle. No one would have seen him bleeding out on the street either, had his attacker succeeded, he realised. It was a well-planned location at least – he would give him that.

'Who the fuck are you?' he growled, fuming. There was no answer. He twisted his arm harder, causing the man to wince. 'No? No answer? That's fine, mate. Not a fucking problem.' His tone was furious. He began marching him towards his car, the knife pressed hard against his side. 'I'd prefer to get it out of you the hard way anyway.'

An hour later, Michael's attacker sat tied to a hard-backed chair in the middle of one of Freddie's empty barns in Essex. They had various empty storehouses like this, dotted around for when things needed to be moved quickly or to hold any excess stock. This one was empty, other than a few pieces of furniture. Underneath the chair Michael had laid out a large plastic sheet, four metres wide and long. The Tylers kept plastic sheeting at most of their rural locations, to make clean-up easier on dirty jobs such as these. It was just practical, as it avoided any DNA traces being left on the floor.

'So,' Michael snapped as he paced back and forth in front of the now-bloodied young man. 'Still not feeling chatty, sunshine?' He pulled back his leather-clad fist and smashed it into the man's face again. Blood spattered across the floor and he spat out a tooth, but still he said nothing.

Dean walked in and shut the big barn doors behind him. 'Alright?' he asked, frowning in concern. He put down his heavy backpack on a nearby desk.

'Luckily, yeah. Wouldn't be if this wanker had got his way.'

Dean shook his head in disgust and turned away to open his bag. Michael swung his attention back to the man tied up in the chair. He was seething with anger. Rather than calming down on his way over here, he had become more and more enraged at the audacity of this no-mark trying to kill him. He was ready to rip his head off right now, but he held back. He still needed to know who he worked for and whether this was a solo vendetta or whether there was a hit out against him.

He studied him. He was shabbily dressed in jeans, a shapeless T-shirt and an oversized, dark-green hoody. He was tall and fairly strong but thin, with bad skin and a short patchy beard. He was no one of note and no one Michael had come across before. Michael had a knack for remembering faces. And he definitely would have remembered this one.

'I'm going to ask you again.' He narrowed his eyes as the man smirked through the black eyes and dried blood on his face. 'Who are you and why were you trying to kill me? I suggest you start talking now, because I don't think you're particularly going to like being tortured.'

The man's eyes widened and focused in on Michael.

'Yeah.' Michael smiled coldly. 'My friend here is very skilled at causing a ton of pain with minimal effort. It's beautiful to watch actually. Personally I'd like to just go ahead, but I'll allow you this one last chance before we get to that.'

Dean turned on a small hand-held blowtorch and began heating the end of a small branding iron. The man in the chair gave them a panicked look before locking his jaw and straining against his bindings. Michael waited, his face emotionless. The branding iron glowed brightly, having reached maximum heat.

Suddenly the barn door was flung open and hit the inside wall with a bang. They all jumped at the unexpectedly loud noise. Freddie flew across the room towards them with a roar, deep red rage written across his face. He swiped the branding iron out of Dean's hand, and before any of them knew what was happening, grabbed the man by the throat with one hand as he slammed the iron down hard onto the top of his thigh with the other.

The man screamed out in agony. Freddie bellowed at him. 'Who the fuck do you think you are? You think you can try to take out my brother and get away with it?' Spittle flew out of his mouth onto the man's face as he shook with anger.

The man screamed again, his face turning white in shock and pain. Freddie squeezed his neck one last time and reluctantly let go, flinging him backward. The chair fell over and he hit the floor.

Freddie sniffed and ran his hand back through his hair, fixing it back into place again. He took a deep breath and straightened his jacket, regaining his composure before he spoke. He turned to his brother.

'Michael,' he said curtly. 'You alright?'

'Yeah, good thanks,' Michael replied.

'Good. What have you got so far?'

'Nothing yet. Dean just got here though, so hopefully something soon.'

'Right. OK.' Freddie nodded, his lips set in a hard line.

He had been furious when he received Michael's call. Freddie wasn't someone who allowed his emotions to get the better of him. His cool head was what had helped him rise to the top and stay there. But his one weakness was his family.

Dean hoisted the chair up so that the man was once again upright. He was sobbing and shaking, blood running down his leg from the big, red burn now on show through the hole the iron had made in his trousers. Freddie handed the iron back to Dean, who once again began to burn it with the blowtorch.

'No, please,' the man begged shakily. 'I'll tell you. Please don't do it again.'

Freddie tilted his head to the side at the sound of the accent. He swung around. 'You're Albanian,' he stated.

'Yes.' The man lowered his eyes away from Freddie's intense gaze. Freddie quickly pieced things together.

'Do you work for Viktor Morina?'

'Yes,' he admitted.

Freddie raised an eyebrow, unimpressed. 'Well, you weren't hard to crack. Not very loyal to your boss, are you? Any one of my men would have shown more balls in your place.' He shook his head. 'What is the world coming to… OK then, why?'

'Why he ask me to kill your brother?'

'Yes, why did he ask you to kill my brother?' Freddie confirmed, his patience wearing thin.

'Because you had him kidnapped and his arm broken. He had to repay you.'

'He had to repay me?' Freddie shrugged at Michael. 'He had to repay me. Right, OK. Well, thank you for that and better luck in your next life.'

'Wha—'

Before he could finish his sentence, Freddie pulled his gun from his inside pocket and shot him in the head.

'Hey, hang on,' Michael protested. 'I wasn't finished!'

'He isn't a toy, Michael.' Freddie wiped down his gun with the bottom of his jacket before taking it off. 'We got what we needed out of him.' He unbuttoned his shirt and threw that on the floor along with the jacket. 'Dean, get my gym bag out of the boot.'

'On it.' Dean disappeared.

'But he tried to kill me,' Michael persisted.

Freddie stopped and looked him in the eye. 'And he's paid for that. Like Viktor will, for ordering the hit. Now burn those' – he pointed to his clothes – 'along with the rest of this shit. And get rid of him. Dean, you help him.'

''Course.' Dean had reappeared with the leather holdall Freddie used as a gym bag.

Reaching into it, Freddie pulled out a white T-shirt and shrugged it on over his head. He slung the bag over his shoulder and put his gun into one of the inner pockets.

'I'll have someone pick Morina up.'

Without further discussion, Freddie left. He stepped out of the barn into bright sunshine and blue skies. It was a beautiful day, but he didn't notice. He drove away with a grim expression. Viktor Morina had stepped way beyond the line. It wouldn't be a broken arm and a warning this time. He had just signed his own death warrant.

# CHAPTER THIRTY-FIVE

Freddie's phone rang, and he closed his eyes in annoyance when he saw who it was. He let it ring a few more times before resentfully picking it up.

'What?' he asked angrily.

'He's been back to the house.' Riley's excitement seemed to override the usual tone of disdain she used with him.

'And?'

'And he's left a voice recorder, with a message from her on it. I've got it in the lab now, being analysed.'

Freddie quickly thought over his plans for the evening. There was nothing pressing that wouldn't wait.

'Bring the recorder and the results to my office at CoCo in an hour.'

'I'll see you there,' she replied.

Freddie clicked off the call and looked at the picture of Anna staring up at him from his screen. He sent her a text.

*Dinner tomorrow night? Zafferano 8 p.m.? X*

He pressed send and waited for her response. It came through a minute later.

*OK. X*

A warm smile temporarily replaced the stress and worry on Freddie's face. She loved that restaurant. They had spent their first

Valentine's Day there, which had not been long after they had both finally escaped the wrath of Tony Christou. It had been an amazing night, their first proper romantic date with no need to hide and no more secrets between them. Perhaps the reminder of happier times would help bridge the gap that was widening between them.

Freddie wished there were still no secrets between them now. He knew Anna deserved the truth, but he couldn't give her that. Not yet. He couldn't put the worry and fear of being locked up and murdered on her head. He just couldn't do that to her. He had to fix it first. He was just hoping that her belief in him was strong enough to hold out until he could. But at this point, he really wasn't sure it would be.

An hour later, Sarah Riley walked into Freddie's office, not bothering to knock. Freddie hid his annoyance and ignored her childish attempt to get under his skin. Sarah sat in the chair opposite him.

'Please, sit down,' he said sarcastically. He took a breath and sat up straighter in his chair, leaning forward. 'So what did they find?'

Sarah slid an evidence bag across the table to Freddie. He reached into his desk drawer and pulled out a pair of latex gloves. He put them on before opening the bag.

'Oh please.' Sarah snorted. 'I'm hardly going to put it back into evidence now, am I?'

'Better safe than sorry,' Freddie replied.

He pulled out the recorder and pressed the play button. There was a crackling noise, then a weak, shaky voice began talking.

*'This is a message for my father. I'm still alive. I'm not dead… yet.'*

The woman on the tape gulped and began to cry.

*'I am very ill. I've been given medication to keep the infection from spreading, but this won't save me if I'm down here much longer. You have to… you… I can't!'*

The sobbing grew louder, and a deep, strange voice murmured something quietly in the background. A louder noise sounded which Freddie couldn't identify, but it seemed to scare the girl into continuing through her tears.

*'OK, OK! Dad… he says you have to trade William's life for mine. He says…'*

She gulped and sobbed again.

*'William must sacrifice himself by his own hand. He must kill himself within the next seven days. He is allowed this week to get his affairs in order and when that time is up, if William hasn't done as requested, I… I will be mutilated and killed. And my body will never be found. Oh God…'*

Freddie heard her voice move away from the microphone and her desperate sobs take over completely. There was a muffled sound and then the recording ended.

Freddie blew out the breath he had been holding and raised his eyebrows in shock. 'Fuck me.'

'I wouldn't have thought listening to the threat of mutilation and murder would unsettle someone like you, Mr Tyler,' Riley replied caustically.

Freddie stared at her levelly. 'Which goes to prove how little you actually know of me, Miss Riley.'

Freddie dismissed her barbed comment. Someone like her would never be able to understand the complex life he led. Yes, Freddie was known as someone not to be crossed. He had tortured and he had killed, but he'd had good reason every time. It wasn't something he enjoyed and something he never carried out lightly. Was he a killer? Yes. But he wasn't sadistic. He would never harm an innocent. DCI Riley would never understand the vast difference between him and Katherine Hargreaves' kidnapper.

'What did your squints find?' he asked, moving on.

'A couple of things. The kidnapper was careful not to leave anything we could use last time, but this time some pollen made its way into the bag. Possibly carried in on his glove.'

'Pollen?' Freddie looked sceptical.

'Yes, but not just any pollen. It was pollen that comes from a rare plant called grass-of-Parnassus. It's not usually found in London, but when it is, it's found in damp areas with old, close-knit housing.'

'Right, so is there some sort of flower fanatic group that keeps track of who grows them?'

'It's a wildflower, so it would be unlikely. But the team are working on narrowing down areas it would be more likely to grow in. I've had a look through what few documented accounts there are and it seems they've mostly been spotted in the older residential areas of the East End, fairly close to the river, or further down south.'

Freddie shook his head. 'He don't have her south of the river.'

'Why do you say that?'

'That's too much hassle. It would have been difficult to get her across or under the river without being picked up on traffic cams or CCTV. Your facial recognition would have picked her up.'

'Unless he had her hidden in the boot of his car.'

'She disappeared without a struggle in a public place. There were no disturbances nearby. If she went willingly, I'd bet he kept her happy in the passenger seat of his car until he reached his destination. Keeps it simple, less risk of being noticed.'

Riley chewed the side of her mouth as she thought it over. 'Possibly. But we can't assume.'

'No, *you* can't assume. I can assume what I want. My instincts haven't let me down yet. What else? What about his voice?'

'She says *"if I'm down here much longer"*, so we're thinking it must be underground somewhere. We isolated his voice and cleared it up as much as possible, but it told us nothing. He's using some sort of voice mask. All we can gather is that the kidnapper is male, which we already knew from her message and that he probably has a deep voice.' She shrugged. 'It could be half of London.'

'What about the recorder itself? Where sells it?'

'Loads of places. It's cheap, sells in most gadget shops, and it's also a bestseller on Amazon.'

Freddie pinched the bridge of his nose. That wasn't much to work on, and now the clock was ticking faster than ever. In one week, if he didn't find the girl first, one of Ben Hargreaves' children would be dead. And Freddie was lined up to pay the price. The pressure lay heavily across his shoulders.

Sarah placed the recorder back into the bag and slipped it into her jacket pocket. She stood up and looked down her nose at him. 'One week, Tyler. Find her.'

She turned and walked out, leaving the door open behind her. Freddie stared after her, lost in thought. He needed to start thinking about drastic measures. His time was running out.

# CHAPTER THIRTY-SIX

Club Anya was closed for the night. Anna sat down on the small sofa in her office and, slipping her feet out of her stilettos, pushed them to one side. She curled up comfortably and looked through the folder in her hand once more.

Tanya had asked her if she wanted to partner up on buying another house to rent out. Anna had enthusiastically agreed, relieved to have something else to take her mind off her sinking relationship, and they were now sifting through options. She paused on the third house in and chewed her lip thoughtfully. It was a great location, a four-bedroomed house in West Hampstead. The price was about a hundred thousand more than the top end of their budget, but they both still really wanted to buy it.

Anna knew that she had only to ask and Freddie would give her the money, but that was something she wasn't prepared to do. She had never accepted a penny from him before, or any of his offers of help. Having spent years stripped of any independence by her psychotic ex, she still found it hard to allow anyone else to assist her now. Her business was her own, as were her finances. She would never allow anyone the opportunity to take that away from her again.

She knew Freddie was nothing like Tony. She knew he wasn't the sort of person to ever try to take what was not his. But still, old habits die hard. And lately, with how things had been between them, Anna wasn't sure she wanted to form any more ties that would be hard to undo if things fell apart. Now more than ever, she would be keeping her ranks firmly closed.

There was a soft knock at the door.

'Come in, Carl.'

'It's not Carl,' came the reply.

Anna looked up to see Michael walking through.

'He let me in; he's just leaving. Hope that's OK?'

'Oh! Hi, of course it's fine. Come on in.' Anna smiled up at him, glad of the distraction from her thoughts of Freddie. 'This is a surprise. Everything OK?'

'Yeah… everything's fine.'

The way he said it made Anna frown. He seemed slightly agitated, but she didn't press it. If he wanted to talk, he would. His expression changed and he smiled at her, his blue eyes twinkling. She was reminded of how similar he looked to Freddie. The same, dark, brooding good looks and the same cheeky smile that could melt a heart of ice. She smiled back fondly. He was a handsome young boy. No doubt he was already breaking hearts.

Michael held up two glasses and a bottle of wine. 'Swiped these from behind your bar and left the money by the till. Could really use a drink. Have one with me?'

'Sure, OK.' Anna was surprised. They saw each other frequently around the rest of the family, but Michael had never dropped in on her before. It was a nice surprise though. Now he had grown up, he was working a lot closer with Freddie. It would be good to spend more time with him and get to know him better.

He sat down next to her on the sofa and poured them each a glass. Taking hers, Anna closed the file she had been looking at.

'So, long day then?'

'Hmm?' Michael seemed distracted.

'You said you really needed a drink.'

'Oh, yeah. Well, most days you need a drink in our line of work. I guess Freddie's the same.'

'Yes, we usually have a glass or two in the evenings. You usually go for one with Paul, don't you?'

'Usually, yeah. But he's been busy a lot lately. Don't seem to have time for it no more.' Michael's tone held a tinge of resentment.

*Ah*, Anna thought. *He was lonely.*

'I never see you with girls. Do you not get much time to date, working with Freddie?'

'It's not that, it's just… None of the single girls I meet are the right sort, you know?'

'Yes, I do.' Anna had to agree. Most of the women who threw themselves at the Tyler brothers were cheap and shallow, just looking to bag a bad boy with some status.

'I need someone with brains. Classy, interesting. Someone who grafts. Someone I can respect.' His clear blue eyes were steady as he stared at her, his expression unreadable.

'That sounds like a good list of attributes. And there are plenty of those women around too. We just need to find them.'

'Are there?' he asked. 'I can't say I've met many that meet that description.'

'Well, I have.' Anna grinned brightly. 'And I tell you what, I bet you I could set you up with someone within the week who you would actually like.'

Michael looked sceptical. 'I doubt it,' he replied.

'Well, why don't you give it a try? You have nothing to lose. And I have a really nice girl in mind for you already. What do you say?' Anna smiled, excited by the idea forming in her mind.

Michael paused and drank some of his wine. 'OK,' he replied reluctantly. 'If it'll make you happy, I'll meet her.'

'Fantastic!' Anna replied enthusiastically. 'I'll text her and let you know what she says.'

'OK. I have to go, only popped in on my way through. Got to meet Freddie.'

'OK, have a good night then. See you soon.'

'Laters.' Michael left and Anna was alone again.

She stared at the wine glasses thoughtfully. What had that been about? Michael seemed really down in the dumps. At least he had agreed to the blind date though. She really did have a nice girl in mind for him, someone she really liked. It would be a great match. Hopefully it would lift his spirits, and he wouldn't be quite so glum.

Michael's last words finally registering in her head, Anna sighed. There was little chance of Freddie coming home tonight if Michael was only just off to meet him. Her heart sank, and her eyes rested on their favourite picture on the wall. What was Freddie up to? she wondered. Was it truly the beginning of the end for them? Was their time as a happy, honest, open couple nearly up?

# CHAPTER THIRTY-SEVEN

Freddie pulled up at a tall terraced house in East London. The road was quiet, and several of the houses around them were abandoned. He walked in and made his way through a dark, narrow hallway into the lounge at the back. Two saggy brown sofas sat against the walls, with three men casually slouched in them, smoking cigarettes. The ancient carpet was badly stained and burned around its dark green and orange swirls. Freddie hid his disgust. It was a horrible place. Mollie would have a fit if she saw the amount of filth that had accumulated over the years.

In an empty corner of the room there was a man seated on the floor, his mouth gagged and his wrists and ankles bound. He was eyeing the men around him angrily.

'Reggie, Dean, Simon.' Freddie nodded at each of his men in turn.

Freddie unbuttoned his jacket and took it off, laying it neatly on the back of one of the sofas. Dean stubbed out his cigarette, rolled up his sleeves and stood, having received his cue.

Freddie faced the bound man, who was now beginning to show signs of panic.

'It was one thing trying your luck with my business, Viktor,' Freddie began. 'It was stupid, but I let that go. I let you off very lightly. You should have thanked me for only ordering a broken arm and been on your way. Because it is another thing entirely' – Freddie's voice was deadly – 'to try to kill my brother; my flesh and blood. See, I value family over everything. I value family over money, property, even over my own life. I would do anything for those I care about. And I do mean anything.' Freddie signalled to his men with a wave of his hand that he was ready to begin.

Simon moved a wooden chair into the middle of the room, and Dean hoisted Viktor up onto it. He bound his wrists to the back so that he wasn't able to stand. Viktor kicked out and squirmed, but he was a small man and had no muscle. He got nowhere.

Freddie leaned down until his face was level with his captive's. With one hand he pulled the gag down. Viktor immediately screamed for help. The men in the room began to laugh, and Freddie shook his head.

'Screaming won't get you anywhere here, mate. Half the street is derelict, and the other half wouldn't grass me out if I was the last person standing between them and heaven.' Freddie waited as this sank in and Viktor stopped screaming. 'Well, now that's done with, let's get down to business, shall we?'

'It wasn't me, Freddie. I would never order hit on your brother. We had little disagreement, yes, but that is finished with.' Viktor's voice trembled as he tried to squirm his way out of the situation. He knew he had fucked up, big time. He had thought he was big enough to take the Tylers on. He had seen himself waltzing in and taking what he wanted, with no opposition. He hadn't realised until far too late that the fat, lazy scumbags he employed might be good at doing the dirty work, but they had no real skill, and they were about as loyal as a bunch of hyenas.

'Please,' he begged. 'I don't want make enemy; I want to make up for my poor judgement before. Perhaps you would be interested in one of my whorehouses? As gift to you, to show my humble gratitude and friendship at your mercy?' His eyes shot from one to another of the men around the room. No one was listening to him except Freddie, whose look of anger had only deepened.

'Listen to me, you jumped-up cunt!' Freddie shot forward and grabbed Viktor by the throat. He lifted him so that he was slightly off the chair, his face turning deep red as he squeezed. 'I don't take kindly to bullshit, so you best start owning it, straight up like a man, or I will make this ten times worse for you. I hold little respect for liars.' He unclenched his hand from Viktor's throat and dropped him back into the chair. Viktor coughed and spluttered as he drew oxygen back into his lungs.

'OK, fine. It was me. But you started war with me – I could not ignore. I will, though, if you let me go. I will show you respect and do whatever you want. Please, I beg of you. I have wife and children.'

'You should have thought of that before trying to murder my brother. I can't accept that. You know the score. You ain't leaving this room alive. But I'll give you one merciful option. You give me some information on how I can find Katherine Hargreaves, the girl I came to you about. If you do that, I'll make it quick.' Freddie looked at his watch. 'You have ten seconds to start talking. There will be no second chance. Go.'

Viktor's mouth flapped open as he flailed. 'I – I don't have information. Please, Freddie, I don't know anything about her. That is the truth! Please don't do this!' he begged.

'Five, four…'

'Please, I would tell you if I knew. Maybe I can find out! If you let me go, I will put all my men on her trail. I will find her! Freddie, please!'

'One.'

'Wait, no, Freddie, I will find her for you. I can talk to people, have my men search, no, please!' His cries turned into loud screams as Reggie and Dean held him down in his chair. Dean passed Freddie a thick plastic bag. Freddie walked behind the hysterical man.

'Freddie, no, please, no! I will do anything…' His voice trailed off into a gargle as Freddie placed the bag over his head and pulled it tight around his neck. He yanked back hard and pulled against the struggling man with all his strength. A small bubble of air in the plastic moved in and out of his gaping mouth as he tried and failed to breathe. He kicked out, struggling against the strong men who held him in place. Freddie's mouth set into a determined line as he held fast to the plastic behind Viktor's head. No one spoke. No one batted an eyelid.

Rules were rules. In this game, if you try to kill someone like one of the Tylers, you pay with your own life. It was black and white.

Viktor's struggles were becoming weaker, his body convulsing as it became desperate for air. The bubble in the plastic was moving in and out at a much slower rate. It became slower and slower until finally it just stopped moving altogether and Viktor's body slumped down, no longer fighting for freedom. Freddie held on for a few moments more, just to be sure. Then he let go. He stepped back and rubbed his hands. Dean moved forward, putting two fingers on his neck to check for a pulse.

'He's done,' Dean confirmed.

'OK.' Freddie pinched the bridge of his nose. He suddenly looked tired.

It had been a heavy week on the body-count front. It wasn't often that Freddie had to take a life, and it wasn't something he did lightly. But that was the punishment for trying to take out a Tyler. It was a dog-eat-dog world, and he would always do what was needed to stay on top and keep his family safe.

Bidding goodbye to his men, he turned and walked out. Now that this issue was dealt with, he needed to get back to finding the girl. He had one week to find her, or all he cared about would be lost.

# CHAPTER THIRTY-EIGHT

William Hargreaves walked through the door of his spacious, top-floor flat in Chelsea. He threw the keys into a bowl on top of the oak dresser in his hall and stared at himself in the mirror hanging above it. He looked awful. His face was haggard, and he looked as though he hadn't slept in a month. In reality, it had only been one night of sleeplessness so far, but he doubted it would be the last. He ran his hand though his floppy, wavy hair and pushed it over to one side in an attempt to look less unkempt. It didn't work. He closed his red-rimmed eyes and sighed.

His father and the police had played him the message over and over. What on earth was he supposed to do? In six days, some psycho would kill his sister unless he took her place. He felt sick. The police had come up with nothing. There were no solid leads. They had been on the case for weeks. He knew this wasn't a good thing – he watched the detective programmes. They always said if a missing person wasn't found in the first few days, their chances of finding them alive were slim at best.

The police had tried to convince him to go into something they called a 'vulnerable peoples unit', but he had refused. What would be the point? Clearly whoever had his sister did not want to harm him themselves – they had ordered him to take his own life. He was just as safe at home as anywhere else. They had grudgingly let him go, unable to force him, and given him a phone number for a crisis team. He had almost laughed. What would a shrink at the end of the phone do for him now? Either he or his sister would be dead soon, and he had to decide which. Fishing the number out of his pocket, he screwed it up and threw it towards the wastepaper basket.

William slipped his loafers off and padded through to the lounge. He needed a drink, something strong. Reaching the tall wooden drinks cabinet, he opened the glass front doors and just stared at the bottles.

'I'd go for a whisky personally. Takes the edge off.'

William jumped in shock at the unexpected voice. He yelped and turned round, his eyes wide with fright. There was a man sitting in one of the chairs against the wall, beside the door he had just walked in through. His eyes flickered back towards it as he wondered if he should try to run.

'I wouldn't if I were you.' The stranger signalled towards the small, black gun in his hand.

William began to shake, a million thoughts running through his head. Why was he here? Why did he have a gun? Was this his sister's kidnapper? Had he come to do it himself after all? He didn't know what to do. He looked at him properly. The man was older than him, maybe early thirties. He dressed well, his suit was of good quality and fitted his muscular physique flatteringly. His voice was deep and with a thick East London accent. He didn't look angry – this was hopefully a good sign.

'Wha— who are you? What are you doing?' William heard his voice shake as he spoke.

'Pour yourself a drink and sit down. I'm just here to talk.'

William hesitated for a moment, then fixed himself a drink with a trembling hand, never taking his eyes fully off the stranger with the gun. He closed the cabinet and sat down nervously on the edge of the sofa.

'Are you going to kill me?' he asked, finally.

'No. Like I said, I'm just here to talk.'

'Then why have you got a gun?' William asked, barely containing the panic that was threatening to spill over.

'In case you didn't want to talk. Drink your whisky. You'll feel better.'

William did as he was told and downed the fiery drink in one. He coughed, and his eyes watered as he put down the glass. He didn't usually drink the stuff, and when he did, he sipped it. But as he felt the warm liquid reach his belly, he slowly began to calm down.

'What do you want to talk about?'

'Your sister.'

'You could have just asked,' William said crabbily. 'Knocked at the door, called me and set up an appointment.'

'I don't have time for bullshit. Now why do you think the guy who took your sister wants you dead?'

'I don't know! I have been through this already. I spent half the night in the station answering questions. I have no idea what's going on!' William was frustrated.

'Watch your tone,' the other man snapped.

William closed his mouth, remembering his precarious position.

'Who are you?' he asked. 'You're not with the police.'

'No, I'm not. I'm just someone trying to get your sister back. And I need every single bit of information I can get my hands on to do so. You need to tell me everything. Especially the stuff you can't and wouldn't have told the police. I'm no threat to you on that side of things.'

'What do you mean?' William was confused.

'I mean, you need to tell me everything you've done that's less than legal. If you have underground business dealings, I need to know. If you fucked off your weed dealer, I need to know. If you killed your neighbour's cat because it was pissing on your doormat, I need to know. I need to know everything that has any link to anyone that might have decided you needed to be taught a lesson.'

William frowned. 'I haven't done anything illegal at all. I work in investment banking, for God's sake. I have to be cleaner than soap!'

'You're telling me that you've never done anything even slightly underhand?'

'No! I smoked a bit of weed at high school for a few months, but that was years ago and hardly the crime of the century.'

'What about at work? Have you lost someone a lot of money lately? Swiped someone else's client? Do you have any enemies at all, for any reason?'

'No, I really don't. I only started a couple of months ago. I'm a junior handler still; I don't get near the big accounts yet. And I've done pretty well on the small ones.' William slumped back on the sofa, his exhaustion taking over. 'I don't have enemies. I get on well with everyone, and aside from the odd girl I haven't called back, I can't think of anyone I've done anything to.'

They both sat in silence.

Freddie contemplated the man in front of him. He was just a kid, twenty years old and finding his way in the world. Everything he said just backed up what Freddie had already found out. An intelligent boy, he had graduated early from university and walked straight into a big firm. Nothing on his record, no serious dating history, liked by everyone. The young man was clearly at a total loss as to what was happening. He stood up.

'I'll leave you to it. Have another whisky and get some sleep. You look like you need it.'

'That's it?' William stood up too. He wanted to make sure this man was really gone and double lock the door before he tried to rest.

'That's it,' Freddie confirmed.

They walked to the door together, and William opened it.

'Can I just ask… if you're not anything to do with the police, why are you looking for my sister?'

Freddie have him a hard look. 'Because yours isn't the only life that rides on this.'

He walked out and disappeared before William could ask anything more.

# CHAPTER THIRTY-NINE

Anna sat down opposite Freddie in the restaurant and forced herself to relax. She placed her clutch bag on the table and folded her arms in front of her. She loved it here and so desperately wanted to enjoy the evening. The food was amazing, Michelin star. But it was more than that. This was the first place they had come together on a formal date, as an official couple. It was a brand-new start for them, finally both understanding who the other was after the revelations of that fateful night when Tony had kidnapped Anna. Tony was finally out of their lives, and they were free to enjoy their new-found love. It had been such a happy time.

Freddie reached over and squeezed Anna's hand. 'You look amazing, as always.' He gave her an admiring look.

'Thank you,' she answered, smiling.

'Champagne?' Freddie began pouring her a glass. Anna looked at the label. It was Cristal, her favourite. He was pulling out all the stops tonight. Usually this would make her happy, but tonight it just unnerved her. With Freddie being so secretive and disappearing all the time, she had no idea what to expect.

'Have you had a good week?' she asked, her voice carefully casual. 'I haven't seen you in a few days.'

Freddie sighed internally. 'I've just been really busy lately. That's why I thought it would be good for us to take a night off and spend some quality time together.' He stared at her, his eyes beseeching. He needed her to stick by him at the moment, even though he knew the war that must be raging inside her. Anna had been damaged long before he met her. He knew her natural instinct would be to pull away from him now.

Anna cast her eyes down. It was eating her up inside now, knowing there were things he was keeping from her. She knew everything about his illegal businesses and even men he had murdered, so what on earth could there be left to keep from her? The only answer, no matter how much she tried to find another, was that it was another woman.

She watched as Freddie lifted his champagne glass, waiting for her to lift hers. She put her fingers on the stem and paused. This was killing her. If she didn't ask him now, she never would.

Sitting up straight, she looked him determinedly in the eye. 'Freddie. Is there someone else? Are you having an affair?'

Freddie's eyebrows shot up in shock. 'Are you joking?' came his immediate retort.

'Sadly no. There's nothing that you haven't been able to tell me before.' She leaned in. 'And I really mean *nothing*.' She emphasised the word heavily. He would know what she meant. 'But now you're keeping secrets from me. You're holding something back, and you're away even more than usual.' Anna kept her voice low and her expression straight but couldn't quite contain the tears that began to spill down her cheeks. 'We've spent three years together without a single thing between us. And so now I really don't know what else to think. I won't go through this, Freddie. I won't live with secrets and lies. I won't be made a fool of again, not by any man.'

Freddie leaned forward, mortified to have caused her so much anxiety and pain.

'Anna, stop. Anna, here take this.' He handed her a serviette, and she quickly dabbed the tears away, annoyed with herself for crying. She lifted her chin and tightened her jaw.

Freddie sighed and closed his eyes for a second. 'There is no one else. There will never be anyone else. You know that,' he said strongly. 'You are everything to me.' Freddie grabbed one of her hands and squeezed it. 'There is something going on, yes. It's to do with one of my clubs. I know that this doesn't make sense to you right now, but I can't discuss it with anyone. If I do, it'll just make the situation worse.'

Anna frowned and shook her head in frustrated confusion.

'I know. It won't make sense yet, but I really need you to just trust me and stick with me. Can you do that? I would never do anything to hurt or disrespect you – ever. That I can promise you. And I also promise you that when this is all over, I will tell you everything.'

'And when will that be, Freddie? Because this is all really difficult to swallow.'

'Well, one way or another, in about one week.'

'A week?' Anna looked sceptical.

'A week,' Freddie confirmed, his heart sitting heavily in his stomach. There wasn't enough time. God, if only she knew.

There was silence as Anna took a deep breath. She lifted her glass to his, her face still sombre.

'OK. You have one week. But I'm warning you now, Freddie, if you don't come clean then, there will be no future for us.'

Freddie chinked his glass to hers and drank some of his champagne, his eyes never leaving hers, his heart heavy.

He would never do anything to purposely hurt her – that promise was the truth. He just wished he could control the nightmare he had unwittingly dragged her into. Because in one week's time, if he didn't find this girl, Anna might well be taking her last, terrified breath. And there would be nothing he could do to save her.

*

Tanya scowled at the woman barging past her down Oxford Street. She had completely forgotten that it was the school holidays when she made her way down there for a weekday shopping spree. She had counted on fewer tourists bumbling around, getting in everyone's way.

'Fuck sake!' she complained loudly, securing the knocked shopping bags in the crook of her arm. A pious looking woman in an 'I love London' T-shirt gave her a snotty look. 'Oh, you can piss off an' all, love.' Tanya rolled her eyes and swept onwards towards the Tube station. She couldn't wait to get back to her apartment and try on the new lingerie she had just bought for her next date with Daniel. She flicked her long, red hair back over her shoulder. It was baking out – she should have tied it up to stay cool.

She reached the Tube and swiped her Oyster to get through the barrier. Following the crowd to the stairs down to her platform, her mind drifted, wondering whether she had enough ice at home to make frozen cocktails.

As she took her third step, Tanya felt two hands press against her back, through her thin camisole top. Before she could move, they shoved her forward with force. Her feet lost contact with the ground and she began plunging downward through thin air. Her arms flailed around helplessly. The shopping bags flew off to the side as she loosened her grip, their security no longer a priority. Tanya began to scream as she realised she was going to land face first at the bottom of the steep, tall set of steps. People moved out of her way automatically, trying not to get pushed down themselves by this human cannonball. It all happened so fast, yet Tanya felt like everything was moving in slow motion.

Suddenly all the wind seemed to escape her lungs as a vice-like grip stopped her fall with a hard jolt. Her body swung around, and she nearly carried on falling backward, but a second burly arm quickly encased her. Tanya grasped the big manly arms around her as if they were a lifeboat. She gulped in the air around her in huge, panicked gasps.

'It's OK – I've got ya.' The voice came from the man holding her up. She looked up at him and immediately stood herself up. He let her go but kept one hand on her arm, worried in case she started to fall again.

Tanya looked back up the stairwell to the top, where she had been pushed. She had fallen quite a way – she was now more than halfway down. If she hadn't been caught… she stared at the hard concrete floor at the bottom and shuddered. *Best not to dwell on that*, she thought. A few people slowed down, concern on their faces, but no one stopped.

'You OK?' the man who had caught her asked.

'Yeah. Sorry. Thank you.' Tanya was shaken up.

'That's OK. Er, let's get out the way.' He guided her down the rest of the steps and over to a less-crowded area. He looked at her drawn face, concerned. 'You sure you're alright? That was a pretty hefty fall.'

'It wasn't a fall,' Tanya replied heavily. 'Someone pushed me.'

'Yeah, it gets crazy round here sometimes—'

'No.' Tanya shook her head. 'Someone purposely pushed me.'

'Really?' He looked back to the stairs, frowning. 'Did you see who?'

'No.' Tanya suddenly looked at him, realising she was sharing things with a complete stranger. She plastered a smile over her face. 'Maybe I'm imagining it. Don't worry. I'm fine. I really do appreciate your help. Thanks, mate.'

'Any time. Just glad I heard you coming.'

Tanya laughed. 'Yeah, well, I was never the quiet type.'

He grinned at her, and she was struck by how attractive he was. *In a rugged sort of way anyway*, she thought. His brown eyes twinkled. She might have been interested were she not already in a happy relationship.

'Hang on a minute.' He left her and went back to the side of the stairs, collecting her fallen bags. She cringed as he picked up a lacy red garter and dropped it back into the bag. To his credit, he said nothing as he returned them all to her.

'Listen,' she said, 'it's not much but I would like to repay you for saving me from a face full of concrete. I own a club over on Greek Street. Club Anya. Pop down sometime – bring your mates. I'll get you a good table and drinks are on me all night.'

'I thought I knew you from somewhere,' he cried. 'I worked on that construction site opposite the club, a couple of years back. My mates used to wolf whistle you, every time you came into work.'

'What, and you didn't?' She laughed and pretended to be offended.

'Nah, it ain't classy to whistle a lady. And you always looked like a proper lady.'

Tanya found herself warming to his open charm.

'I'm Tom, by the way,' he said, holding his hand out.

'Tanya.' She shook his hand.

'And you don't have to do that, really,' he said.

'No, I want to. Please. I insist. I'll be insulted if you don't come.'

'OK, well I don't want to insult ya.' He rolled his eyes jokingly, backed into a corner. 'I'll come down sometime. Thank you.'

'Great. Well…' She looked round. 'I'd best get on.'

'Yeah, me too. I was on my way up. I'll see you later.'

'Yeah, bye.' Tanya waved awkwardly as he left.

*What a nice guy*, she thought. Her eyes lingered on the top of the stairs well after he disappeared from view. Her mood darkened and a quiet anger flashed across her face. She had definitely been pushed, and it was no accident. Whoever had done that to her meant business. She remembered the feel of their hands, both hands pressed deliberately across her back before sending her flying. From that height onto the concrete below, she could have died. At best, she would have been hospitalised had Tom not caught her.

This was no longer a few sinister texts. Whoever was following her was out for blood.

# CHAPTER FORTY

Thea sat sipping her coffee outside the little café in Brixton, eying the empty property opposite with interest. It would make a good tea room, with its old-fashioned windowpanes looking in on a spacious room with wooden pillars dotted around. It would be a simple front business for Freddie, if the rent wasn't too high. She jotted down the agent's number in the little notebook she kept in her pocket. Slipping it back into the pocket of her denim jacket, she raised her hand and waved at the tall, awkward young man making his way towards her. He waved back and they smiled in greeting to one another.

'Ready to go?' Dominic asked gaily as he reached her.

Thea downed the last dregs of her coffee and stood up, grabbing her backpack. It held her camera and all the related accessories she needed inside.

'Yeah, definitely. Well excited.' Thea smiled, and her eyes twinkled brightly. She loved photography and was relishing the challenge she had set herself. She had dressed comfortably and casually, not knowing how long they would be out and not wanting to draw attention to herself. Stalking her brothers would be no easy task.

'Where do we start?' Dominic asked.

'My brother Paul mentioned popping over this way for a meeting this morning, so I followed him in. He's up the next street, but his car is parked down there.' She pointed to the other end of the street. 'I was thinking, you could position yourself at that corner and pretend to be taking shots of the street. Then you can get him walking towards you. I'll come from behind and shoot at another angle so I don't sit in your shot. But I can get him walking away, maybe even some side face if I can keep well enough hidden.' She looked around. 'There.' She pointed to a narrow alleyway between two buildings. 'I can shoot from there.'

'OK.' Dominic grimaced slightly at the look of the alley. Bin bags were piled up high, and flies swarmed around over the top in the summer heat. It didn't seem like the most pleasant position. But if that's what she thought was best, he would go along with it. He greatly admired her dedication to the art of photography.

'Let's start with that then and see what we get. He should be coming out soon, so we had best get into position. I showed you his photo, didn't I? You know what he looks like?'

'Yes, I remember,' Dominic replied, nodding.

Thea grinned and, hoisting her bag higher on her shoulder, walked determinedly into the mouth of the foetid alley. She pulled a face as she set her bag down on an upturned bucket. It stank down there. Perhaps she hadn't thought this through. She wrinkled her nose and peered further in. A dead, half-eaten mouse lay just beyond the bins, and a cat prowled at the other end, shooting her a resentful look. Clearly she had interrupted its meal. She raised her eyebrows and shrugged apologetically at the mangy feline, before turning back to her bag. She pulled out her camera and took the cap off the lens. Pointing it out into the street, she took a couple of practise shots and tweaked the focus.

They didn't have too long to wait. Paul came into view about ten minutes later. Sticking her head out before he got too close, she signalled his arrival to Dominic. She stepped back and began taking photos, making sure to focus on her brother rather than the environment around him. He looked as though he was deep in thought as he walked, his expression sombre. His thin, summer suit jacket was open and flapped about as he walked. He carried a brown bag that looked as though it carried some sort of takeaway food, clearly his lunch.

As Paul passed Thea held her breath, even though he was much too far away to hear something as quiet as her breathing on this busy London street. He didn't glance her way. He didn't seem to see anything in fact. He looked far too distracted. Thea frowned and wondered what was wrong. Still in photographer mode, she stepped back out and kept shooting. She would have to work out how to subtly ask him if he was OK another time.

*

Freddie took a deep breath and knocked on the hotel-room door. It opened after just a couple of seconds and he walked past DCI Riley without giving her a second glance. He wasn't here to see her. He was here because he had been summoned by Ben Hargreaves.

The man was seated on the small sofa in the middle of the room, looking utterly deflated. Freddie looked him up and down critically. Even just in the past week he seemed as though he had lost half his body weight, his suit hanging off his small frame. His hair was a mess and his tie loose. He held a tumbler in his hand and a half-empty bottle sat on the table in front of him. His eyes looked hollow, as though he had not slept in a decade.

'You summoned me?' Freddie asked flatly. While he felt for the man's plight, he did not take kindly to the corner he had been forced into, or the threat to Anna's life that hung over him like a ten-ton weight.

Ben looked up at him with dead eyes. 'You heard the tape,' he replied. 'We have less than a week until my baby girl is dead. Or my son,' he added. 'One of the two. What have you found?'

'Nothing that your pigs haven't already,' Freddie answered. 'I've looked. I've asked about. I've gone through every avenue I can think of. I've had men stationed around possible sites where the bastard could be coming through, on his late-night visits to your house. I've talked to your son—'

'William?'

'Yes, William. I talked to him in case there was anything he could tell me but not the police, but I got jack shit.' Freddie held his arms out in the air. 'Short of scaling London inch by inch, there ain't a lot more I can do for you. If there was, I would. Trust me – I want you lot out of my life as soon as possible.'

Ben stared at him, and his eyes narrowed hatefully.

'She got taken outside your club,' he said through gritted teeth. 'I know it wasn't you, but I also know who you are. I know the sort of people who frequent your clubs. Men like you. Criminals. So let me make myself clear once more.' He pointed his finger at Freddie. 'You find my daughter and you get her back to me before her time is up. Because if you don't, I swear to God, you will spend the rest of your life behind bars and that little girlfriend of yours will be history. I'll make sure she doesn't even make it through her first night in prison. I will take everything from you, and I will keep going until there is nothing more in this world you even remotely care about.' He shook with exhaustion and emotion.

Freddie clenched his teeth and said nothing. He had never wanted to hurt someone so badly before. But there was no point. Ben was on the edge of a breakdown and it wouldn't do Freddie any favours if he was tipped over.

'Just do your job, Tyler,' he barked. 'You're running out of time.'

Freddie's concern deepened. Grief-stricken or not, there was something not quite right with this bloke. For an intelligent man, he wasn't hearing anything that Freddie said. There was no reasoning anymore. He looked like he was losing the plot. Freddie stared at him for a moment, then turned and left without another word. As he made his way down the hall he rubbed his jaw tensely. Things were heating up, and he suddenly wasn't sure that he was holding all the pieces of the puzzle.

*

Michael walked into The Black Bear and took a seat next to Sammy and Freddie. He signalled over to the barmaid, who nodded and began pouring him a pint.

'Michael,' Freddie said in greeting.

'What's 'appening?' he replied.

'Not a fucking lot,' Sammy said glumly.

'Had another little meeting with Hargreaves today,' said Freddie.

'Oh? Junior or Senior?' Michael asked, his attention gained.

'Senior.' Freddie gazed off into space thoughtfully. 'There's something not quite right there. The way he's acting… it's very erratic. Abnormally so, even for someone who hates us.'

'Well, he is under a lot of strain; he's probably not sleeping or eating. The guy's probably going a bit mad,' Sammy offered.

'Nah, it's beyond that. I think we need to put a tail on him, do some digging. Because I'm beginning to wonder if he knows more than he's letting on.'

'Really?' Michael looked surprised.

'Yeah.' Freddie leaned in and looked at them both – hard. 'There's something about Ben Hargreaves that isn't adding up, and if we're going to get anywhere with finding his daughter, we need to work out what that is and fast.'

Michael and Sammy nodded their agreement and Freddie sat back, picking up his pint. Perhaps he had been looking too far out this whole time. Perhaps the culprit was a lot closer to home than he had originally thought.

# CHAPTER FORTY-ONE

Tanya stared into the bathroom mirror with a grim expression. She still couldn't shake off the heavy feeling of dread she'd had since yesterday in the Tube. She hadn't told anyone. All they would do is worry, and no one could help her anyway. She wondered whether she should have taken Freddie's offer more seriously, but it all just seemed far too dramatic and over the top. Much as she had a flair for the dramatic herself, she didn't need some bodyguard following her round like she was Whitney Houston.

She sighed and tried to push the worry out of her mind. Daniel was here, and she wanted to be able to enjoy the evening. Their schedules had both been so busy over the last week that they had only managed one quick coffee date. To her surprise, she had actually really missed him. He was fast becoming a permanent fixture in her life, and for once she was happy to go with it. She had spent a long time doing it all on her own and having fun with the wrong guys. Tanya felt ready to commit to the right person.

Running her hands through her thick red hair and pouting to check that her even brighter red lipstick was perfect, she left the bathroom and returned to the kitchen. Daniel stood behind the counter cutting up the peppers for the crudité plate, her apron tied around his waist over his crisp, white shirt. She stood in the doorway drinking in the sight for a moment. Her lip curled into a content smile. Daniel looked up and saw her.

'Ah, there you are. Can you pour the wine?'

'Shouldn't we wait?' she asked.

'We can have a quick one before they get here, can't we?' His eyebrows crossed for a second and Tanya realised he was anxious about meeting her friends. She grinned.

''Course,' she replied.

Tanya poured the chilled white wine into two glasses and placed one next to the chopping board for him. She squeezed his arm affectionately before pinching one of the carrot sticks, neatly stacked on one of her serving plates.

'Hey, not until your guests arrive,' Daniel chided, laughing. 'It's rude.'

'Mm.' Tanya nodded through a mouthful of carrot. 'It is. But more importantly, there's something we need to discuss.'

'Oh? What's that, then?' Daniel continued chopping, unaware of the cheeky twinkle in his girlfriend's eye.

'Your attire.'

'What's wrong with this?' He looked down at himself, confused. 'I've just come from work, you know that.'

'Yes, but I personally think you should remove everything except the apron. I think that would look very good indeed.'

'Oh, do you now?' Daniel put the knife down and grabbed her by the waist, pulling her to him.

Tanya laughed, and he leaned in for a slow, passionate kiss. She melted into him.

The doorbell sounded and Daniel pulled away, releasing her. 'Saved by the bell,' he joked.

'Mm, I wouldn't call it saved,' she grumbled. She winked and left him to open the door.

Freddie burst in first, brandishing a bottle of champagne. 'I come bearing gifts,' he announced jovially.

'Yeah, is that from my club?' she asked, raising an eyebrow.

Freddie looked back at Anna, who nodded. 'Yeah, it is actually,' he said.

They all laughed. Anna stepped forward and grasped her best friend and business partner in a warm hug. She was excited to meet this boyfriend that Tanya was so head over heels about.

'Is he in there?' Anna heard Freddie greet Daniel and the two men start talking. 'Ooh, let me through!' She pushed past and Tanya closed the door, her heart singing.

She was having a double-date night in with her best friend and her new love. Freddie was in a great mood and seemed to be chatting animatedly to Daniel. She hoped they would be fast friends in no time. Things couldn't be going better.

Her phone chimed in her pocket, and she pulled it out to see who it was. As soon as she read it, her elated mood plummeted.

*Your time is running out.*

Tanya's heart turned to ice as she stared at the text, reading it again. Her time was running out. Whoever had tried to kill her on the Tube wasn't going to give up. She shivered. Something told her that next time they wouldn't be taking any chances.

'Tan? You joining us?' Freddie walked back into the hallway with a champagne flute. He stopped when he saw her ashen face. He lowered his voice. 'You OK?'

Tanya bit her lip and made a decision. She couldn't risk the phantom texter succeeding in their next murder attempt. Not wanting to tell the others, she whispered back shakily, 'No. I'm not OK. I need your help, Freddie.'

*

There was a knock at the door, and Freddie looked up from his desk in the office at Ruby Ten, the club where Katherine had gone missing.

'Come in,' he said.

The door opened and a middle-aged man in a grey tweed jacket walked in. He smiled at Freddie, though the lines of stress and worry never left the area around his eyes.

'DI Fraser, to what do I owe this pleasure?' Freddie asked. He offered the man a seat. Although he had little respect for the filth on his payroll, his relationship with this particular man had been of great value over the years.

'Freddie, you're looking well.' He sat down. 'I've come to share some bad news, I'm afraid.' He frowned, and the worry lines on his face deepened. 'I know you've been under Hargreaves' spotlight lately, what with his daughter and everything. I don't know what you've done to piss him off, but he pulled me into an off-record meeting yesterday. He's told me that in five days, unless I hear otherwise, I'm to arrange a raid on your house.' He shifted his weight uncomfortably. 'He wants me to fit you up with enough gear to put you away for a long time. Not just you either – Anna too. Which I don't understand one bit.' He sighed. He had been dreading coming down here, but he knew he had to tell Freddie. 'There's nothing I can do to get out of it. He's the Secretary of State for Justice.' He held his arms out helplessly. 'If I refuse, I lose my job, and he'd just find someone else to do it anyway. The only thing going in our favour right now is that he has no idea of my relationship to you. At least I can warn you and give you enough time to make arrangements or get away. I'm sorry, Freddie.'

Freddie nodded gravely as he took the information in. 'That's OK, Fraser. I knew it was coming. I just didn't know what direction from or when exactly. So thank you for that.'

'If things change, if he tells me otherwise, I'll let you know straight away.'

'I appreciate that. Just do me one favour.'

'Of course, what is it?'

'If it comes to it… raid Club CoCo first, not my home. Then give me an hour before anyone hits Club Anya.'

'Sure.' DI Fraser nodded. 'I can do that. I'll let you know in advance too. Give you more time.'

'Good man.'

DI Fraser nodded and got up to leave. He knew Freddie's time was valuable; he didn't want to take up too much of it.

'I'll hopefully be calling you to tell you there's been a change of plan instead. See you later, Fred.'

He walked out, and Freddie sat back in his chair, staring at the door. So it had begun. The final wheels were in motion. His brain began whirring, ten to the dozen. It was time to put his back-up plan into action.

# CHAPTER FORTY-TWO

Thea walked into the large gymnasium and looked around. It was full to the brim with people eager to see the fight. Freddie and Sammy had been working with some local lads, training them up and getting them ready for some of the lower-league boxing matches. This was the first big fight for one of their boys, and Thea knew it was an exciting night for them. They had exclusive gambling rights here, the gymnasium being in Freddie's territory, so their men stood at stalls around the room, taking bets.

Freddie had asked her to cover the event and get photos for the press and for future advertising. She had been more than happy to accept. Thea wandered around and found a nook at the side, with a great view of the ring and her brothers. She could kill two birds with one stone tonight. She could get the boxing shots for Freddie and some candid shots of her brothers for her project.

The room was full of activity. They had gone all out for this fight. They had multiple vendors around the edges, selling all sorts of delicious-looking food and drink. She eyed up the Prosecco stand. Maybe later, once she had finished her work for the evening. It would be nice to hang out with all of her brothers together for once. They were all so busy these days she hardly saw them.

The ringleader stepped out and began to fire up the already excited crowds. Thea sat and watched, snapping away as each fighter came out and the rounds began. She was thrilled with the photos she got of her brothers as they watched the fight. Freddie was tense and wired, and Michael was overly excited, the emotions playing out strongly on their faces. Paul watched with a critical eye, but he still seemed slightly distracted to Thea.

The third round came and went, and Thea saw a huge change in Freddie. He stood up and began frantically cheering their fighter on. His smile broadened as the boy came at his opponent again and again, never letting up. Eventually, the other man stayed down, and after he was counted out by the referee, the crowd went wild. The ref held up the winner's hand to signal victory. Thea moved around and quickly grabbed some shots of the big win. She was thrilled that Freddie's bet on this boy had paid off. She went back to her original position and took photos of the celebrating crowds.

Staring through the lens at her brothers, she realised that Paul had disappeared. Thea looked up, frowning. She scanned the room and eventually found him paying for two lots of fish and chips at one of the stands. She watched him pick up the food, expecting him to return to his seat. Instead, he looked over his shoulder and checked that Freddie hadn't noticed his departure before slipping out of a nearby exit. He disappeared from view and the door closed behind him. Thea blinked. What was he doing? They were all on a family night out. They were all together for once, except for Mollie who didn't enjoy boxing. It was a big night for her brothers though – the first big win. Where could he possibly need to go? And who, she wondered, was the second meal for?

*

Michael walked into Club Anya and, nodding to Carl as he passed, walked straight through to the back office. He knocked but didn't wait for a response before he entered.

'Anna.' He smiled at her as he closed the door behind him.

'Michael, oh, you're early!' Anna was surprised as she looked at the time. She needed longer to work on the new marketing campaign she had put together. But she could finish it a bit later, she reasoned with herself. This was more important. A gleam appeared in her eye as she smiled back at him.

'Yeah, traffic wasn't as bad as I'd expected,' Michael replied. 'All the more time to spend with you though, so I'm not complaining.'

Anna laughed. 'Why thank you, but save your compliments for later.'

'Later?'

Anna didn't hear him – she was busy tidying away the mess of papers strewn across her desk.

'I was pleased you texted,' Michael continued. 'I enjoyed hanging out before, especially now Paul's never around.'

'Me too – it was nice to spend some time with you,' Anna replied warmly. 'We're all so busy these days, aren't we?'

'Yeah I guess.' Michael sat down across the desk from her and waited for her to finish tidying up. 'I was thinking about you the other day actually. I passed this shop and in the window there was this scarf that I thought would look perfect on you. I know that sounds stupid,' he said, laughing, 'but I just couldn't help noticing. So I picked it up for you.' He pulled a small package out of his pocket. It was wrapped up smartly in purple tissue paper.

Anna hesitated, and her smile faltered into puzzlement.

Michael hastily continued. 'I felt bad that I didn't get you a gift for your birthday,' he explained, 'so I've been on the lookout for anything you might like.'

'Oh, how sweet,' Anna replied. 'You really didn't need to. I didn't expect anything.'

'Well, I got it now anyway. So here, have a look.'

Anna took the small package and unwrapped the delicate tissue paper. She noted that he had purchased the gift from Liberty, one of her favourite shops to wander round. A slim silk neck scarf slid out into her hands, and she opened it out. It was a beautiful thing indeed, she thought. It was a deep blue colour, somewhere between royal blue and navy, and had a subtle pattern running through it that reminded her of running water. It was exactly the sort of thing she would have chosen herself.

'It's beautiful, Michael. I love it,' she said sincerely. Smiling, she stood up and moved to the mirror on the wall by the door. She placed it around her neck and tied it at the side. It suited her. *What a lovely gift*, she thought. Michael really was growing up into a very thoughtful young man.

'And I was right,' Michael said, smiling. 'It looks great on you.'

Anna pulled the scarf off and wrapped it back in the tissue paper.

'Thank you. It will go with loads of my outfits,' Anna said warmly. 'A really thoughtful gift for a sister-in-law.'

'Not yet,' he replied.

'Hmm?'

'Well, you're not married to Freddie. So we aren't in-laws yet,' he said.

Anna shuffled some papers about awkwardly as she tried to think up a response. Marriage was not a subject she relished discussing at any time, especially now that her relationship with Freddie was so strained.

'Well, anyway,' she blundered on, flustered, 'Shall we go through to the bar and get that drink? I'm done in here for now.'

Anna opened the door and held it for Michael, her smile bright. He grinned.

Walking through the bar, Anna thought about how much Michael had grown and changed since he had arrived home three years ago. He was only twenty, but he already seemed so much older, so much more confident than his tender years. She guessed that was down to his role in the Tyler empire. It was a harsh world Freddie and his family lived in. There was no room for the weak. 'So, what would you like to drink?' she asked, squeezing his arm warmly.

'I'll go for rum and Coke.'

'Great. One rum and Coke and a Pinot Grigio for me, Carl.' Anna sat down on one of the bar stools and Michael sat next to her. 'So, you're still definitely free for an hour or two, aren't you?'

'Yeah, nothing on until tonight. Unless Freddie calls me for something.'

'Great, well, in that case…' Anna looked over his shoulder and beamed at the young woman who had just entered the club. 'Perfect timing!' she cried. She kissed the pretty blonde on each cheek in greeting as she reached them. 'Sophie, this is Michael, my… Freddie's brother.' She stopped herself from using the term 'brother-in-law'. 'And, Michael, I would like you to meet a good friend of mine, Sophie.' Anna stepped back and watched as they assessed each other.

'Oh, OK. Hello.' Sophie laughed nervously. Anna felt a small stab of guilt. She hadn't told either of them that this was a set-up. She knew Michael wasn't super keen on the blind-date idea, despite agreeing to it, and she hadn't been sure what Sophie's reaction would be. Sophie was a charismatic, interesting, beautiful girl, but she could be quite shy when it came to people she didn't know.

'I was actually hoping to catch up with both of you, but I've had something come up…' Anna lied. She pulled an exaggeratedly annoyed face. Michael shook his head at her from behind Sophie. He knew what she was up to. She purposely ignored him and directed her apologetic smile at Sophie. 'So sorry. Why don't you guys grab a drink? I'll see if I can wrap things up quickly and get back here so we can still catch up. Would that be OK?'

'Sure, no problem,' Sophie said in an understanding tone. 'I'm not up to much for the rest of the day anyway.'

'Michael, you'll look after Sophie for me, won't you?' she asked him, her expression innocent.

'Sure.' His tone was bemused, but he smiled at Sophie and offered her a seat. 'Guess we'll see you later then.'

'Mm.' She nodded.

Anna squeezed both of their arms and left them to it, making her way towards the exit. She breathed in and let herself relax, making plans in her head to go and enjoy the sunshine for a while. They wouldn't be seeing her later, but they wouldn't know that for at least an hour, at which point she would text to make her excuse.

'Just call me Cilla,' she muttered to herself humorously as she stepped into the outside world and away from her club.

# CHAPTER FORTY-THREE

Freddie swirled the whisky around in the glass he was holding. It occurred to him that he had been drinking more and more frequently lately. The stress of the so-far-fruitless search for Katherine was getting to him more than anything ever had before. Perhaps it was because he had so much to lose this time. Nightmares woke him frequently. They were always the same thing, a vision of Anna screaming and struggling as one of Hargreaves' lackeys bent down to slit her throat in a cold, dark jail cell. His freedom didn't matter to him anymore. It would mean nothing without Anna to share it with. She was the only woman he had ever loved, and the only one he ever wanted to. If he lost her, it would kill him. And it might already be too late.

He sighed heavily and knocked back the golden liquid. He signalled to the bouncer standing at the rope separating him from the dance floor to order him another. He looked around at the busy club. People were dancing, drinking, having fun. This was where it had all started, this nightmare that he was now trapped in.

A couple of young women stood gossiping just the other side of the rope, shooting him appreciative sideways glances. He knew they were wondering who he was, the mysterious man seated at the top VIP table all alone. He smirked without humour. They would assume he was some minor celebrity or a trust-fund kid spending his inheritance. They would never guess that he was the head of one of the largest criminal organisations in London. They would never imagine that he was a killer, someone who ended the lives of people who tried to cross him. He wondered what they would do if he told them he had suffocated a man to death, just days ago. They most likely wouldn't believe him. If they did, they would run screaming. It took a certain amount of darkness in your soul to swallow the sort of life Freddie led. Even Anna, as good a person as she was, was tainted with past horrors which had darkened her forever.

The bouncer opened up the rope and Michael marched in, throwing his jacket on the end of the luxurious, curved sofa before sitting down next to Freddie.

'Sorry I'm late.'

'Yeah, you should be,' Freddie replied. He didn't much like being left alone with his own thoughts at the moment. That was why he was down here, instead of in the peace of his office. He needed the noise. Michael ignored the comment, assuming Freddie was joking.

Freddie shook off the self-pity and turned away from the party girls to face his brother. 'Three days, Michael. That's all we've got now. It's not looking good.'

'It'll be fine.' Michael brushed it off as though it were nothing.

'No, it won't, Michael. Hargreaves is coming for me and Anna, and he'll make sure we go down. And if I go down, they'll most likely pull you and Paul down with me. They know it's a family business. I doubt they'd let such a golden opportunity slip through their hands.'

Michael blinked, his face suddenly serious. 'Fuck,' he said after a few moments. He looked over at his brother and let what this meant to him soak in. For once he had nothing else to say.

'Yeah, exactly,' Freddie said wryly.

The barmaid arrived with two fresh glasses and an open bottle of the whisky Freddie had been drinking. She had seen Michael come in. Michael thanked her and she hurried off, acutely aware that her boss was not in the best of moods this evening.

Freddie looked at Michael and frowned. 'Where's Paul? I thought he was with you?'

'He was.' Michael's tone was tinged with annoyance. 'But he buggered off again. He keeps doing that lately.'

'Yeah, I've noticed that. What's going on with him, do you know?' Freddie asked. He was pissed off. He needed to be able to rely on his brothers more than ever right now and Paul, his right-hand man, never seemed to be around.

'No, he don't tell me nothing these days…' Michael trailed off, deep in thought.

They sat in silence for a few minutes. After a while, Michael sat up, and his eyes flickered towards Freddie. He bit his lip. Staring at the floor, he began speaking slowly, as if unsure whether or not to share his thoughts.

'It's been since the girl disappeared, I've noticed.' Michael carefully poured them each a whisky and slid one across to Freddie. 'Paul's disappearances.'

'Yeah, which is exactly what's so fucking annoying,' Freddie replied, exasperated.

Michael stroked the stubble on his chin before delicately continuing. 'What I mean is… the timings are a bit odd. I noticed too that he was pretty certain from the off that we wouldn't find her. He always talks as if it's futile…' Michael stopped talking and let it sit for a moment.

Freddie's forehead creased deeply as he turned to his younger brother. He didn't like where Michael's thoughts were heading.

'What are you saying?' he demanded.

Michael blew out his cheeks as he exhaled slowly. 'I don't know what I'm saying. I'm just saying it seems odd, that's all.' He sat back and drank his whisky, moving his gaze to the dance floor. He had said enough. He didn't need to continue.

Freddie's frown deepened as he mulled it over. He didn't like what his brother was insinuating. Paul was their flesh and blood.

He was one of the Tyler brothers. There were a lot of dark things Paul would do for the sake of the family, but he would never do something like this. And he would certainly never put Freddie into this sort of position. He was the most loyal person Freddie had ever known. Wasn't he?

Freddie studied the side of his younger brother's face as he watched the dance floor. Michael was flesh and blood too. He was as much one of them as Paul was. Michael spent a lot of time with Paul these days. Should he be concerned at the suspicions Michael was having? Should he be taking them seriously? Surely not. Freddie closed his eyes. His head hurt. He rubbed his forehead as he warred with a decision that went against the grain of everything he had ever stood for. He felt as if he had aged a decade in a matter of minutes when he opened his eyes.

'You really think there's something in it?' he asked heavily. 'I need you to be sure, Michael. This isn't the sort of thing you say lightly.'

'I think the sudden absences and his attitude towards the issue have been very odd,' Michael repeated carefully.

Freddie stared at him long and hard before eventually nodding.

'I'll deal with it,' he said curtly. His expression was full of tense disappointment as he resigned himself to what he had to do. Whether he felt that disappointment in himself, in Michael, or in Paul, Freddie wasn't quite sure. He stared into the bottom of his glass, not really seeing. Guilt began to settle uncomfortably in his stomach. Because after the suspicion Michael had just shared, he was going to have to cross a line that couldn't be uncrossed. He was going to have to put a tail on his own brother.

# CHAPTER FORTY-FOUR

Tanya cut a line of cocaine on the desk in the back office. It wasn't something she did much these days, but lately she hadn't been sleeping and she needed a pick-me-up to get through her shifts at the club. She pulled her thick, long hair over one shoulder and leaned in. Holding the rolled-up twenty-pound note delicately between her fingers, she sniffed the fluffy white powder up through it. She sat back upright, shook her hair back out behind her and sniffed a couple more times to make sure it had all gone up. Blinking, she rubbed the end of her nose to make sure all visible traces were gone, neatly stowed the little bag back into her purse and with her finger dabbed up any traces still on the desk and rubbed it into her gums. They immediately went pleasantly numb. She pulled a face of approval. It was good stuff.

She walked through to the bar and leaned on it, waiting while the bouncers escorted the last of the rowdy crowds out for the night. Her phone vibrated in the back pocket of the tight black jeans she was wearing. She pulled it out and read the text. It was from Simon, her bodyguard for the night. He was stuck in traffic and was still half an hour away. She sighed, resigned, and replied to tell him it was no problem.

Since she had confided in Freddie, he had made sure one of his men was present to escort her to and from work and that someone was stationed outside her flat at night. She had to admit, it had made her feel much more secure. And to his credit, Freddie hadn't told a soul, not even Anna. She felt guilty about that. She knew how much Anna loathed secrets, and she hated herself for adding to them. But this one was for her own good. Anna had enough to worry about without Tanya throwing her problems into the mix.

Freddie had looked into the Tube incident for her. He had managed to get hold of the tapes somehow, but the angle had been off, and with such a large crowd of people there was no way of telling who it was that had pushed her. They had gone through the faces on the footage, but there was no one who Tanya recognised or who looked particularly suspicious. Her ghost was still a ghost.

Carl began to wipe down the tables as the last waiter left for the night, and Tanya took a deep breath as the line of cocaine she had just taken kicked in. A rush of energy soared through her, and she jumped up from the bar. She licked her lips. Man, this stuff was strong. She knew the initial buzz would wear off in a few minutes and leave her feeling a more normal level of awake, but right now she just needed something to do.

'Hey Carl, I'll do that,' she offered merrily.

He gave her a quizzical look. 'You want to do the clean down?' He didn't sound convinced.

'Well, not all of it,' she admitted, laughing. 'But I'll do the tables.'

Carl laughed with her. 'OK then, you crack on. I'll sweep.' Carl yawned. It had been a long day.

'Why don't you leave it till the morning?' Tanya offered. 'It won't hurt. You look cream-crackered.'

'You sure? I am pretty done in,' he admitted.

'Yeah, go.' Tanya waved him away. 'My ride won't be here for another half hour, so I'll do these and leave the rest for you tomorrow.'

'Alright.' Carl threw his cloth to her. She caught it. 'Catch ya later, then.' He grabbed his jacket from behind the bar and left through the side door.

Tanya smiled fondly after him. He was a great guy, Carl. Both she and Anna had spent many a night with him in here. She thought of him as a bit like an older brother, always there to lend an ear and some advice. He was reliable too and worked harder than anyone she knew. He deserved an early night.

She set to work scrubbing the tables, putting all of her sudden excess energy into it. It didn't take long to do the first few, then she paused to catch her breath. The buzz was beginning to settle into a normal pace and she needed to slow down. She laughed at herself suddenly. What on earth was she doing here late at night, coked up, scrubbing tables? This would certainly be something to laugh about on her next girls' night in with Anna.

A noise resounded through the empty club, and Tanya immediately stopped. She held her breath, all her senses on high alert. She strained her ears, listening hard but there was nothing else to hear. Tanya shook herself. She was being paranoid. It was probably just a water pipe clanking somewhere in the building. Still, she decided to check all the doors were firmly locked before she carried on with the tables.

Walking through to the front of the building, the only sound was that of her high heels tapping on the hard floor. She stared through the glass panel in the front door and was soothed by the sights and muffled sounds of the still-busy London street outside. She shook the doors. They rattled slightly, but the sturdy locks held fast. Tanya checked the side door, which was locked just as tightly. Satisfied that everything was as it should be, she walked back through the inner doors into the club and picked up where she'd left off.

She wasn't sure what it was that made her look up, some kind of sixth sense maybe, but as she did, she caught sight of the thin, brunette woman standing across the room, staring at her with deep venom in her eyes.

Tanya stifled a scream. She put her hand to her chest in an attempt to calm her racing heart and stared at the small woman with wide eyes, not knowing what to do next. The woman just stood there, not moving. Small though she was, the dark anger in her expression and the tense way she held herself made her incredibly menacing.

Tanya slipped her hand slowly towards her back pocket, her fingers reaching for her phone, but it wasn't there. Her eyes flicked over to the bar and her heart dropped as she realised she had left it there earlier. She knew without asking that this was the woman who had been sending her all those texts. She knew without doubt that, for some reason, this woman was the one who had tried to kill her.

# CHAPTER FORTY-FIVE

Tanya swallowed the dry lump in her throat as she tried to figure out what to do. A fresh wave of bitterness rippled across the woman's face, and Tanya wondered what she could have done to her to cause such anger. She had never seen this woman before, that much she was sure of.

The woman was dressed in leggings and a long plain top. It was hardly club attire. How had she even got into the building? Her knee-length boots were flat and simple, and her overcoat was thick and grey. It was this which caught Tanya's attention. Why would she be wearing a winter coat in the middle of summer? Her eyes moved down to the large pockets, which the woman's hands disappeared into. *Ah*, she thought, her fear increasing. Large pockets were perfect for concealing small weapons.

Their eyes met once more, and Tanya suddenly couldn't bear the heavy silence any longer.

'What do you want?' Tanya heard the false confidence and authority in her voice. She had learned long ago to style things out. Fake it till you make it.

The woman shook with rage, her face turning red, but she didn't answer.

'OK.' Tanya swallowed. 'Well, who are you, then?'

'Who am I?' the woman suddenly burst out, her voice louder and stronger than Tanya would have expected from such a small person. She stepped back slightly. 'You know exactly who I am,' she continued, her cultured voice shaking with emotion. 'You whore.'

Tanya frowned, utterly confused. 'I have no idea who you are, lady,' she replied, beginning to get angry herself now that the shock was wearing off. She stepped forward again. 'But I would very much like to know, and I would also like to know why exactly you're harassing me like this.'

The woman took a few steps towards her, and Tanya backed away again, her eyes warily settling on the woman's hands stuffed inside her coat pockets. She wished again that she had her phone to hand or that she had left the door open for Simon to come in when he arrived. But that wasn't the case. It was just the two of them, and Tanya would have to deal with this alone. She looked around in her peripheral vision, trying to locate anything within reach that she could use as a weapon to defend herself. There was nothing. Just empty tables. Even the glasses were already back behind the bar.

Tears began to run down the woman's face, and she wiped them away angrily. 'You make me sick,' she spat. 'People like you, you're all the same. You think you can waltz in and take what you like and that there will be no consequences. Well, there *are* consequences. And I'm here to show you exactly what those consequences are.'

She stepped towards Tanya, her face dark and determined. She pulled something out of her pocket, and Tanya stepped back. She lost her balance as her heel slipped in a small puddle of water, and she fell back against the table, losing her small window of opportunity to get out of her crazed stalker's path. She threw her hands out in front of her in defence, not sure exactly what to expect. Cursing herself for not running earlier, Tanya squeezed her eyes shut and waited for the worst. Seconds passed and she held her breath. Was it a knife, or a gun? Was the woman waiting for her to open her eyes before she did it?

Tanya blinked and looked up. What she saw shocked her to the core. It shook her more deeply than the sight of a gun could ever have done.

The woman held the small photobook out in front of Tanya's face like a cross against a vampire. It was open on the middle page, and the picture spread across both pages may as well have been a punch to the gut. There he was in perfect colour. Daniel, hugging two children who looked like his miniatures and this crazed, brunette stalker was standing right behind him, her loving arm draped across his shoulder. Daniel had a family. And this was his wife.

Tanya slowly stood up and took the album from Daniel's wife's hand. She flicked through the pages, feeling more and more sick with each second that passed. The album was of a family holiday to Disneyland. They all looked so happy. The children looked up at their father adoringly and full of trust in the more candid pictures. Tanya shut the book. She didn't want to see any more. She gently handed it back to the woman and pulled one of the chairs out from the table behind her. She needed to sit down.

How could he do this? How could he lie to her, after she had let him in, after she had given him her trust? Tanya was crushed. She had spent years comfortably behind the emotional wall in her heart. No one had hurt her – no one had been allowed the opportunity. She had let Daniel through, allowed him into her life and her home and introduced him to her friends.

Tanya looked up and just shook her head in shock. How could he do this to his wife? To his children? She saw the anger and hate still burning in the other woman's eyes and realised that she assumed Tanya knew.

'I didn't know,' she said quietly.

'Of course you did,' the woman shot back. 'How could you not? He must have left you after most of your dates; he never spent weekends with you. You must have known. I read your texts.' She started pacing and held her arms around her stomach as though she were in pain. 'I found his phone. His second phone, that is. The one he uses for you.' Her dark brown eyes closed for a second before she continued. 'Several times he mentioned the fact he was unable to see you at weekends. You replied saying you understood the situation.' Her voice heightened into a humourless laugh.

'Listen... what's your name?'

'My name is Amanda, Tanya. Amanda Sharp.' She emphasised her last name haughtily and Tanya breathed out heavily.

'OK, Amanda. Daniel told me that he had only become successful because he had given up weekends to see all the clients who could never spare time on weekdays. That this was where the real money lay. And I believed him.' Tanya's tone was sober as she explained things as simply as she could. 'It seemed perfect. I run a club. Weekends are my busiest times.' She shrugged and then dropped her shoulders, defeated. 'I thought I'd finally found someone who wouldn't mind not going out on a Saturday night or cosying up on a Friday together after a long week at work. I was so happy to find someone in the same situation.' Tanya's voice quivered and she stopped talking. She still couldn't believe this was happening.

Amanda's hard gaze faltered, and she hesitated before speaking again.

'You honestly didn't know?' she questioned. 'You didn't know he had a wife or children waiting for him at home?'

'No, I didn't,' Tanya said. 'I had no idea. I wouldn't have touched him with a bargepole if I had.' She looked Amanda up and down. The woman was clearly upper middle class and well educated by the sound of her voice and her appearance. Someone from Daniel's own background, Tanya realised with a pang of jealousy. Something she would never have been.

'You don't know me. You don't know what kind of person I am, or what morals I live by. You've just assumed I'm the sort of person to happily wreck a family. You've assumed, based on the fact that I speak and look different to you. You've come into my life, you've followed me, sent me abusive messages, even tried to kill me. You stand here now, in my club, talking down to me. And you think I'm the one who should be judged?' Tanya raised an eyebrow and let out a long breath, trying to work out where to go from here.

Amanda had the good grace to at least look embarrassed at Tanya's words. Her face reddened, and she shrank back, her initial, blind rage diminished. Tanya chewed the inside of her cheek and studied the woman.

'Sit down. I'll get us a drink. Clearly we need to talk.' Tanya's tone was flat. She walked tiredly to the bar and, after eyeing the shelves, grabbed a bottle of cherry vodka and two glasses. Placing them on the table between them, she poured some into each glass and gave one to Amanda, which she took gratefully. They eyed each other warily for a few seconds before Amanda began talking.

'I didn't mean to push you that day.' She sighed unhappily and looked down into her glass. 'I was following you, yes. I never meant to do anything. But then you were strolling along, so carefree, so happy and I knew that it was my husband who was making you feel like that.' Her voice cracked, but she continued. 'I got angry. You were getting looks from every man you passed. And why wouldn't you? You're beautiful.' A tear slowly rolled down her cheek. 'Something just came over me. And in that split second, you were in front of me, and I just pushed you. I didn't even think about the fact we were on the stairs. I've felt terrible ever since. I was glad you were OK. Whatever I thought you were doing to me, no one deserves that, and I'm sorry.'

Tanya's eyebrows shot up in surprise. She hadn't been expecting that. Whether or not it was true, she couldn't tell, but Amanda seemed genuine enough, so she accepted it for now. She nodded and topped up their glasses, both already empty.

'Guess I was just lucky that day then,' she replied wryly. She looked around and frowned. 'How did you get in here?'

'I was already here. I hid in the storage cupboard next to the toilets when they did the rounds to check everyone was out.'

Tanya made a mental note to tell the staff to keep that locked in future. 'What was your plan exactly? Just to show me your pictures?'

'Well, initially I was hoping to meet you another way. When I started looking into who you were, I quickly realised that you were in business with an old friend of mine, Anna. We went to uni together. We hadn't seen each other in years, but I got in touch, managed to find out some more about you.'

Tanya gasped at Amanda's admission. Things started clicking into place.

'She doesn't know of the connection,' Amanda continued. 'I had hoped to take her up on her offer of a girls' night and confront you then. I thought you knew about me and the children already. I guess I was just hoping that seeing the children might make you feel bad. That maybe you might leave him and the affair would end. I hoped it would embarrass you, the secret coming out in front of your business partner.' She began to cry in despair. 'Oh God, things are so messed up.' She folded her arms on the table and lay her head face down on them as she cried her heart out.

Tanya stared at Amanda, her eyebrows raised in shock. This was the old friend Anna had been worrying about lately, the one whose husband was a cheat. It was all too much to take in. She had just found out that Daniel was cheating on her. Or rather, that she was his mistress rather than his leading lady, and now it turned out that his actual leading lady, his *wife*, was Anna's friend too.

Amanda was still crying. Tanya sighed a long, heavy sigh. She had her own whirling emotions to figure out and deal with; she couldn't pick Amanda up too. It seemed she had no choice though. She shook her head in disbelief and refilled their glasses. She was going to have to mop up this mess whether she liked it or not. She cursed Daniel, pain and anger beginning to boil to the surface.

'Amanda? Amanda!' she snapped.

Amanda sat up and wiped her tears with the back of her hand.

'I'm sorry. I'm just so tired. I'm so tired of putting up with shit like this,' she said miserably.

'Then leave,' Tanya said. 'I know it hurts, but if he's treating you and your children like this surely you don't want to stay?'

'No, I don't want to stay. I don't want to pretend things are OK any longer. I can't even bear him touching me, knowing he's out there with other women.'

Tanya looked down, uncomfortable at the position she found herself in. She tried not to think about herself for now.

'So what will you do?' she asked.

'That's the problem.' Amanda laughed sadly. 'I'm trapped with him.'

'What do you mean?'

'When we were married we both had good jobs, but Daniel always earned more than me. He had me sign a prenup that stated that if I ever left him of my own will, I would get nothing. He said it was his way of protecting himself from being used.'

'Wow, what a dick,' Tanya replied.

'Yes, well, it's more complicated than that now. If it were just me, I would walk away. But I have my children to think of. My youngest is just three. I've been at home with my children for five years. I have no income. I could get a part-time job, but I wouldn't earn enough to keep us all and give my children the life they're used to. And we would have to leave the family home – it's in his name. I can't do that to them. I can't uproot them from everything they know.' She rubbed her eyes tiredly. 'I know Daniel. He's all sunshine and light when he's getting his way, but he's a very selfish man at heart. If I left, he would make damn sure I got as little from him as possible.' Amanda downed the next glass of vodka and then topped it back up herself.

Tanya sat back in her chair. She could see Amanda's problem. Things were infinitely more difficult when children were involved.

'A friend of mine went through a divorce last year,' Tanya said. 'The court allowed her to stay in her home for the kids' sakes and she was given fifty percent of everything.'

'Which I would no doubt be awarded, had I not signed the prenup.'

'And there's no way around that?'

'No. I've taken it to a solicitor. He said if I can prove Daniel is having an affair, the contract is null and void, but that the phone and the texts aren't enough. They could be anyone. It wouldn't stand up in court,' she said hopelessly.

'And what would?'

'I would need a solid case. Incriminating photos, witnesses and even receipts from dates. I tried to get photos of you, but although I have you together I never got photos of anything romantic.' She pulled an apologetic face at the admission.

'Wow, OK.' Tanya decided to overlook the stalking. It was understandable, after all. She pondered the situation. 'Look… Obviously I want nothing more to do with that bastard now,' she said strongly. 'But I also don't want to let him get away with this. He's mugged me right off, and that ain't something I take lightly.' She leaned forward. 'If you really want to leave him, if you're sure you're ready to go down that road, then I think we can get what you need.'

Amanda frowned. 'But you don't want to see him now, you said.'

'I don't. But I'm a good actress.' Tanya thought back to her days as a stripper and the lows she used to go to for extra money. Her lips formed a hard line. 'I'll organise one more date and get the photos. He won't find out I know until we have everything. I'll talk to Anna. She'll stand as a witness if I ask her. And as for receipts, I do happen to have a few still.' Tanya turned pink and looked away. 'I kept some as keepsakes. In this box. First date and things. It's stupid.'

'It's genius.' Amanda's eyes gleamed with hope for the first time. Perhaps she really could escape him after all. She grasped Tanya's arms and pulled her forward into an unexpected hug.

'Oh, Tanya, I don't know what to say. If you really can pull that off, it would mean a whole new future for me and my kids.' Her voice wobbled. 'I thought I'd never get rid of him. I thought I'd just have to keep chasing all these women away.'

'Wait, has this happened before?' Tanya asked.

'Yes. Twice,' Amanda replied. 'One of the affairs fizzled out by itself, and the other woman ended it after I introduced myself.'

'Yes, well…' Tanya pulled a face. 'I'm not surprised, now that I'm familiar with your introductions…'

Amanda laughed – a real laugh this time. Already she seemed as though all the weight had been lifted from her shoulders. Tanya watched her as she thought about what she was going to do. She was going to go and get her revenge and hit that son of a bitch where it hurt.

*

Anna looked at the screen of her buzzing phone and sighed. It was her parents, ringing for a catch-up. Pressing the silence button, she focused back on the staff rota. Anna had been avoiding her parents lately, unable to give a strong-enough performance that everything was OK. Her mother would see through the fakery in an instant, and she didn't want to talk about it. Whatever was going on, it was between her and Freddie – it wasn't something that could be fixed over a cup of tea and a chat with her parents. They didn't even know what Freddie really did. They knew about the clubs and the properties he owned; everything legal. But they had no clue who he really was. Anna had worked hard to keep it that way over the years.

Anna's eyes glazed as her mind wandered back to her troubles. One week, Freddie had said. Anna had been working through all the possible reasons for this time frame, but there was nothing solid that she could reason with. It was driving her crazy. *What are you doing, Freddie?*

'Hey, Anna.' A gentle voice broke through her thoughts. Anna swivelled round, her frown swiftly turning into a warm smile as she saw Sophie approaching her.

Sophie was dressed to train, in soft yoga trousers and a sports top. It was only lunchtime – they wouldn't be open for another few hours. She often came at this sort of time to practise her sets on the hanging rings that Anna and Tanya had installed.

'Hi, how are you?' Anna asked. 'Fancy a coffee?'

'Yeah, OK, go on then.' Sophie dropped her bag on the floor and made herself comfortable on the bar stool next to Anna.

Anna walked behind the bar and poured a mug for Sophie. Sophie took it gladly and wrapped her hands around it.

'It's just one of those days today,' Anna told her.

'Oh no, everything OK?' Sophie's expressive face crumpled in concern.

Anna was reminded how lovely the girl was and immediately felt guilty at her self-pitying comment. She shook away the dark cloud she had been allowing to fester and put her troubles to the back of her mind.

'Yes, everything's fine. Sorry, just tired. I'm not sleeping very well.' She grinned brightly and sat back next to her employee and friend. 'Ignore me.'

'Have you tried lavender oil on your pillow? Or some manuka honey in warm milk? Might sound odd, but if ever I have trouble sleeping I do both and it always helps me drop off,' Sophie offered.

Anna laughed. If only her sleep troubles could be fixed so easily. She envied Sophie her simple solution. 'Perhaps I'll try it,' she said, not wanting to offend her. 'Anyway, enough about me, how are you? How did your drink with Michael go?' She grinned wickedly.

'Oh yes, I was going to mention that,' Sophie said, rolling her eyes.

'Well, how did it go?' Anna asked.

'Well…' Sophie bit her lip as she searched for the right words. She didn't want to offend her boss but didn't want to be untruthful either. 'Michael isn't really my type. He's a bit too… intense for me.'

'Intense? Oh, in what way?' Anna was disappointed. She had hoped the pair would hit it off. Sophie was just the sort of girl that Michael needed in his life.

'Um, I don't know, it's hard to explain. I think we're just not really compatible. I prefer someone a bit more laidback.' She grimaced apologetically.

Anna hid her disappointment and shrugged with a smile. 'No worries. Was worth a try! I shall just have to improve my matchmaking skills.'

Sophie laughed. 'He's a big boy; I'm sure he'll be OK finding someone himself.'

Anna smiled in response but kept her thoughts to herself. She wasn't sure Michael would be able to find someone on his own. He seemed so lonely lately, and Anna didn't want him to have to suffer their kind of life alone. Her resolve deepened. She would make it her mission to find him a nice girl to date, no matter what. At the very least, perhaps the distraction would stop her driving herself crazy.

# CHAPTER FORTY-SIX

Sammy pulled up on the side of the road, facing a small block of flats in Romford, and cut the engine.

'And this is where he keeps coming to?' Freddie asked.

'Yeah. Last three days he's gone in there, stayed a while then left. Here are the times.' He handed Freddie a small notebook.

'Do you know where in the building he goes?' Freddie asked.

'Not exactly, but I do know it's ground floor. The lift is directly in front of the front door. He always skirts around it and disappears.'

Freddie nodded and stared at the door. 'How do you know he's on his way over? There's no pattern to these times.' Freddie's eyes searched over the notebook again.

'I planted a tracker app in his phone after you called me. It hasn't been that many years since I was bottom of the pile nicking wallets. I've still got skills.' He grinned, trying to make Freddie laugh. It didn't work. Sammy took the hint and allowed the quiet to take over.

The pair sat in silence in the dark car for another ten minutes until eventually they saw Paul's car pull up outside the front of the building. He got out and took a cursory look around. Not noticing his brother and friend in the dark car down the road, he reached into the car and pulled out a full brown-paper takeaway bag. Securing it under his arm, he locked the car and walked up to the building.

'Well…' Freddie took a deep breath. 'It's now or never. Stay here – I need to do this alone.' Pulling his leather gloves on, he reached for the door.

'The code for the buzzer is one-zero-two-three,' Sammy said.

Freddie nodded, left the car and walked silently up to the building. He keyed in the door code and slipped inside. Skirting around the lift in the middle of the hallway as his brother had done, Freddie took a look around the back. It wasn't deep, the building. A few feet down the corridor there were just two doors, one on each side. Flat one and flat two. Both doors were closed. He looked around. There was nowhere else to go, aside from a small window at the back that looked as though it hadn't been opened in a decade. He had to be behind one of these doors.

Moving to the right, Freddie put his ear against the first door and listened. He stopped breathing and strained his ears. There was nothing. No one was in.

Moving across the hall to the left, he repeated the action. As he listened, muffled sounds began to make their way through. A bag rustled, and some footsteps sounded on a hard floor. A man began talking quietly. Freddie couldn't make out what was being said, but the deep tone was almost definitely Paul. He exhaled heavily and drew in a calm breath before continuing. He tried the door. It was unlocked.

Pushing the door open slowly, Freddie peered into a dark, rectangular hallway. Several doors led off it. He stepped forward, careful not to make a sound. The hallway was fairly bare, just a few pairs of shoes neatly lined up to one side and a coat stand with Paul's jacket hanging on it. A picture hung on one wall depicting a paradise of white sands and palm trees. An ornate mirror hung opposite it, at head height. Freddie listened again, trying to work out which way to go. There were two voices talking together now. One was definitely Paul, but the other man Freddie couldn't identify. It wasn't someone he knew.

Footsteps began to move towards Freddie from the other side of a door on his right. He braced himself and waited for whoever it was to come through. He would use the element of surprise to his advantage and hopefully find out what was happening here.

The door opened and a tall, slender man in his thirties walked through holding a full plate and a glass of red wine. As he caught sight of Freddie standing in the shadows, he screamed in shock and dropped everything he was holding. The plate and glass shattered, covering the hallway in food and broken shards. The man looked terrified and held his hands up, shaking.

'Please, take whatever you want,' he squeaked.

Within a heartbeat, Paul lunged into the hall like a bull. He yanked the young man out of harm's way and brandished a large carving knife, thunder on his face. He opened his mouth to yell at whoever was there but then stopped and stepped back in shock.

'Freddie?' he asked, his voice angry and confused. 'What the hell?' He lowered his knife, and his jaw dropped as he tried to understand what his brother was doing there. 'What are you doing here?' Paul demanded.

Freddie hadn't moved. He was trying to work out who the other man was, who was at this moment hiding behind Paul. Paul looked annoyed and upset. Freddie's lips pressed into a determined line. It was time to get to the truth, once and for all.

'Where is she, Paul?' Freddie's voice was low and dangerous.

'Where's who?' Paul's confused frown grew deeper.

'Katherine. Where is she? You've been lying to me, disappearing, acting shady ever since she was taken. You were there that night, the night she disappeared. You even knew the blind spots on the CCTV. No one knows the blind spots, Paul. No one except us. I didn't want to think it of you, and if I'm honest, I still can't.' Freddie warred with himself. This was the hardest thing he had ever done. 'But I don't have any other explanation for all that's been going on, so I'll ask you again – where is she?'

Paul barked a humourless laugh as what Freddie was saying finally dawned on him. He seemed to deflate, and he smiled sadly, shaking his head and exhaling loudly. He looked up at the brother he had followed all his life and the sadness Freddie saw there nearly killed him.

'You really think that I would kidnap some young girl? For what? Some random boy to kill himself for me? I don't even know William Hargreaves.' Paul's voice was quiet and full of pain. 'I don't know Ben Hargreaves. I don't know any of them. I'm just a normal bloke, living his life. I'm your brother.' His voice cracked, and he swallowed the lump in his throat.

Freddie hesitated. He looked down at the mess around their feet. He suddenly felt as though he'd aged ten years, and seeing his brother's reaction, he felt like a total wanker. He should never have even entertained the idea that it was possible.

'No,' Freddie said soberly. 'I don't think that. Really. But I do think you've been lying to me, and I need to know why, Paul. Because right now time is against us, and we need to stick together more than ever. I don't trust anyone anymore. Whoever it is doing this, they're always one step ahead of us.' He put his arms out to the side helplessly. 'They know our every move. They even managed to get around our men, to Hargreaves' house. They know what's coming and are leaving us nothing.'

Paul tried to process everything, now that the shock had worn off. He was hurt that Freddie could even have considered him to be the kidnapper, but considering the logic of the evidence Freddie had displayed and the pressure he was under, he could grudgingly understand how he came to that suspicion. He had been disappearing a lot and lying to him. He had been lying to everyone for some time, in fact. But now that Freddie was here, he wouldn't be able to keep his secrets for much longer. It was time to be honest with his brother. Whatever the consequences may be. Sighing he turned to the man standing silently behind him.

'James, this is my brother, Freddie. It's OK,' he said encouragingly, 'he isn't going to cause trouble.'

James stepped forward and stood next to Paul, nodding politely but still looking wary.

Paul faced Freddie and braced his shoulders tensely. 'Freddie…' He paused, worry marring his face. 'This is James. James is my partner.'

'Your partner?' Freddie asked slowly.

'Yes. My partner. And no, not in the business sense.' He held his head high. 'I'm gay, Fred. Bent as a nine-bob note. Have been for a long time.'

Freddie stared at Paul in shock. That was the last thing he'd been expecting to hear from his big, burly, hard-man brother. He racked his brains, trying to think back to the last time he had seen Paul hook up with a woman. He couldn't think of a single instance, at least not since he was a teenager. Paul chatted to women easily enough, but he'd never had a girlfriend. Freddie thought it was just because he didn't want the hassle. They led busy, complicated lives – it was often easier to stay single.

'Well, bloody hell, Paul, you kept that quiet!' he eventually exclaimed. 'Why would you hide that from me?'

'Are you joking? You know this isn't good for business, Fred,' Paul replied. 'I've tried to keep this side of my life separate, so it wouldn't affect anything. I didn't want to be the reason things went south.'

Freddie nodded his acceptance of this. He had to agree with Paul on that front. A lot of the people they worked with were old school and narrow-minded. It could affect them. But it wouldn't be the end of the world. And business, though important, was not his highest priority – family was. He was surprised by the news, yes. He really hadn't had the slightest clue before now. But he felt sad that Paul had felt the need to hide it from him. He didn't give two shits that Paul liked blokes. It changed nothing.

'So what?' Freddie held his arms out and shrugged. 'Who gives a shit if a few old faces want to take their ball home. We'll figure it out. But you shouldn't be hiding like this.' Freddie frowned. 'You should have told me. I don't care what floats your boat – you're my brother.'

Paul felt a wave of guilt flood through him as Freddie talked. He should have known Freddie wouldn't care. Freddie had been watching his back since the day he was born. It had been Freddie who'd beaten the bullies who jumped him when he was six. It had been Freddie who'd taught him and Michael how to grow into men, since their dad had died when they were all young. It was Freddie who'd pulled their whole family up from nothing into underground royalty. Everything he had ever done was for the safety and happiness of his family. Paul felt terrible for thinking that Freddie might have turned his back on him now.

Freddie switched his attention to the man standing silently beside Paul. 'Nice to meet you, James,' he said. 'I'm sorry for arriving like this. This is not how we should have met.' His last remark was a casual dig at Paul, but Paul accepted it gladly.

Paul was overjoyed that Freddie had not disowned him. He could have done. Their empire had taken them years to build, but they all knew how fragile it was. It could all fall around their ears in an instant. If that happened though, he knew Freddie would sit down next to him and watch it crumble. Because they were family. He should have just told Freddie years ago, even if they'd kept it between themselves.

He had met James six months before, and in the last couple of months they'd become pretty serious. He cared for him a lot and wanted to spend as much time with him as he could. It had become increasingly difficult to cover all his absences. It seemed, though, that he hadn't been as covert as he had thought.

James smiled warmly at Freddie, accepting the sudden change of pace.

'Well, yes. Quite. On that we can agree!' He squeezed Paul's arm and moved back towards the kitchen. 'How about we all get a drink and start again, yes?'

'Sounds great,' Freddie replied politely. He lowered his voice as he passed Paul. 'I am really sorry, mate. This was all a huge mistake. I hope you can forgive me.'

''Course,' Paul said. 'It's forgotten. And I'm sorry I lied to you. I should have told you a long time ago.'

'Yeah, well…' Freddie said, rolling his eyes. 'A heads-up would have been nice! Might have saved me bowling in here looking like a right twat. You hid it well – I had no idea.' He looked through to the kitchen where James was pouring more wine. 'As long as you're happy, I'm happy. I don't care who it's with. We are who we are – it don't change nothing. Not with me anyway.' He pressed Paul's arm to strengthen his point. 'Blood's thicker than anything, mate.'

# CHAPTER FORTY-SEVEN

Anna walked through her front door and kicked off her shoes. She was exhausted. It had been a long night, and instead of coming home when the club had closed, she had sat talking with Tanya into the early hours. She was shocked to learn about Daniel and upset for both women. What a mess. Tanya deserved someone amazing, and Daniel had seemed like he might have been that guy. But all the time he had been a lying, cheating rat. And to top it off, he happened to be Amanda's lying, cheating rat. Both of them deserved so much better. Anna was more than happy to help bring him down and had readily agreed to being Tanya's witness. She just hoped that her evidence was enough to help Amanda get what she deserved from the divorce.

Anna walked down the long hallway to her bedroom, her toes curling in the thick carpet. She wanted nothing more than to cosy up into her covers and fall asleep. She turned the light on and jumped as she saw Freddie sitting in the armchair in the corner of the room. She put her hand to her chest.

'God, you scared me! Why were you sitting in the dark?' Anna asked.

Something was wrong. Freddie had never looked so drawn and tense. He looked up, and she saw something in his eyes that she had never seen before. It looked like… defeat.

'Anna, I need to ask you something.' Freddie said hoarsely.

'Sure, what is it?' Anna hurried over and knelt down in front of him, putting her hands in his, her face full of concern.

Freddie was silent for a moment as he tried to find the right words. Anna waited.

'There are some things going on right now that are out of my control. And there are some influential people who are threatening to take down everything we've got.'

'But they can't.' Anna frowned, her eyes searching his face. 'You've been careful. Haven't you? Surely they don't have anything solid on you.'

Freddie squeezed Anna's hands. 'I have been careful, yes. I always am. But these people don't need real evidence. They plan to plant it. And they can. Easily.'

Anna's quick brain worked through what Freddie was saying. 'They're police? But you have police of your own, in your pocket.'

'Not at this level,' Freddie replied, his voice flat. 'Look, Anna, I've gone at this from every angle in my head and there's no way out for me if they go down this route. Not this time. Clean pigs I can work with – I can always stay one step ahead. They have to follow rules. But dirty coppers this far up the food chain, those I can't fight.' Freddie stared into Anna's eyes. 'There's only one option I have left to take. If it comes to it, I'll have to leave, and I won't be able to come back.' Freddie paused to let that sink in. He purposely left out the threat to Anna in his explanation. He wanted to find out her true feelings before she knew that she had no choice.

Anna felt herself go cold as she realised what he was saying. 'Right,' she heard herself say faintly.

'What I want to ask is, if I have to go, will you come with me?' Freddie asked the question, hoping against hope that she would say yes. If she said no, he would have to tell her that she too was in danger and that, actually, she had no choice but to leave if the shit hit the fan. He so desperately wanted her to say yes of her own free will. That way she would never have to know how close she'd been to her own death, and also it would give him hope for their future. He hadn't been sure lately that they had one. 'I know it's a lot to ask. I know it will mean leaving everything and everyone else behind, and I hate that I have to put you in this position. But I may soon have no other choice, and I need to know if that time comes whether you're with me or if you'll stay here. I have enough cash to set us up comfortably somewhere else; I've got papers for us already, new identities. We could start again. But we would never be able to return.'

Anna sank back onto the floor and looked up at the man she loved so much. He meant everything to her. But she had a life here – family, friends. It would mean leaving her whole life and everybody else that she loved, and she didn't even know why. She knew already that he wouldn't tell her, if she asked. This was all to do with his big secret. Could she really give up everything for love, with secrets still between them? She would be diving into all of this completely blind, at a time when she had never felt less certain.

'You've already had papers made?' she asked.

'Yes.' Freddie picked up a thick envelope from the small table next to him.

Anna opened it. Inside were four passports and four birth certificates. She opened the passports. The first two had hers and Freddie's pictures inside. Hannah and Ted Jones. A married couple. The second two contained Paul and Michael's pictures. She looked at Freddie questioningly.

'If they go for me, they'll bring down the three of us. Even if I'm gone, I have no doubt they'll still go after them. It's up to them what they do, but I can at least arm them with the means to get away if they need to.'

Anna nodded. She traced her finger over the front of one of the passports. She felt torn. If things were normal between them, if there hadn't been all the secrets and strain of late, she wouldn't have had to think twice. But with everything that had been going on, she had begun to question how strong they really were. And now here Freddie was, asking her to gamble her whole life on him without giving her the reasons why.

Anna's brain raced. They had been together for three years and now that she was being pushed to make a decision, Anna couldn't imagine being without Freddie. But then she couldn't imagine being without Tanya and her parents or the club either. But she would have to choose. Freddie was scared. This was serious. Whether or not she wanted to choose between big parts of her life was no longer in play. She had to make a decision. Anna looked around at the stylishly furnished bedroom. Every stick of furniture held memories of when they'd chosen it together. This house, their home, it had been put together with love. Without Freddie, they were just meaningless items. All the money in the world wouldn't be able to replace him.

'OK,' she whispered. 'I'll come.' Her heart broke as she said it out loud, and she looked down at the carpet so that he wouldn't see the extent of the sadness in her eyes.

Freddie knew though, without looking. He hated himself for putting her in this position. He reached forward and pulled her to him, holding her close.

'Pack a bag tonight with everything essential in and leave it in your office. Take the passports and put them in the club safe,' he said quietly. 'Keep anything you want to take in your bag. Because when I get the tip-off, we'll have to leave within the hour. There'll be no time for anything else. We won't be able to come back here.' Freddie buried his face into her hair and squeezed her to him.

A solitary tear ran down Anna's face. 'When will it happen?' she asked.

'It still might not. But if it does, it will be in about two days. I'm still trying to sort things. I'll do everything I can to avoid this outcome. But we must be prepared.'

He felt Anna nod against his chest. Freddie stared out of the bedroom window at the dark, stormy clouds outside as they sat there unmoving. He would try his best, of course he would. He didn't want to leave the life he'd worked so hard to build any more than Anna did. He didn't want to think about what it would do to his family either. But at this point, he didn't see there being any other outcome. The kidnapper was too clever. He knew how to keep off both the police and Freddie's radar, and no matter what way he approached it, there was nothing to go on. Ben Hargreaves was teetering on the edge of madness and he wanted someone to take out his frustration on. Freddie wished it was anyone else but him, but it was what it was, and all he could do now was pray that they got away and out of the country before Hargreaves finally snapped.

# CHAPTER FORTY-EIGHT

Katherine tried to open her eyes as she heard her captor entering the room. Her eyelids felt heavy, just like the rest of her body these days. Her muscles had quickly wasted away, lying there on the foetid mattress day and night. She no longer felt cold. In fact sometimes she felt downright hot. Her mind was swimming in and out of feverish delusion. In her moments of clarity, she knew that she wouldn't last much longer. Her body was full of infection, and she was wasting away.

The torch was switched on and a bag of food thrown onto the bed next to one of her hands. She attempted to reach out for it but didn't have the energy.

'You need to eat.' The robotic voice was matter-of-fact, no care behind the words.

Katherine let a ghost of a wry smile play across her lips. 'Oh please,' she murmured. 'You don't care. How many days left now? Three?' Katherine's breath became laboured. Even speaking took too much effort.

'Two actually.'

She heard him move towards her.

'Eat,' he repeated. 'I bought more penicillin.' He paused and then picked up her arm and checked her pulse. He tutted. 'So weak. Come here.'

Katherine felt him pick her up as though she weighed no more than a newspaper. She probably didn't. He sat down on the bed and pulled her so that she sat propped up against him. Holding her around the waist with one hand so that she didn't fall, he opened the bag and pulled out the cardboard sleeve full of soggy chips. He began lifting them to her mouth, and Katherine made the effort to eat a few. She wasn't hungry, but it would take more energy to fight him on that point.

After a painfully slow feed, Katherine let her head loll against her captor's broad chest.

'Please,' she uttered, 'no more.'

The sudden realisation hit her that this was the closest she had ever been to her captor. She hated him more than she ever thought she could hate anyone, but hate took a lot of energy, and she was too tired to pull herself away right now. Instead she asked him a question.

'Why do you want my brother to die?' She felt him tense before he answered.

'That would be my business, not yours,' he replied tightly.

Katherine felt a sharp stab of anger run through her feeble body. It *was* her business. She had been made to give up her freedom and would shortly sacrifice her life for this business, so of all people she should be given the truth. She gathered what little strength she had and grasped the thick, black ski mask that covered his face. Taken by surprise, he had no time to pull it back before she'd ripped it off his head. She gasped, and her eyes widened in shock as she saw her captor's face for the first time.

'It's you,' she whispered in horror and confusion. Her eyes filled with tears and her thin body shook as she recognised the person who had put her through all of this torture and pain. 'Why?' she asked, the tears spilling down her face.

The last thing she remembered when she came back round was the blow to the head as he knocked her out.

# CHAPTER FORTY-NINE

Tanya narrowed her eyes as the buzzer sounded. Her fingers gripped the handle of the knife she was using to chop tomatoes tighter as she imagined plunging it through Daniel's lying, cheating chest. But she took a deep breath instead and, putting the knife down, plastered a pleasant smile on her face before going to open the door.

Daniel swept in and grabbed her face, kissing her passionately on the lips.

'I've missed you like crazy this week, my red-headed vixen,' he said jovially. 'It's been far too long since I last saw you and that sexy arse of yours.'

'Yes, well,' she said, 'we've both just been so busy at work. Good trip to see those potential clients this weekend?' Tanya looked at him with innocent expectation on her face.

'Yeah, yeah – it went well. Think I've landed us a pretty big fish after taking them golfing. Fingers crossed.' He shot her a winning smile.

Tanya gave him an excited grin, but as he turned to walk through to the kitchen she shot daggers into his back with her eyes. *Lying snake*, she thought. Her fluffy white cat strolled lazily down the hallway and gave her a quizzical look.

'Oh you wait, Princess,' she whispered conspiratorially. 'I'm going to make sure that this is a night he'll never forget.'

She followed him through to the kitchen, where he was pouring them both a glass of wine.

'What's in the oven? Smells delicious,' Daniel said. He had taken his jacket off and undone a couple of buttons on his shirt. He was ready to relax.

'Mediterranean chicken, to go with the salad.' She pointed towards the small bowl she had been preparing before he arrived.

Daniel frowned at it. 'There's not much salad. Shall I put some more in?' he asked.

'No, no, there's plenty. I'll add to it later.' Tanya lifted her glass to his in a casual toast. There was enough salad for one, which was all she needed. She drank deeply from her glass, never taking her eyes off him. 'Actually, I have a little treat in store for you. A little starter, shall we say.' Her lips curled into a naughty smile and Daniel immediately put his glass down.

'Now that sounds pretty perfect to me,' he said huskily. He moved over to her and put his hands around her waist.

'Aw.' Tanya touched his hair. 'You look really handsome today. Let's take some selfies. I have no decent photos of us to put up on the wall. Come here.' Tanya pulled his face next to hers and took a picture.

Daniel complied, feeling very happy after the compliment and thinly veiled promise of sex. He smiled and posed as she did, while she snapped away on her phone's camera. Tanya kissed his cheek before gently turning his head to hers for a full-on snog. Daniel pulled away laughing as she took a series of photos while they kissed.

'They aren't very wall-worthy. I bet I have about five chins in that last one.'

Tanya winked and pulled him through the house towards the bedroom.

'What about,' she purred, 'if we made some extremely wall-unworthy pictures in here? They can keep you warm when you're away.'

'Now you're talking,' Daniel replied.

Tanya stopped at the door to her room and turned to him, looking up through her eyelashes coyly.

'Now there's one rule, if you want what I've got in here.'

'Oh yeah?' Daniel leaned over her, kissing her neck. 'What's that then?' He was getting excited already.

'You have to do whatever I say,' she replied. 'And I mean *whatever.*'

'You kinky bitch.' Daniel's pupils were dilated as he stared at her hungrily. 'I'm all yours. I will do whatever you say.'

'Good.' Tanya opened the door, and his jaw dropped as he saw the bed. 'Then get naked, get on the bed and lie still like a good boy while I secure the cuffs.'

On each of the four corners of Tanya's metal bedframe, a set of handcuffs was attached. Candles were lit around the room, giving off an atmospheric glow, and next to the bed was an array of sensual instruments. Daniel walked in and eagerly stripped off, watching Tanya undress next to him. Underneath her clothes Tanya was wearing a red and black laced corset, pulled tight. Her breasts sat pert and full in the plunging bra at the top. His eyes slid down her body to the lacy knickers and stockings. She looked so sexy that Daniel could barely contain himself. He just wanted to grab her and fuck her hard, right there on the floor.

As if she could tell what he was thinking, Tanya wagged her finger at him. 'Ah-ah-ahh. Not yet, big boy,' she teased. 'Get on the bed. You promised to do as you were told.'

Daniel exaggeratedly rolled his eyes and moaned in sexual frustration, before climbing onto the bed and lying on his back obediently. He waited and watched Tanya as she tightly secured his wrists and ankles with the handcuffs. When she was done, her eyes glinted mischievously and she mounted the bed herself, kneeling just next to him. Leaning over his face, she allowed Daniel to suck at her breasts while she took pictures of the two of them. Moving lower down the bed, she gripped his penis and took a selfie of herself doing that too. She made sure to get an angle with his face in. Satisfied that she had enough evidence for Amanda, she threw her phone over to a nearby chair.

'Now, what I'm going to do to you tonight is going to blow your mind, Mr Sharp,' she said in a seductive voice. 'That much I can absolutely promise you.'

Daniel moaned, desperate for her. 'Get on me.'

Tanya knelt over him, hovering just above his large erection. He held his breath, praying that she would put him out of his misery. Instead she laughed and moved backward so that she was straddling his thighs.

'Not yet. First I'm going to give you a relaxing massage. Lie back and enjoy. Because you aren't going anywhere.'

Tanya reached over into the top drawer of her bedside table and poured some lavender oil into her hand. Starting at the top of his hard chest, she slowly rubbed the oil into his skin. She leaned over him as she did so and kissed him deeply. Pulling back she ran her hands down his torso and over his muscular stomach. *He really was a fine specimen,* Tanya thought with a pang of hatred as she looked at his body. She made sure to keep her hands above his hips until she had rubbed all of the oil in.

'Oops, run out. Let me make sure I have enough oil on my hands for the, er, main event…' she trailed off suggestively, and Daniel groaned with delight.

Keeping one eye on Daniel to make sure he couldn't see what she was doing, Tanya reached back into her drawer. Ignoring the lavender oil, she picked up a much smaller bottle and tipped the entire contents into her hand. Careful not to spill any, she settled back onto his legs, locked hers around his and with both hands grasped his engorged penis. She quickly rubbed the liquid around the shaft and into the end, making sure to get as much coverage as possible. Some of it trickled down over his balls, but that just made her smile grow wider.

The second Tanya's hands made contact he made a sound of delight, assuming his sexual relief was finally in sight. Barely a couple of seconds later, as his nerve endings registered the heat of the Tabasco sauce, he began to scream in agony.

Tanya steadied herself as he bucked and writhed underneath her in distress. She widened her eyes innocently and leaned towards his face.

'Oh my God, what's wrong?' she asked.

'I don't know,' he wailed. 'Get it off! Get it off me!'

'Get what off you?' Tanya feigned ignorance, wiping her hands on the bedspread to get rid of the excess sauce.

'The oil! Get it off – it's burning! Oh fuck! Fuck, it's burning, help me!' His shouts were getting louder by the second. 'Get me out of these *now*, Tanya!' He strained against the cuffs, but they were strong and the bedframe was sturdy.

'OK, hold on – I'll go find the keys.'

Tanya jumped down lightly from the bed and, grabbing her phone as she passed it, she left the room. As soon as she got into the hallway, she doubled over and began to laugh silently as he screamed. *Good*, she thought. *He damn well deserves it.* She turned her phone to silent and slipped it onto a hidden shelf under a side table in the next room. You could never be too careful.

Pulling the key out of her bra where it had been all along, she sauntered back into the bedroom. Daniel was red in the face and crying. His penis was pretty red too and had shrivelled right up. Feigning clumsiness, she undid his cuffs as slowly as she could get away with. He almost ripped his own arm off as she undid the last one in his haste to get to the bathroom.

Daniel jumped into the shower and turned it on, pushing the showerhead down to his red-raw privates and sobbing loudly as he tried to wash it off. Tanya stood in the doorway and pretended to feel awful.

'Wow, Daniel, I am so sorry.'

Tanya stared at him in wonder. There he was, a fully grown man, weeping in the shower like a baby girl. This was even better than she'd thought it would be.

'What the hell was it?' he asked, between heavy, snotty sobs.

'Tabasco sauce, darling. I don't know how the bottles got mixed up.' Tanya looked at him apologetically and then grimaced.

'It fucking kills,' he howled. 'It's not going away – I think I need to go to hospital. I think this might have done serious damage. Oh God!' He wailed in pain once more.

'Hospital, good idea. Let's go – quickly. The sooner the better.'

Tanya nipped back through to her bedroom and shrugged a casual dress on over her lingerie. Slipping her feet into a pair of pumps, she unceremoniously shoved Daniel's clothes and shoes into a plastic bag and grabbed the dressing gown she had bought him to keep at hers.

'Here,' she said, going back to the bathroom. 'Just put this on for now. I have your clothes. Let's go.'

Daniel stood up with difficulty and let Tanya assist him in putting the dressing gown on. He waddled down the hallway and out of the front door, holding on to his ravaged manhood. Tanya pressed the button for the lift and waited patiently. It arrived with a ping, and Daniel stepped in as soon as the doors opened. He looked back at Tanya as she stood smiling in the hallway.

'What are you doing? Come on,' he whined.

Tanya's smile broadened. 'I think I'll sit this one out. You're a big boy – you'll be fine on your own. I'll tell you what I will do for you though.' The smile dropped, and her face turned cold. 'I'll give Amanda a call, let her and the kids know where you are. I'm sure she'll greatly appreciate this story.'

Tanya watched his red, agonised face pale significantly as her words hit home. She shoved the bag that held his clothes at him. The doors began to close and she waved goodbye to the dripping-wet shell of a man before slowly walking back into her flat. Shutting the door behind her, her shoulders sank and she gave Princess a sad smile.

She had really cared about Daniel, had let him into her life and her heart, and finding out who he really was had cut her deeply. Since Amanda had confronted her in the club, she had held on to all of her anger and her thirst for revenge. But now that part was over. She had got what she needed to make sure he lost out financially. She had put him through possibly the most excruciating evening he would ever experience in his life. And now he was gone. He wouldn't be back – she was sure of that. Aside from the fact that he would soon know Tanya had given Amanda everything she needed for the divorce, she doubted he would ever want to risk crossing her again.

Tanya allowed herself to feel the pain for a few moments. She pulled down the invisible walls around her heart and let it wash over her, closed her eyes and mentally said goodbye to the only relationship she had really thought was going somewhere. Then she drew herself up to full height and fluffed her hair.

With perfect timing, the buzzer on her oven went off. Her dinner was ready. Mediterranean chicken and salad for one. Tanya walked through to the kitchen with her head held high. Onwards and upwards, as Carl would say.

# CHAPTER FIFTY

Thea drove slowly up the long, narrow road full of rundown terraced houses, most of which were boarded up. Some were even condemned, big railings up outside the front. The boards tied to the railings indicated that these were all owned by the same company. Thea guessed that they would eventually pull them down and rebuild something else here instead. Probably flats or offices. That seemed to be happening everywhere now.

She pulled into a space at the side of the road and looked around. She had lost him again. Opening the backpack she took everywhere on shoots, she pulled out a bag of crisps and began to eat. She was starving, having been out shooting nearly all day. Time seemed to run away with her when she immersed herself in her passion. Today she was following Michael, but it was proving trickier than she had accounted for. She had followed him out here a few days before but had managed to lose him then too.

About to give up and go home, Thea suddenly spotted Michael in her side mirror. She chucked the bag of crisps onto the passenger seat and grabbed her camera. Jumping out of the car quickly she locked it using the central-locking button on her keys as she ran down the road. He had disappeared down the next side street and she didn't want to lose him again. She reached the corner and came to a halt, peering round carefully. Her eyes searched the street and locked on to her brother. Bingo!

Thea raised her camera and was about to begin taking shots, but then she paused. She lowered it and watched Michael.

He took a key from his pocket and unlocked a heavy padlock that was keeping the tall railings together outside one of the condemned houses. Locking it behind him again, he walked in through the front door and out of her line of sight. Thea frowned.

As the Tyler who ran all of the accounts, she knew about all of their businesses. There wasn't anything she wasn't privy to. But she wasn't aware of anything they owned over this way. The house he had walked into was very obviously empty, and it was definitely not somewhere that he would ever conduct a meeting either. Which meant that whatever Michael was up to out here, he was doing it on his own. And that meant that Freddie didn't know about it.

This immediately worried her. She knew Michael was part of the firm now, and technically he was all grown up. But he was still her little brother, and he was still the baby of the family. Freddie knew what he was doing – he had been running the show for years. Under his wing Michael had flourished, sure. But Thea knew that he was still fairly new to the business and a bit green around the gills. She guessed that Michael was probably just trying to prove himself, show that he could do something without any help. But Thea knew he could easily slip up on his own. She bit her lip. She should tell Freddie, but she needed more information before she could do that. Walking back to her car she waited for Michael to leave, watching for him in her rear-view mirror.

Barely fifteen minutes had passed when Michael's broad figure came back into view. She waited another five minutes to make sure that he had definitely gone, before she stepped back out of the car.

As she reached the building Thea glanced both ways down the street. There was no one around. The padlock looked pretty heavy-duty so she didn't try to pick it. Instead she quickly scaled the wire fence and jumped down the other side. Thea dusted her hands off, impressed that she had been able to do it so easily. She silently thanked her mother for insisting she did gymnastics at school.

Thea found herself standing in a small, overgrown front garden. The weeds had taken over completely, and even the slabs that lined the front path weren't easy to pick out among them. Treading carefully, she made her way up the path. She gingerly pulled at the rotten front door. It didn't open fully but enough that she could slide in without a problem. Once inside, she squinted and tried to make out her surroundings. It was dusty and dark where most of the windows were boarded up with wood. There was some light making its way in, but not much. Rummaging in her bag, she pulled out a travel torch and shone it around the room.

Clearly no one had lived here for a long time. There was no furniture, and even the carpet had gone. In the corner were a few rags and a ripped sleeping bag, signs that at some point this had been home to a squatter. A thin layer of dust had settled like a blanket over everything. Thea couldn't understand why Michael would come here.

She froze as a thud sounded from upstairs. *What was that?* A second later, the same sound came through again. Ice trickled down Thea's spine. She wasn't alone. There was somebody else in the house. She quickly pulled her bag off her back and rummaged with one hand, until she found her Swiss army knife. She flicked the blade out and held it up in front of her. Just because Michael had been here didn't mean it was safe. She narrowed her eyes and locked her jaw. She may not be one of the brothers, but she was still a Tyler and had the same steely blood running through her veins. She could hold her own, when it counted.

She quietly crept back the way she'd come, to where she'd seen the bottom of the stairs. Carefully, she climbed them, trying to stay silent. Cocking her ear to one side, she could hear a rustling sound coming from one of the rooms. As she reached the landing, she honed in on it. Whatever it was, it was coming from the back bedroom. The door was closed.

With a deep breath, Thea reached forward and pushed the door open, sending it banging against the wall. She jumped forward and scanned the room, ready to face whatever she found there.

The stench of urine assailed her nostrils at the same time her brain registered what she was looking at.

'Oh my God,' she breathed in horror. There was nothing in the room except for a young blonde woman lying on the bare floorboards, her wrist chained to the radiator. She pulled herself up into a seated position, leaning back against the wall in exhaustion, as Thea ran over.

'Jesus, what is this? Who's done this to you? Are you OK?' Thea shook her head. She had never imagined finding this. She tugged at the chains, but they were thick and the radiator pipes were strong.

'No use, I've tried for days,' the girl said, her voice weak. 'Water, please…'

'Yes, of course.' Thea hurriedly reached into her bag and pulled out a water bottle. She held it to the girl's lips patiently, while the girl slurped desperately at it. When nearly all of it was gone, she rested back.

'Thank you. Haven't drunk in two days.'

Thea looked around and realised that the girl was slumped next to a pile of her own excrement and urine. There wasn't even a bucket nearby. She felt sick.

'We need to get you out of here,' Thea said, her eyes darting back to the door. She yanked the chains again.

The girl laid her hand on Thea's and shook her head. 'You need bolt cutters – you'll have to go get some.'

'OK, I will. I'll do that, and I'll be back soon with help, OK? What's your name?' Thea tried to sound calm and confident, but inside she felt anything but that. What was going on here? And what did Michael have to do with it?

'I'm Carla,' she replied. 'Please – hurry.' Carla's eyes filled with tears and her body began to shake. She had been up here for days.

He had taken her here after she'd seen the CCTV in his office; after she'd seen the captured girl on the cameras. Michael had been furious. She had begged him to let her go, had promised never to tell, but he hadn't listened. He had chained her here and left her to rot. The slow death of starvation and thirst was her punishment for disobeying him and prying into his office.

She hadn't been able to believe her luck when she'd heard someone else walking through the house. She'd known it wasn't him – could tell by the softer sounds and lighter footsteps. She had used what little strength she had to bang on the floor with her leg. She thanked God it had worked.

'I will, I promise, Carla. I'll be back really soon.' Thea stood up to leave, but Carla stopped her.

'Wait, there's something else.' Carla's expression was full of fear. 'He has another girl. I think she might be here too, because he comes in and out. It looked like a basement on the camera, no windows.'

'What?' Thea was horrified. What on earth had she stumbled into?

'You need to find her. She don't look so good.' Carla closed her eyes again, lethargic from several days without food.

Horror gripped Thea's heart. This couldn't be happening. She stood up and backed out of the room. 'Just wait here, OK. I'll check the house and be back soon. I'll get you out of here.'

Almost falling back down the stairs in her haste, she ran through the abandoned house to the kitchen at the back. This was where the entrance to the basement would be, if there was one. She whirled around, looking for it. There was a door, a smaller one next to the one she'd come in through. There was an arc on the floor underneath it, clear of debris and dust. It had been opened recently. She closed her eyes for a second as her heart fell heavily into her stomach.

Without hesitation, Thea swung open the door. Just inside was a set of old, brick stairs that seemed to lead down to some sort of cellar. She ran down to the thick, wooden door at the bottom. The door seemed as old as the stairs themselves, and the handle creaked as she tried to open it. She pushed against it, but it held fast. Thea looked down and realised there was a key sticking out of the lock. She turned it and heard the lock click open.

She swung it open and the smell hit her like a brick wall. It was awful. It smelled like something had died down there. Ignoring it, she squinted and tried to make out what was inside, but it was pitch black. Running her hands up the brick wall just inside the door, Thea felt around for a light switch. She prayed there was still a working bulb down here. The walls were damp, and she pulled a face as her fingers made contact with it, but they quickly reached an old, round light switch. She flicked it on and with a tired buzz, a weak bulb woke up and lit the room.

Her hands shot to cover her mouth, and her eyes grew wide in horrified shock.

At the back of the room stood a broken bedframe with a thin, rotting mattress. But it was what was on top of the mattress that made Thea want to cry. On top of the mattress lay the dirty, thin, lifeless body of another young woman.

Thea jumped as the body stirred, and she realised in amazement that this girl was still alive. The girl blinked awake, in the weak light. She locked eyes with Thea, and Thea saw surprise finally register on her face. It was a slow reaction. This girl was in a very, very bad way.

'Am I dead?' the girl whispered after a long few moments.

Her words seemed to spur Thea into action. She rushed forward, dropping to her knees, and grasped at the chains attached to the ropes around the girl's wrists. 'I'm going to get you out of here, OK? Both of you. It's going to be alright.' Thea wasn't sure who she was trying to convince more, as fear tightened its grip on her heart.

With shaking hands, Thea used her Swiss army knife to try to saw through the ropes. She looked the girl over as she worked. Gaunt to the point that she was skeletal, her eye sockets were sunk into her head, the skin around her eyes dark as though bruised. She had cracked, white lips, and her hair looked as though it might be blonde, but it was filthy and matted to her head, so Thea couldn't be sure.

Thea stifled a gasp as she saw the girl's ankles. They were raw through to the bone at some points, and the torn skin around them was angry and red with patches of rotting, dead tissue. This was where the stench of death was coming from. The girl's feet were black from the ankles down. Thea didn't need to be a doctor to tell that she would never have use of them again.

Bringing her eyes back up to the girl's face, she could see she'd passed out again. 'Wake up,' she said, alarmed. 'Please – wake up. I need you to stay with me.'

The girl's eyelids fluttered, and her eyes opened again with a small frown.

'Come on, love, please,' Thea begged. 'You need to help me get you out of here, OK? Can you sit up do you think? Can you get your arm around my shoulders?'

The girl mumbled incomprehensibly.

Thea stood up and pulled her phone out of her pocket. There was no signal – she was too deep underground.

'Shit,' she cursed. 'Listen, I'm going to go and get help, OK? I'm coming back – I'll get you both out, I promise.'

Thea ran up the stairs two at a time and fled back out of the house the way she'd come in. Bursting through the stiff front door she fell to her knees amongst the weeds and proceeded to be violently sick. She heaved again and again until the entire contents of her stomach were out. Tears streamed down her face as the full realisation of what she'd just uncovered hit her. She wiped her mouth with the back of her hand and, ignoring the full-on panic attack she was having, she pulled her phone out and quickly made a call. It was answered by the third ring.

'Freddie,' she sobbed, 'you have to come. It's bad. It's really, really bad.'

# CHAPTER FIFTY-ONE

Freddie and Paul sat side by side on the small grey sofa in Michael's flat, both in complete silence. They had never seen Thea so shaken up. As soon as they heard her story and saw the girls, they could understand why.

Freddie could see straight away that the girl in the basement was Katherine. Even through the dirt and the extreme deterioration of her body, he could tell it was her. He had been staring at her picture for so long now, he could tell even just by her bone structure. He had been hard pushed to keep his lunch down at the sight of her and the realisation that it had been Michael all along. He closed his eyes now, thinking about it.

After they'd cut Carla loose, she'd told them what she'd found in Michael's flat, and how he had left her chained up to die. It was unthinkable. And yet it was happening.

Paul leaned forward and rested his head in his hands. Freddie knew he was torturing himself. He knew Paul was wondering what had gone wrong, how he hadn't picked up on it, what he could have done to stop Michael doing something so horrendous. He knew all of this, because he was wondering the same. He was blaming himself for this too. Perhaps, though, it really was his fault.

He thought back to the angry boy Michael had been three years ago, when he'd first returned home. The anger and hatred that he'd spewed at Freddie had been deep. Michael had blamed his older brother for the torture he'd been put through at school.

The prestigious private school that Freddie had proudly sent him off to without a thought for how he might fit in. It had taken months for Michael to calm down and come back into the fold. Freddie had kept him close ever since, brought him into the business, taught him everything he knew. Perhaps that had been a mistake. Perhaps Michael had never truly forgiven him and had been biding his time, waiting to get his revenge. If that was the case, he'd done a good job, Freddie thought sadly. If Thea hadn't stumbled across the house, they never would have found Katherine, and in a few days Freddie and Anna would have been fugitives, never able to return. Freddie sighed sadly. Whatever his reasons for doing this, Michael was their brother, their flesh and blood.

When they'd arrived at the abandoned house earlier, Freddie had carried the unconscious Katherine out in his arms. She had lain there in his grip, limp and barely holding on to life, her breath shallow and her skin deathly pale. Freddie hadn't been sure she would make it. He had driven her straight to hospital, praying the whole way that they'd found her in time. He couldn't take Katherine directly into A&E, as he would be questioned, so carefully keeping out of the way of the cameras, Freddie had driven round to one of the side doors and laid her on the steps. It was a busy hospital – he knew she would be found in minutes.

Paul and Thea had helped Carla walk out of the house. Physically she would be OK; she was just weakened and stiff from her days chained up. Mentally, Freddie wasn't so sure. The girl had been left to die – slowly, painfully and with all dignity taken from her. Freddie doubted anyone could endure that fate for a few days and walk away unscarred.

Leaving Thea to tend to Carla back at his flat, he and Paul had come straight here, to Michael's little sanctuary. Freddie knew this would be where he would go tonight. It was just a question of when. They'd been here a couple of hours already, and Freddie couldn't bear to carry on much longer with so many unanswered questions. But he would have to. He didn't want to alert Michael to their presence until he was inside the flat. He'd hidden the car on the next street and jimmied the lock with two pins to get in. Now he realised why Michael had never let any of them have a spare key. He hadn't wanted them to stumble across the cameras he used to keep tabs on Katherine.

Freddie knew that he was going to have to tell Hargreaves something, but what that something was he hadn't decided yet. He knew that it should be the truth, but he needed to see Michael himself first before he could make a solid decision. All he had relayed to Hargreaves so far was that he had found Katherine, that she was in a bad way but still alive and where he'd left her. He had closed the call off before he could be asked any questions.

The noise of Michael's key in the door sounded through the flat and Paul stood up. They waited as their youngest sibling came through and watched as surprise registered on his face.

'What are you two doing here?' He gave them a confused half smile. 'How'd you even get in?' His eyes flicked quickly to the door of his office, an action Freddie would have missed had he not known what was in there.

Paul walked across the room and stood behind him, closing the front door softly. A look of annoyance flashed across Michael's face as he realised what Paul was doing.

'What's all this about? You don't need to do the fucking round-up on me! What would I run from you two for?' he asked scornfully, taking offence.

Freddie stared at Michael, his handsome, well-built, suave little brother. He suddenly had no idea who he was, this man who could do such terrible things to innocent women. A man who could put his own brother in such a terrible position.

'There's only one day left on the clock now,' he said huskily. 'One more day until Hargreaves fits me up. I'll have to disappear – Anna too. You and Paul will be taken in, not long after.'

Michael gave him an odd look. 'We still have a whole day to find her then. This isn't over yet – you shouldn't let yourself get so down.'

The concern in Michael's face and voice nearly pushed Freddie over the edge. It enraged him. It was all lies. It had all been lies from the start. 'Well,' he said, keeping his voice level, 'we still have no clue as to who it might be.'

Freddie watched as Michael slid his gaze sideways, subtly eying Paul before giving Freddie a meaningful private look. That was what did it. Freddie lost control and leaped off the sofa, punching Michael in the face with all his strength.

'How could you?' he yelled as he bent over Michael, who sat stunned on the ground. Freddie moved away and ran his hands over his head. 'How could you?' he repeated quietly, his voice breaking, defeated. 'How could you do this to us? You tried to make me believe that it was Paul! You've had me putting together contingency plans to stop Anna being fucking killed by Ben Hargreaves! You took an innocent young woman from outside my club, raining hell down on my head and ruining her life! You tortured her—' Freddie searched for the right words but none were bad enough. 'You've had her chained up all this time! That girl, she will never recover from this. Hargreaves, her dad, when he sees what you've done… God, Michael, he ain't going to let that lie. What have you done?' Freddie shook his head from side to side in disbelief. Grief clouded his face. 'Why would you do it?'

Michael stared levelly at Freddie until he'd finished. He wiped the blood from the side of his mouth and slowly stood up, straightening his jacket and brushing it down. His expression was calm but cold.

'How did you find her?' he asked.

'That doesn't matter. Answer my questions. I'm not messing around, Michael. This is serious.'

Michael walked into the open-plan kitchen and picked up a glass and a bottle of whisky from the side.

'Want one?' he asked, raising a questioning eyebrow at each of his brothers.

Paul shook his head gravely. Freddie considered it for a moment. He had never wanted a drink so badly, but he knew that he needed a clear head if he had any chance of sorting this mess out. He declined. Michael took a large gulp of his drink and sat on one of the stools at the breakfast bar. There was a long silence, which Freddie eventually broke.

'Why, Michael?' he asked flatly. 'Was it to get back at me?'

'Get back at you?' Michael seemed genuinely confused. 'Why would I want to hurt you? You're my brother. You've taught me everything. I appreciate that.'

'When you came back three years ago, you hated me. You told me then that one day you would overtake me. I thought that was all behind us, but I've never forgotten that.'

'Oh, I will overtake you. One day. But not now, and hopefully when I do it will be with your blessing. That's something for the future,' Michael explained.

Freddie frowned. That wasn't how things were done. They were the Tyler brothers – they ran the firm together and in sync. It was also an unspoken fact that Freddie would always be the head of the family. Not only was he the eldest, but he was the one who had spent blood, sweat and years building their empire up from nothing. This wasn't some corporate rat race where you stepped over people to get to the top, but it sounded like that was exactly what Michael thought it was.

'This has nothing to do with either of you,' Michael continued. 'But it does have a lot to do with how unhappy I was back then.' His face clouded over. 'They really did torture me at that school, you know. One boy especially.'

Freddie froze as he remembered Michael's explosive outburst when he'd arrived home angry, in shame and expelled.

'William Hargreaves…' Freddie said in shock, as he finally made the connection.

It had been Hargreaves' son who had made Michael's life a misery at boarding school. He had bullied him mercilessly, and Michael had kept quiet about it, right up to the point he was expelled for dealing drugs. It had affected him badly, but Freddie had thought that was over and done with.

'Bingo,' Michael replied.

'What?' Paul asked, looking at Freddie.

'William was at school with Michael – he bullied him,' Freddie updated Paul before turning to Michael. 'But, Michael, that was years ago. You were kids. He was a cunt, sure, but that doesn't warrant all this.'

'Bullied!' Michael snorted. 'Such a weak word for what he put me through,' he snapped, glaring at Freddie.

Michael's controlled mask had slipped, and Freddie was shocked at the look he saw in his brother's eyes. It was almost feral and eerily absent, like Michael wasn't even there anymore.

'That piece of shit put me through hell. Not only did he and his friends beat me up every single day, but he belittled me and tore me down in front of anyone who was there to watch.' Michael snarled at the memory.

Freddie realised that this was what had cut Michael so deeply. Michael didn't take well to small jokes that were made at his expense. For someone to ridicule him and laugh at him like William had would be unacceptable. But even so, this had been taken way too far.

'I wanted him to feel some of the helplessness that he made me feel,' Michael said. 'He adored his sister. It'll have killed him, knowing she was suffering. He deserves it. It didn't take much to find her,' he said, a cold smile on his face. 'She's quite the social butterfly. All it took then was a couple of compliments at a bar one night and we got to chatting. I told her she should come to the club, that I would make sure she got in free. I knew I could take her undetected from there. The club really isn't that well covered by cameras, you know. I always thought that. You should probably look into that actually, when you get a chance.'

Freddie shook his head in amazement. Michael was talking to him as though everything was normal suddenly.

'And what about your demands that William kill himself, Michael? When were you going to put a stop to that?' Freddie asked.

'Put a stop to it? Why on earth would I do that?' Michael laughed as if that amused him. 'He needs to die,' he said earnestly. 'He has to pay for what he did to me. And what better way than by his own hand, saving someone he loves? That way, he really has atoned for his sins.' Michael nodded as he talked. He clearly believed wholeheartedly in everything he was saying.

Freddie was horrified. The man in front of him right now, the honest and true Michael, was a madman. There was no regret in his eyes. There was no remorse in his words. Michael thought, even now, that he was going to go through with his plan. Freddie realised in disbelief that Michael still actually thought his brothers would be on his side. He stared at Paul, whose horrified expression surely mirrored his own. What on earth were they going to do?

'Michael… This isn't going to happen. There's no way I'm letting you go forward with any of this madness. I've already dropped Katherine to the hospital, and I pray to God she lives. Hargreaves already knows she's safe. William won't be topping himself for you any time soon.'

'No!' Michael's enraged cry resounded through the minimally furnished room. His face contorted as he tried to process this disaster. 'What have you done?' he yelled.

'You can't murder that girl, or her brother – or Carla either, who we also found chained up like an animal. They're innocent people!' Freddie shouted.

'You murder people all the time. I got rid of two bodies last week alone!' Michael retorted.

'I do not murder people all the time. Last week was unusual, and you fucking know it!' Freddie yelled. 'In this line of business it happens, yes. But never to innocent people. The only people I ever take out are those who are a serious threat to me and mine. That's it. They're bad people with bad intentions, and even then I leave them to it until I have no choice. So don't you dare compare that to this.' Freddie fumed. He was always sensitive on that subject. He thought Michael understood his reluctance to kill.

'One rule for you and one for the rest of us, eh, Fred?' Michael said sarcastically.

He narrowed his eyes at his older brother. He had thought that now they knew, they would help him finish the job. He was always on hand to help finish their jobs. This was no different.

Michael knew *he* was different. Death didn't bother or affect him at all. In fact it excited him. He enjoyed that part of the job. This was something he saw as a strength. He wasn't weak like the others, who killed as quickly as possible and turned their eyes away when they were done. He didn't get affected by the feeble emotions of his prey. Fear, sorrow, love. No, he was stronger. He was built to thrive and conquer in their world. If only everyone else could see that.

Paul had been quiet as they talked, but now he stepped forward. 'I can't see a way out of this, Fred. He won't stop if he stays. We can't protect him like this.'

Freddie nodded. Paul was right. If Michael had made a mistake and had kept her out of fear, if he had been scared and remorseful, Freddie would have defended him to the end. He would have figured out a way of getting him out of it. But seeing him like this, still so hell-bent on revenge and seeing no wrong in his actions, Freddie couldn't help him. If they covered it up, Michael would still go after William, and then they would all be done for.

'Yeah, I know.' Freddie took a deep breath. 'I'm telling Hargreaves that it was you, and I'm going to tell him why,' he said to Michael. 'We'll just have to take it from there.'

'What?' Fear crossed Michael's face for the first time. 'You must be joking?'

'You'll be staying here with Paul,' Freddie said. Paul pulled a handgun out from his pocket and took a seat at the dining table. Michael's eyes flickered towards the bedroom.

'I wouldn't bother,' Freddie said. 'I already took it out from under the bed. There are no knives either. Sit down on the sofa and don't move until I get back.'

Freddie walked out of the flat, leaving Michael with his mouth gaping open. He needed to tell Ben now, while he still had the guts to do it.

# CHAPTER FIFTY-TWO

Night fell, the darkness washing over London like a blanket. The sky was clear, meaning that from the Portakabin by the docks Freddie could make out a few stars, as their light fought against the constant orange glow shining out from the city centre. It was here he stood, his heart heavier than it had ever been in his life as he waited for Hargreaves and Riley to arrive. When he had told Ben that Michael was the one responsible, he had demanded that Freddie take his life. He had also demanded that it be done in front of him, so that he could watch and be sure that his demands were carried out. Freddie knew he couldn't refuse them. If he did, Michael wouldn't just go to a prison for the rest of his life – he would be tied up in an asylum. That was no life for anyone. And he and Paul would be living out their days in maximum security, or if they somehow managed to be quick enough, under a new identity a million miles from home. No, Freddie had no choice. Especially as he knew Michael would just continue on the same path if he didn't make him face up to what he'd done.

The warm summer breeze drifted up over the river to where Freddie stood. It rippled through his hair, but he didn't notice. All he could focus on was the quiet sound of an engine turning off on the road at the top of the cobbled path behind him. He heard two muffled thuds as the doors were closed. Freddie waited for them to walk down to him. As they neared, he turned and gave Alan the nod. Alan disappeared into the Portakabin. He returned with Paul. Michael's hands were tied together with rope in front of him, and he had tape over his mouth. Paul stood Michael next to a pile of plastic sheets at the water's edge, away from Freddie, and waited for Hargreaves and DCI Riley to reach them.

Ben's face was as black as thunder as he caught sight of the trussed-up Michael. He made a beeline for him, determined to take out all his frustrations, but Freddie stood in his way and put his hand against his chest.

'Out of my way, Tyler,' he snarled.

'Not a chance,' Freddie replied strongly.

Ben blinked and looked at Freddie, surprised by his response. Freddie took the opportunity to step forward, forcing Ben to move backward.

'I've held up my end of things. I've found your daughter, and I told you who had her. You've demanded I kill Michael for what he's done, and I've accepted your right to that request. But he's still my brother.' Freddie eyed Ben – hard. 'I've done all you've asked, but I will not let you touch him. Do you understand me? You can accord me that respect, considering.'

Ben warred with himself. He wanted to push this low-life scumbag out of the way and beat ten bells out of the man who'd hurt Katherine. But there was a look in Freddie's eye that reminded Ben just how dangerous Freddie Tyler was, and it made him hesitate.

Sarah Riley stepped forward and gently pulled Ben back by the arm.

'Sir, it would be safer for you not to touch him, in case the body is found. Any trace of DNA will link you to the murder. That's definitely something you don't need.'

Freddie was struck again by how calculated Riley was. His dislike of her intensified. She was as crooked as they came. Someone who should never have been on the police force.

Ben took the out that Riley had given him and nodded his acceptance. What she was saying made sense, if he was honest.

It wasn't easy to hold himself back, but he would. At least the psychotic bastard would be dead soon. And he would be here to watch it happen. He hoped that might go some way to soothing the anger that was ripping him apart inside.

'Well, go on then. Do it,' Ben said, through gritted teeth.

Freddie signalled for Paul to put Michael in position. Michael's eyes burned into Freddie's as he stood there, waiting to be shot. His breathing was heavy with adrenaline, and his face was red, but he didn't try to struggle. He stood tall and braced himself.

Freddie stepped forward and lifted his gun. Pointing it at his brother's heart, he cocked the trigger. There was a moment of silence as everyone waited for what was coming with bated breath. Freddie's heart felt heavier than it ever had before, and he swallowed the hard lump in his throat. Taking a deep breath, he blinked away the mist forming in his eyes.

'God forgive me,' he whispered. Freddie squeezed the trigger and a single shot cracked through the silence around them, followed by a dull thump as Michael's body hit the ground.

# CHAPTER FIFTY-THREE

Anna opened the small safe in her office at Club Anya and her fingers rested on a thin A4 file underneath the package with the passports. She pulled it out and opened it up. Inside were the documents that she'd hastily had drawn up by her solicitor only the day before. It was a document that moved Anna's part-ownership of the club to Tanya. She had signed it and left it in the safe along with a note. It was all she could do at such short notice to make sure that if the worst happened, her friend and their business was protected.

Tanya didn't know any of this. She had no idea of the turmoil going on in Anna and Freddie's lives. In truth, Anna hadn't really known much about it either. She had been completely flummoxed when Thea had turned up at her door with Carla the night before with half a garbled explanation about kidnap and Michael. She had helped Thea with Carla, gently washing the exhausted, trembling girl in the bath as she wept inconsolably, before feeding her and putting her to bed in their spare room. Freddie had sat down with her this morning and finally spilled out the whole story. She had listened in shocked silence as he told her everything, from when he disappeared on her birthday right up to the night before on the docks. Grudgingly she accepted his reasons for not telling her. She wished that she'd known all of this was going on, wished that she could have shouldered some of the heavy burden for Freddie. Her heart broke for him as he told her what he'd had to do.

Taking the contract and letter out of the file, Anna stored it away in her personal file safe. She liked to keep hold of things, even though she wouldn't be needing those documents anymore. Freddie had told her they were in the clear again. They wouldn't be running off to start new lives in South America after all. Anna was relieved. She had been dreading getting the call telling her to run.

The news was on quietly on the small TV on the wall. They were now discussing Katherine Hargreaves, so she tuned in.

'… was found barely breathing but alive on the south steps of the hospital by Dr Markham. It was touch and go whether Katherine Hargreaves would make it after her ordeal. Doctors have fought tirelessly for the last forty-eight hours to stabilise her condition. Our on-site journalist Karim Ali reports.'

'Yes, thank you, Holly. It was a bad state indeed that Katherine arrived here in, but I'm glad to report that, as of this morning, she has finally begun to stabilise and has even been able to give her statement to the police. Katherine has no memory of how she came to be on the steps, and there is speculation that perhaps her kidnapper had a moment of guilt, but as it stands the police still have very little to go on.'

'Is it true, Karim, that the police profiler has concerns that this may be a serial kidnapper and that they won't stop here?'

'That is correct, Holly – they are concerned about that. The behaviour displayed by the kidnapper towards Katherine has highlighted some big red flags in the psychotic department. They believe the individual behind this needs serious help…'

Anna switched the television off and shook her head sadly. There would be no help for Michael now. She shivered as she remembered the photos Freddie had shown her of that cold, damp basement and of Katherine Hargreaves when he'd found her. He had kept them, in case he ever needed them should something come back to bite him in the arse. Anna couldn't believe that the sweet young man she had known, the man she had thought of as a younger brother almost, could be capable of such things.

But he was, and he had been caught, and Freddie had done what needed to be done.

Anna sat down suddenly as her tears began to fall and rested her head heavily in her hands. How could he do it? How could he put another person through such horror? Memories of the torture she, herself, had endured at the hands of her ex came flooding into her mind. She couldn't help but compare them, now that she'd found out who Michael really was. It took a special kind of evil to put someone through such abuse. It took a very sick mind not to feel empathy, to not care or feel bad about doing such terrible things. It wasn't something she would ever be able to understand.

Anna wiped the tears away and with difficulty closed the door on the painful memories of her past. She couldn't bear to keep thinking about the monster Michael had turned out to be. She closed her eyes. The world really was never what it seemed.

*

Freddie opened the double doors of the bright, cheerful pub with a bang. He stepped in and nodded towards all the shocked faces looking at him. They all knew exactly who he was, but they couldn't understand for the life of them what he was doing in a pub like this.

'You lost, Freddie?' a middle-aged balding man asked jokingly.

Freddie gave him a small smile. He knew Ted Sparrow well. Ted had been on his payroll for years. He came in handy for the odd bit of information and made sure that any speeding tickets were disposed of before they reached his doormat.

'Nah, I felt like having a pint with one of my close friends. You seen her? Tall, built like a bloke and a personality that would turn milk sour?'

A few of them glanced towards the back corner of the pub where Sarah Riley sat red faced, nursing a large gin and tonic.

'Ah. There she is… Thanks, boys.'

The pub was a well-known social hub for policemen and women. It was situated right by the station and was even called The Pig's Head, much to Freddie's delight. It was as much of a contrast to The Black Bear as you could possibly get and somewhere Freddie normally chose to avoid. Today, however, he had a reason for coming here.

'Wily-Riley…' Freddie's cold smile didn't reach his eyes as he looked down at her. He sat down at her table. 'And you are a little wily, ain't ya, eh?' He raised his eyebrows in question.

The man who'd been about to join Riley at her table thought the better of it and stayed at the bar instead.

'What the fuck do you think you're doing?' Riley hissed. 'We are most certainly not friends,' she continued, acid in her tone.

Freddie's eyes flashed, and Sarah caught a glimpse of the naked hatred in his eyes.

'No. We're not. You and I are going to have a little chat. We can either have it here or you can be at Land's End in ten minutes. Choose. Now.'

'Land's End,' she replied quickly. 'Now fuck off.'

Freddie immediately got up and left, nodding at Sparrow as he walked out the door. Everyone stared at DCI Sarah Riley and suddenly began to question her loyalty to the force. How did she know Freddie Tyler? Why were they on such familiar terms? And what had she done to piss him off so much that he would walk in here?

Sarah fumed in her seat, absolutely furious. In the space of two minutes Freddie had started a chain reaction that would take no time at all to undermine her trustworthiness with everyone on the force. She could already see it in their faces.

Slamming her chair back against the wall, she picked up her phone from the table and stormed out. She didn't care if he was still grieving. She was going to give Freddie Tyler a piece of her mind.

*

Freddie watched as she flew in through the door of the more neutral pub like a hurricane. He almost smiled, but not quite. He hated her too much to find her amusing.

'How dare you come in there like that? Do you know what you've done?' she said angrily.

'Sit down,' Freddie demanded. His hard voice brooked no nonsense, and his eyes flashed dangerously.

'No thanks,' Sarah replied. 'I've just come to warn you to stay the fuck away from me, or I'll bring you down regardless of what your agreement with Ben was.'

'Oh, I don't think you will. I don't think you'll be bringing anyone down again, in fact,' Freddie replied. He watched her hesitate, curious as to what he meant. 'Sit down,' he repeated.

Sarah looked towards the door that she so badly longed to walk out of, but she needed to know what Freddie was talking about. She sat down and glared at him over the table. The barmaid brought over Freddie's pint, and he thanked her politely before continuing.

'There's this funny thing about people. They never really change. I mean, they might get fit or dye their hair, go on some Buddhist retreat, but they never really change deep down. There are very few things in life that actually do change us, for better or worse. Which means when we display a trait, its usually something that's been there all along.'

'What, like your little brother?' Riley taunted.

Freddie clenched his jaw but didn't rise to it. His level stare began to make her feel uncomfortable.

'There's a calculatedness and instinct for self-preservation in you that I've watched with interest throughout our encounters lately. You have no problem going against the law you swore to uphold, as long as it covers your back or lines your pockets. And given the ease with which you did it, I was pretty sure this wasn't your first time. Your spending habits gave you away too.

Like I said before, the designer gear, the expensive jewellery, your lifestyle – they don't come easy to a pig on a salary. Not even at your level. But the money had to come from somewhere, didn't it? So, I did some digging. It's amazing the things you can find out when you're someone like me.' Freddie paused to take a deep drink from his pint glass.

Sarah was distinctly worried now, and it showed on her face.

'Turns out, I was right. But, of course, you know that, don't you?' Freddie said coldly. 'I picked up some details of a very interesting job that went down about five years ago. Do you remember that bank job in Holborn? I do. In fact, my good friend Bill was the one who put together the plan. Not that this can be proved of course, because he never actually physically went on the job – the CCTV footage that was stolen along with the money that day would never have picked him up. Thing is, though, rather than destroying them, Bill kept hold of those tapes just in case he ever needed them down the line.'

Freddie paused to take another slow drink. After all she'd put him and his family through, he was savouring the look of downright fear that was now spreading across her face. 'You were the first plod on the scene that day. It was your patch. You even got awarded for bravery when you chased the thieves out and saved one bag stuffed full of cash. How very noble. Except that wasn't actually what went down, was it?' Freddie lifted one eyebrow in question. 'No. When you got there, no one was in the vault. They had already scarpered and had accidentally left *two* bags of cash behind. They probably meant to go back but had seen you arrive and thought better of it. The camera, though, that picked you up taking a bag full of cash back out to your car before returning and playing the hero. There was somewhere between eighty to ninety grand in that bag, and you, the noble policewoman, stole it from the Bank of England. Now what is that about?'

Freddie sat back and waited for her to respond.

'There weren't any tapes there that day,' she said slowly. 'I checked.'

'Oh, there were. But Bill had a friend on the inside take them out after the fact and slip them to him down the side alley. He was watching over everything from outside.'

Sarah's face paled, and she shrank back into her seat. She swallowed the lump in her throat before replying in a fearful whisper, 'What are you going to do?'

'Me? Nothing. You, on the other hand, are going to walk back into your office, hand your notice in with immediate effect and walk right back out again. You will never work in the police force again. Because if I hear even a sniff of it, I'll send these tapes to every news station this side of fucking Mars. And the second that gets out, you're looking at a minimum of ten years inside.' He leaned forward with a triumphant gleam in his eyes. 'And you wouldn't last ten minutes in prison.'

Riley floundered as she realised in dismay that she had no choice but to do exactly as Freddie was saying. And it was entirely her own fault.

*Game, set, match*, Freddie thought. He had won.

Without a word, Sarah stood up and left the pub, her face still set in an expression of shock. Freddie watched her leave and felt a deep sense of peace wash over him. She was done in this life. He would never have to think of her again.

Bill stood up from his seat, two tables away and sat down next to Freddie, watching the DCI's retreating back through the window.

'Thanks for that, Bill,' Freddie said to his old friend.

'Any time. Especially if it gets rid of scum like her. Shall we go get a proper drink?' Bill eyed the weak beer with disgust. He had never much liked the stuff.

'Yeah, let's go. I could do with something stronger myself.'

Freddie felt a wave of appreciation hit him as he and Bill left the pub. He wouldn't know what to do without his men. They were as loyal as they came. And there was nothing more valuable than loyalty in this world.

# CHAPTER FIFTY-FOUR

Tanya, Anna and Amanda chinked their shot glasses together as they sat in a line at the bar of Club Anya.

'Well, here's to a new start for all of us, with no more secrets,' Anna said.

'Hear, hear!' said Amanda happily. She was like a whole new woman now that she'd kicked Daniel out. Her solicitors had told her that things were going to be fine, and she finally had her future back. Her relationship with Anna was as close again now as it had been ten years before. Even though she had only sought Anna out after realising her relationship to Tanya, she was really glad that she had, and Anna had forgiven her after she'd apologised for hiding her intentions. She had even begun to really like Tanya too, and their friendship was beginning to blossom. She felt happy and hopeful for the first time she could remember.

'Yes. No more secrets please,' Tanya said emphatically.

Anna squeezed her arm and gave her a sympathetic look. She knew how hard Tanya was taking the whole Daniel thing. She had spent years with her guard up, and the moment she'd let it down, it had been to let in a snake. Anna knew as well that Tanya was finding Amanda's sudden interest in her difficult to handle. But Amanda would not be put off easily, so it seemed Tanya was stuck with her new friend whether she wanted it or not.

She looked fondly at her best friend, noting the sad droop of her eyes and mouth, even through the forced smile. She hoped that she wouldn't close herself off again. Tanya needed someone who would really love her. She deserved it.

The door opened and more customers came in; a group of men geared up for a lads' night out. She took no notice, expecting the hostess to take them over to a table soon, but then she saw, out of the corner of her eye, one of them walking over. She turned and frowned, assuming they were looking for someone to help them, but the hostess was already there with the rest of the group. The young man who'd walked over had slowed to an awkward halt beside them and was smiling at Tanya, trying to catch her attention. Anna studied him. Who was he?

'Tom!' Tanya said in surprise. 'You came. I'm so glad!' Tanya's face brightened up immediately, and she beamed over at Anna. 'Anna, this is Tom, the guy I told you about. The one who saved me eating concrete on the Tube, when, er, well—' She glanced at Amanda whose face coloured as she grimaced apologetically. 'Well, that's all in the past now, but this was the hero of the hour.'

'Ah, you're the big, muscular hero we keep hearing about,' Anna said cheekily. No one answered. This was an interesting turn of events. Tanya was eyeing Tom up like he was a fillet steak, and Tom clearly had a crush on Tanya, judging by the eager way he was looking at her.

'Come on, I'm putting you guys on the VIP table tonight,' Tanya said, leading Tom away. 'All drinks are on the house.'

'Are you sure? Like I said, you don't need to. I just fancied seeing you again, to be honest.' Tom answered.

'No, I insist,' Tanya bossed.

Anna saw how her cheeks turned pink and her eyes sparkled with excitement at Tom's admission that he had wanted to see her again. *Well*, she thought, signalling Carl to pour them another shot, *perhaps I've no need to worry about Tanya's bruised heart after all.*

'There she is,' Freddie's voice sounded behind her, and Anna turned to find him walking towards her. Paul and another man she didn't know were with him.

'What are you doing here?' She reached up for a kiss.

'Thought we might pop in for a drink. Paul has someone he wants to introduce to you.'

Paul looked nervous, Anna thought. She wondered why.

Tanya walked back over to them, to get some drinks for her guests. 'Alright guys, what happ'ning?' she greeted them fondly.

Paul stepped forward and shifted from side to side awkwardly. He had never been someone who enjoyed direct attention. He cleared his throat.

'Er, yeah. So, this is James. My partner,' he said.

'Nice to meet you,' Anna immediately replied, smiling at James.

'Yeah, good to meet you. Fancy a shot?' Tanya offered with a grin.

There was silence. Paul shot Freddie a look, not sure the girls had understood. Freddie stepped forward to explain the situation to them.

'Yeah, partner as in… you know, his boyfriend,' he said. Freddie stepped back to stand beside Paul, showing his support for his brother.

Anna and Tanya glanced at each other.

'Yeah, we got that,' Tanya said. 'Do boyfriends not drink shots or something then?'

'Doesn't have to be a shot,' Anna added. 'What would you guys like to drink?' She waited for their answer.

Paul and Freddie looked taken aback by their easy response. Paul scratched his head, confused. James hid a smile.

'You aren't surprised?' Freddie finally asked.

Anna frowned. 'About what? Paul?' She and Tanya looked at each other and they burst out laughing. 'Have you only just found out? Oh, Freddie! Christ, we've known since… well, always. That's not news.'

'You donut,' Tanya shrieked. 'Call yourself a brother? Jesus.' She shook her head, laughing at the surprised expressions on the two brothers' faces. 'I've got to go, but you guys have fun. Nice catch there, Paul!' She winked. 'He's a hotty. Great to meet you, James.'

'Likewise,' James called after her with a laugh. He liked these girls already.

*

The young man stepped out of the airport in Rio and looked up at the bright blue sky through his glasses. It was roasting hot with not a cloud to be seen. Pulling his one solitary bag along behind him, he looked around for a taxi.

A young boy in shorts and sandals came running up to him.

'Can I help you, mister? Can I take your bag? Get you car? Where you wanna go?'

'OK, fine. Let's go.' He let the boy take his bag and walked alongside him.

'Where you wanna go, mister? What's your name?'

'Monroe. Steven Munroe. And just take me down to the busiest part of town.'

'OK, Mr Munroe, whatever you say.'

The young boy loaded the bag into the boot, and the man sat down in the back of the car, thankful for the air con. He looked out of the window at the landscape as he passed. It was rundown in a lot of areas, but he had to admit it was beautiful too. Whatever his opinions, he would have to get used to it for now.

When Freddie had taken the call informing him of Hargreaves' intent, he had set this new plan into motion. Pulling out a fake passport he'd already had set up for Michael, Freddie booked him a one-way flight to Rio and gave him a carry-on bag with concealed compartments that held enough money for Michael to live on for quite some time. Freddie had staged Michael's death using a blank and fake blood. It had been hard to stay so quiet and still, but he'd managed it. Freddie had not allowed Ben to get anywhere near him. From that distance in the dark there was no reason to suspect foul play. Paul had wrapped him in the plastic and moved him to a waiting boat straight away.

Michael still couldn't understand why Freddie was angry with him. If anything, it should be him who was pissed off at his brothers for letting him down and grassing on him. His anger bubbled just under the surface as he thought about it again. Their family, their life, their work, it all balanced on loyalty and teamwork. He had done all the dirty jobs that Freddie had required, and now, when he'd needed his help in return, he was killed off and sent away in disgrace. He was livid that Freddie could do this to him and annoyed at himself that he hadn't seen it coming.

He calmed his angry, racing thoughts. It was OK. Freddie would pay for what he'd done. They all would. Every dark debt that he was owed, he would collect. Everything that was rightfully his, he would claim once and for all. He owed them nothing now.

He would stay here for now, out of the way, and lie low. He would be seen to tow the line and bide his time patiently. But one day soon, when London had all but forgotten him, he would be ready. And when that day came, they wouldn't know what had hit them. He was underworld royalty. He was a Tyler. And though no one seemed to realise it yet, he was the most dangerous Tyler of all.

# A LETTER FROM EMMA

Dear Reader,

Firstly, thank you so much for choosing my book and entering into my little world for a while. I hope you enjoyed reading it as much as I enjoyed writing it.

For those who would like to hear more about my future novels, please sign up here. You can unsubscribe at any time, and your email address will never be shared.

www.bookouture.com/emma-tallon

The first book in this series, *Runaway Girl*, was a very personal story for me. When I started writing it, I had no plans to publish it. Back then, writing was just something I enjoyed and an emotional vent. But when the story started to really take shape and develop, I fell in love with the characters I'd created, and I knew I couldn't just leave it there. Anna, Freddie, Tanya… they are all so strong and so vibrant. Their stories needed to go on! That is when *Dangerous Girl* began forming in my mind.

The new challenges that our characters have faced in this book have revealed even more of their inner strength and just how unbreakable some bonds can be. It has shown us, too, that in the world they live in anything can happen. You never know what's coming next.

In book three, which I am working on currently, we will see our characters face their biggest threats yet. I'm really excited for what's in store next. I'm not leaking any spoilers here, but if you enjoyed *Runaway Girl* and *Dangerous Girl*, I hope you'll join me on a journey through the third instalment in the series.

If you enjoyed *Dangerous Girl* please do leave me a review! I take the time to read all the reviews that get put up online. I love to hear what my readers have to say. And if there's something you're particularly looking forward to reading more about, please do add that into your review too!

Thank you again for all your support – and keep your eyes peeled for the release of book three!

Best wishes,
Emma x

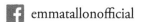 emmatallonofficial

 EmmaEsj

www.emmatallon.com

# ACKNOWLEDGEMENTS

I want to say a huge thank you to everyone at Bookouture who's helped me take the second instalment in this series from just an idea on my laptop to a beautifully finished book that my readers can enjoy.

In particular I want to thank my editor, Helen, who has been with me all the way – from the first rounds of edits, to the hundreds of random emails I send her, right through to the end.

And lastly, I want to thank all my amazing readers – the people who buy my book and immerse themselves in the world that I have created. Knowing that you enjoy my stories and love my characters as much as I do spurs me on. So, thank you. Your support is appreciated more than you know.

Milton Keynes UK
Ingram Content Group UK Ltd.
UKHW021921161123
432711UK00012B/914